THE
BIG FREEZE

Also by Michael J. Katz

Murder off the Glass
Last Dance in Redondo Beach

THE
BIG FREEZE

Michael J. Katz

G. P. Putnam's Sons/New York

G. P. Putnam's Sons
Publishers Since 1838
200 Madison Avenue
New York, NY 10016

Library of Congress Cataloging-in-Publication Data
Katz, Michael J., date.
The big freeze / Michael J. Katz.
p. cm.
PS3561.A772B54 1991   90-8712 CIP
813′.54—dc20
ISBN 0-399-13558-8

Printed in the United States of America
1 2 3 4 5 6 7 8 9 10

This book is printed on acid-free paper.
∞

Thanks to Glenn Leopold for special consulting

Prologue

The manuscript turned up on Andy Sussman's doorstep at ten o'clock on a snowy March morning—dropped ingloriously by a rookie postman, who could have stuck it inside the storm door or possibly even rung the doorbell, both permissible under postal regulations. Instead, he left it upside down on the welcome mat, so that by the time Andy opened it, the snow had seeped through the Jet-Pak mailer and was forming watery ringlets around the cardboard box.

Sussman put his coffee down and stared blearily at the package. He had just flown back from the West Coast, and his senses were still in Los Angeles, where it was barely seven—why hadn't he stayed an extra day? He'd still be sleeping, and when he did wake up it would be coffee and Danish on the beach, where it was a toasty seventy degrees, instead of this wet, freezing, miserable excuse for a climate.

Andy tried to make out the return address, which was now hopelessly stained. J something. Cranston . . . Realty? He looked at the postmark: Sunburst, Colorado. His network was televising a World Cup ski race from there in a few weeks. Some real estate shark must have gotten his name from a mailing list, and sent him what would assuredly be a once-in-a-lifetime opportunity to purchase a deluxe alpine condo with hot tub, sauna, and wet bar, only minutes from the slope. A bargain for three hundred and fifty grand. But which soon-to-be-fired intern had given out his home address?

Sussman tossed the Jet-Pak envelope away and looked at the cardboard box, sealed tight with Scotch tape. His name was scrawled across it in blue Magic Marker: ANDREW "HOOPS" SUSS-MAN.

That explained it.

Only Murray used that name. He'd tagged Andy with it years ago, when they both attended the University of Wisconsin and Sussman was broadcasting Badger basketball games over the student station. The name hadn't exactly stuck in anyone else's mind, but Murray Glick was not one to be dissuaded by the public's tardy recognition of his genius. Now, fifteen years later, at the peak of a career that had taken him from the broadcasting hinterlands of Madison and Green Bay all the way to New York, where he was currently doing network play-by-play of NBA games, he was still "Hoops"—to Murray, anyway. And to no one else.

Andy peeled the tape off the box, expecting to find another of Murray's notorious promotions for Glick Investigations. You had to give him credit, Andy thought. His buddy had taken a basically seedy and low-rent occupation and given it a facelift for the nineties. Murray had begun the makeover several years before, when he had relocated his office in the second level of a glitzy shopping mall in suburban Chicago, a few doors down from Neiman Marcus. Now he had his own "Crimestoppers Column" in the suburban newspapers. He'd organized Murray Glick Mystery Cruises in the Caribbean. He advertised on the Home Shopping Network. He was considering franchising out the whole operation. And somehow, every once in a while, he even found the time to actually solve a crime.

Andy grabbed a letter opener—the box was wrapped up like a mummy. He was expecting a stack of four-color brochures, or possibly Murray's Detective Swimsuit Calendars, or maybe even a videocassette promotional tape. What he found was . . . pages. One hundred and twelve of them.

Andy emptied the box, to make sure this wasn't some half-baked marketing scam of Murray's, with a pop-up, battery-charged gizmo lurking at the bottom. There was nothing, save the manuscript. The typing was messy but readable. Murray had a state-of-the-art computer in his office, and a slightly less than state-of-the-art secretary, but it didn't look like he'd taken advantage of either one.

Andy scanned the first few lines, sipping on his tepid coffee.

He decided almost immediately that the manuscript was going to require a fresh cup, not to mention an easy chair, with some Willie Dixon blues turned low in the background.

And slippers—the soft, warm, fur-lined slippers that Susie had given him for his birthday, with the note that he could lounge around the house all day in them while she was trapped in Manhattan, slaving away at her law practice. It was meant as a joke, of course, but in truth, his wife WAS in Manhattan, presumably slaving away—she had left the house at six in the morning, in a driving snowstorm, so she could get to the train station in time to stand outside freezing for an hour before riding the commuter train into work, part of which consisted of representing him in contract negotiations with the network. It was bound to be a trying day for her, and Andy thought it would be an awful show of ingratitude if he didn't at least wear her slippers.

On the other hand, Susie would surely disapprove of her gift keeping his toesies warm while he read anything with Murray Glick's name on it. In what Andy regarded as one of those odd, unexplainable female quirks, his wife steadfastly misinterpreted Murray's inventive, entrepreneurial nature as the trademark of what she called (charitably she thought) "that pompous, scheming, chauvinistic sleaze." About the best thing Susie could say about the entire production of pulling up roots and moving to New York after their wedding last September was that they had left Murray Glick in Chicago.

It was what Andy missed most about the place.

Oh well, Sussman mused, as he pulled on his slippers and settled into the leather recliner, I'll just keep it out of her sight. Slip it in between the *Sports Illustrated*s, she'll never see it.

Andy put his blues record on the stereo. He stretched his legs and looked out the window. It was a rotten day; he had nowhere to go. He poured a few drops of Jack Daniel's into his coffee. On second thought, he poured in a whole shot.

He picked up the manuscript and began to read.

PART ONE

PART ONE

1

You could tell she was trouble in the twinkling of an eye, and boy, did those eyes twinkle. They were baby-blue peepers, slightly tinted by designer contacts. Long wavy lashes bounced over them like Rockettes, backlit by sea-blue eyeshade, melting gently into sleek, jet-black brows. They were starlets' eyes, models' eyes, manufactured to close a client—they could knock you over with one cockeyed flutter if you didn't know better.

I knew better.

Because in my line of business that twinkle may be all the time you have to make a judgment, and it had damn well better be the right one. Maybe she was just another gorgeous suburban mom, jogging in from Lord and Taylor's with a new fifteen-hundred-dollar outfit on her way to aerobics class, flashing you a mysterious wink and a smile, casually wondering whether the old man really is playing bridge at the country club every Tuesday night. Or maybe I was staring into the eyes of a trained killer.

I'm paid to know the difference. I'm Murray Glick, private investigator. The mall is my beat.

"I'm new at this," the woman said, nervously tapping her fingers in a way that told me she wasn't. Her name was Barbra Kaplan. She crossed her long, sleek legs in front of me, batted those lashes again, and licked her lips, and when I didn't melt away like a cup of cheap margarine she continued. "I was referred by Carol. Carol Berman; you helped her with little Josh."

"Sure, right," I said, flipping through a file. Not that I needed any reminders about Carol. Tall, leggy, a bleach blond, women's tennis champion at Birchmoor Country Club three years straight. Had a sixteen-year-old kid running with the wrong crowd, so she thought. Late from school, gone on the weekends. Fatigue, listlessness, telltale signs. Turns out he'd been doing volunteer work at a country vocational center downtown, part of the Outreach Program at New Trier. Fell hard for a social worker from Hoffman Estates. A helluva long commute, it was wearing him down; the poor kid never had a chance. Truth is, it wore me down too, but it was a gig and Carol and I had a fun stakeout while it lasted. We work in a tennis game every now and then, to keep the reflexes sharp.

"Carol said you'd be discreet about this; it's very important that my husband doesn't know about it."

"Discreet is my middle name."

Barbra glanced up at my P.I. certificate on the wall behind my desk. "Your middle name is Arthur," she said, flashing me a knowing smile, and for a moment I wished we were both ten years younger, although to be truthful thirty-five isn't really so old, and since I moved into Northbrook Court I've done a hell of a lot better than I ever did, even in my salad days. So I guess I really just wished that she was ten years younger, although experience does count for something and Barbra Kaplan looked like she could do things with those long legs that Mary Lou Retton hadn't even begun to consider.

"It's about my daughter," Barbra said softly. She trapped me in her hurt pussycat gaze for a few seconds, then took a photograph out of her purse and set it on my desk, touching my hand as she let it fall. "Her name's Dani. She's nineteen."

"Aha." I looked at the Polaroid snapshot. The girl had honey-blond hair, several shades lighter than her mother's. She had a thin-lipped smile, her right arm was wrapped around a tall, dark-haired kid with a rugged, Colorado tan; she glanced at the camera like it was a temporary distraction. "They do grow up fast," I said. "Dani?"

"Short for Danielle."

"What about him? Or does it matter?"

Barbra's eyelids drooped for a second; I thought there might be a few telltale lines around the edges, but it would take an archeologist to find them. "Casey Wright. He's a ski instructor at Sunburst. Are you a skier, Mr. Glick?"

"Former quartermaster of the Hoofer's Bacchanalia Express."

"Excuse me?"

"The University of Wisconsin ski club. Known for its marathon bus trips to exotic locales. We did Jackson Hole my senior year—I was in charge of refreshments."

Barbra smiled at me. She was wearing a scarlet and black pantsuit and it didn't take much imagination to picture her in a tight-fitting ski turtleneck. "I take it you can afford to fly these days?" she said, her eyes measuring me for a pair of polypropylene long johns.

"Makes it a little easier. You do lose that sense of the land, though."

"We have a condo at Sunburst. Three bedrooms, pool, and sauna. Sam and me and the kids. It's where Dani and Casey met."

"Private lesson?"

"Group. He picked her out."

"Ski instructors have that knack," I said, and felt a pang of envy for a moment, thinking of all those pretty young lasses that stroll past my office each day on their way to the Rekord Rak or the Slice O' Pizza. Easy pickings for the Casey Wrights of the world, but jailbait for me. I closed my eyes for a moment and tried to believe that ten years from now Wright would be an apathetic, washed-up ski bum, wandering aimlessly around Hollywood, looking for a guest shot on "Knot's Landing." It made me feel a lot better.

"I've got nothing against a little romance," Barbra said, and I believed her. "I mean what's a parent supposed to do? She was a freshman in college, I'd given up trying to run her personal life. Thank God she still spent a few weeks with us."

"But it became more than a little romance, didn't it?" I knew what was going to come next. Runaway suburban daughters fall just behind wayward husbands and surprise anniversary presents among my clientele.

"A lot more. She spent last summer with him at Sunburst. This fall she quit school and went out there to live with him."

"Where'd she go to college?"

"Northwestern."

"Sounds like a bargain for you."

Barbra batted those bright-blue peepers at me and tried to suppress a smile. A year's tuition at Northwestern could put us both in Saint Moritz for the winter, but neither of us were packing our bags. I reached for my leather cigar cannister and pulled out one of Fidel's finest. "Mind if I smoke?"

"Not at all." Barbra leaned back on my plush-leather guest chair and gazed admiringly as I puffed a chain of perfectly circular smoke rings toward the vents.

"So Dani and Casey find a cozy loft in Sunburst. He spends his days turning glitzy Easterners into schuss-boomers while our future lawyer/mom and director of the women's tennis ladder at Birchmoor ends up making Indian jewelry and bussing Coors empties at the Antler Inn."

Barbra pursed her lips. She pulled out a container of Tic Tacs and popped one in her mouth. "Tsk, tsk, Mr. Glick. Dated any Jewish girls since your bar mitzvah?"

"A few. And call me Murray, please."

"Look, Murray, Dani was no princess. Straight A's her first year; she was studying art history. Taught tennis in the summer, paid for her board."

"Maybe the pressure got to her. Maybe she'll take a semester off, then come back. She's as bright as you say, she'll see him for an over-the-hill ski rabbit soon enough, be back in Evanston faster than you can say BMW."

"She already left him."

I took a long puff from my cigar and stared at Mrs. Kaplan. "You don't look happy about that, Barbra."

She shook her head. "I don't know where she went. She never told me anything, she just cleared out. She's been missing ten days—"

"How'd you find out?"

"I called. The phone was disconnected—there was no forwarding number. I tried the ski school. Casey was gruff; he didn't want to talk to me. He said she'd walked out—they'd broken up."

"When?"

"A couple of weeks before."

"It took you that long to find out?" I tapped an ash from my cigar. Dani Kaplan may have left the nest, but I knew Jewish mothers. I couldn't believe Barbra would let two Sundays go by without calling her daughter, even if she'd run off with Attila the Hun.

"Sam and I were in Majorca for three weeks. We sent postcards."

I glanced sadly at my snow-dusted overcoat. "And when you came back, your daughter had disappeared off the face of the earth?"

"As far as I can tell."

"And what did your husband have to say about all this?"

Barbra's lips tightened, her eyes sunk into a look of extreme disgust. I had the feeling that poor Sam Kaplan had had about as much fun on Majorca as Robinson Crusoe. I balanced my cigar on an ash tray and blew one last smoke ring toward the air conditioner. "I do have to ask the obligatory question regarding the presumed notification of the authorities and the proffered assistance of our law-enforcement agencies."

"Out of the question." Barbra sat up straight now; a steely gaze shone through the tinted contacts. "Sam wouldn't allow it if he knew, and I don't want him to know." She hesitated, edging closer to my desk.

"Do continue, Mrs. Kaplan."

Barbra dropped her voice. "Sam was furious when Dani ran off to Colorado. He wanted to cut her off completely. He wouldn't talk to her on the phone—my God, he wouldn't even let her call collect."

"Serious business," I said, knowing that the words, "Will you accept a collect call from your daughter?" have achieved biblical status in our modern-day faith. "So you never talked?"

"I had to go next door. For three months I was buying the Wolfes' groceries, just to cover the phone bill."

"And what did you discuss on the phone all that time that kept the Wolfes in fresh produce?"

I thought I saw a blush filter through Barbra's cheeks, but the signal was faint. "Girl talk. Mother-daughter talk."

"Nothing to indicate a falling out with darling Casey?"

Barbra shook her head. "She was crazy about him. Casey was going to be head of the ski school. Casey was getting into marketing. Casey was going to be a very big man at Sunburst."

I picked up the Polaroid again and looked at the young girl

clutching Wright's waist. She had a look of total devotion, but I knew how fast that could change. "Where'd your daughter work at Sunburst, Barbra? I assume she did work."

"She clerked at a little grocery store in the village. I never got the name. She did some volunteer work at the art center. Dani was a good photographer; she had some prints exhibited once in high school."

"Right." I tapped another cigar ash. "Nikon camera, I take it? Gitza tripod, the whole getup?"

Barbra winced; she shook her bangs back smartly. "No, she used a Brownie. We dressed her in rags, she saved up her allowance and spent it on surplus cheese. Would that make you happy, Mr. Glick?"

"Easy there," I said, taking Barbra's hand; I'd gotten a rise out of her, I could feel her trembling.

"Listen, Murray, the world's tough enough as it is. We struggled for years building a foundation for our family. Am I supposed to apologize for providing them with the best?"

"Not at all, Barbra. That's why you're here, after all."

"I want you to find Dani," Barbra said, retrieving her hand and taking out her pocketbook. She filled out a check payable to me, leaving the amount blank. She tore it out and placed it on my desk. "I don't want the police in on this. I don't want Sam to know."

"Mum's the word."

"You're welcome to use our place at Sunburst. I've already covered it with the rental people." She took a white business envelope out of her purse. "The keys are inside. There's a map, maintenance information, a list of restaurants, and tourist information—"

"I'm sure I won't have time for entertainment, Barbra." I placed the envelope, the check, and the Polaroid in my desk drawer. "I don't suppose you'll be making a visit anytime in the next few weeks?"

Barbra smiled and gave those eyelids one last flutter. "I've got my own key." She closed her purse and pushed her chair back. "Find my daughter, Mr. Glick."

"Absolutely Mrs. Kaplan." I got up to show her out. "Thanks for stopping by. Don't forget the shoe sale over at Naylor's."

"I'm late for tennis. Send me a gift certificate." Barbra Kap-

Ian headed for the door. "We'll talk later," she said, without turning around.

I hurried to open the door for her, but she was already outside. By the time I'd followed her through the front office she'd disappeared into the walkway and down the escalator, lost in the faceless march to Neiman Marcus.

2

Tuesday, 12:35 P.M. I leaned back in my desk chair, my feet kicked up on my blotter, polishing off a frozen treat from 31 Flavors—I figured it would be weeks before I'd be able to eat another ice cream sandwich without looking over my shoulder. Peggy, my receptionist, waltzed in with my airline tickets from the travel agency on the first level. She set them down on my desk, next to a parka I'd bought at the sporting goods place downstairs, a ski sweater from I. Magnin across the corridor, and some thermal undies from Eddie Bauer, three stores down.

"Too bad you can't get the plane to taxi up to the parking lot," Peggy said, glancing at my skis and ski boots and the luggage I'd bought at Lord and Taylor. "You might actually have to hit fresh air between here and Sunburst."

"No problem, my dear, I've got to acclimatize myself to the mountains sometime."

"Make sure the limo driver opens a window."

Peggy gave me that sweet, bewitching laugh of hers. She's a tall redhead, with freckles from head to toe, begging to play connect-the-dots. She's been my girl Friday for five years now—starting the day after she divorced the assistant state's attorney. I must admit I considered that useful experience at the time; she'd gleaned all sorts of tidbits from the County Building that made life easier for a fledgling PI, and the way she modeled Magnin's sweaters didn't hurt either. But the truth is, this is one relationship that's been strictly business from square one. There's not one shred of information that I won't share with her—she knows where I am twenty-four hours a day, and she's got the key to the safe. I'm a loner, sure, but even when you write your own ticket you've got to trust one person in the world, and Peggy's my choice.

"You sure you don't need an assistant on the slopes?" she said, giving me a quick back massage and fitting a new blue-and-silver stocking cap over my ears.

"Someone's gotta mind the store."

"Lock your office. Hire a temp to shoo the customers away."

"Sorry, Peg, there's work to be done. We need business data and tax info on Sam Kaplan. He's at Kozlo Realty; get an update on their holdings—"

"I'll deliver it personally. Just tell me which run you'll be on, and we'll rendezvous at the top of the chairlift—"

"No sale. Our customers get a special feeling of security from your voice on the telephone."

Peggy put both hands on my stocking cap and breathed a long, trenchant sigh. "Boss," she said, pulling the hat over my eyes, "have I ever mentioned that I'm madly in love with you and we should run away to Acapulco for the winter, maybe forever?"

"Last time it was Kauai."

"The travel place has rates to Mexico."

I pulled the hat off. I stood up and kissed Peggy on the cheek. "Sorry, kid. No work for gringo PI's at the Princess. Here, enjoy." I gave her a month's worth of coupons for the Orange Julius and stuffed the parka and long johns into my suitcase. Peggy helped me with the zipper, then stuck the airline tickets in my pockets and tossed me my overcoat.

"Murray," she said with a sardonic grin, "I can't live on dreams forever."

"Take lots of vitamin C and have a drink before dinner." I gave her another kiss and hauled my luggage outside.

"Murray, hang on!" she shouted as I wandered into the mall, clattering my skis behind me. I stopped and turned around, just as she caught up to me. "Murray, don't you think you should pack some heat with you to all that snow?"

"Miss Terrell, begging doesn't become you."

"That wasn't what I meant." She turned her thumb and index finger into a derringer and stuck it in my ribs.

"Don't worry, Peg. Just a missing kid, no reason to bother all those nice people at airport security. Any problems, I'll call—you can FedEx it."

"You sure?"

"Absolutely."

"Just be careful, boss."

"Careful's my middle name."

"Arthur's your middle name."

"I'm having it legally changed." I tenderly placed Peggy's derringer back in her holster, then picked up my skis and headed for the escalator. "See ya, kiddo," I shouted. A few minutes later, I was gone, Peggy was back at her telephone, and the Colt .38 was in my bottom desk drawer.

Something told me I shouldn't be leaving either one behind.

3

It started to snow a few minutes after I touched down at the little airport a few miles north of Sunburst, Colorado. By the time I got the papers straightened out on my rental Land Cruiser, the tarmac was cloaked in white; I knew there wouldn't be any more flights arriving that night. The terminal was shutting down; visions of sensational powder skiing danced through the minds of employees and tourists.

Not that I'd forgotten the business at hand. I was just imagining the best possible scenario—a headstrong college kid gets her first serious jilt, crawls into a hole for a few weeks, surfaces in Evanston right behind the Easter Bunny in time for Spring Quarter. I'd chase down all the leads between ski runs, give Casey Wright a lecture on chivalry, maybe rattle his bones a little for good measure. Maybe I'd find a nice ski instructor of the female persuasion, we'd share a bottle of champagne, invent old times. I'd book her on my Christmas Mystery Cruise; we'd be friends for life. Somehow I knew it wasn't going to be that easy.

I hadn't told Barbra Kaplan, but I'd actually skied Sunburst before, back in my college days when it was just a couple of broken-down double-chairs and a T-bar, rising over a deserted gold mine. We'd taken a day off from Aspen; they were giving away two-for-one coupons on lift tickets here and the slopes were still nearly empty. One thing was clear to me now: dropping Real Estate 101 at Madison had been a mistake. Even through the blizzard I could see this place had gone world class. Lights flickered from condos all along the base of the mountain and edged up the slope to the end of the first chairlift. The ghost town had been replaced by Sunburst Village—the crumbling gold veins had been hyped with plastic; you could dine and dance and drink the night away, the only frontier left was your credit limit.

I heard music streaming from a bar a few miles away. I thought about a nice cold brew and a fresh mountain trout, but I had a 4 x 4 full of skis and luggage and besides—I had a feeling that Barbra kept her place well stocked.

I followed the directions she'd left me; the road forked off the main drag up into the hills, then circled into a cul-de-sac. I found her condo; it was a two-unit chalet a kick and a glide from the number 2 chairlift. I slipped my key in the door, flicked on a light, and gazed at my plush accommodations: polished oak floors covered with Indian-weave rugs; teak furniture, crystal chandeliers. An art collection that could have had its own wing at the Louvre.

The kitchen looked like the showroom from Neiman Marcus. Utensils were hanging neatly from a rack beside the range: ladles, basters, tongs, an international spice rack. It was overwhelming for a guy who's used to making do with a can opener and a maid. I opened the refrigerator and knew that Barbra hadn't let me down: inside was a fresh prime T-bone, an onion, and a cold six-pack of Heinekens. Maybe it was my imagination, or maybe it was just a sleuth's intuition, but I thought I detected a whiff of Barbra's perfume. I stole into the bedroom and turned on the light. The linen was fresh, the bed was turned down. There was a bottle of Grand Marnier on the nightstand, but the room was cold and empty. I loped back into the kitchen, heated up the broiler, and emptied a can of beans into a saucepan. Dinner was simmering toward perfection when I heard a knock on the front door.

It was midnight, a little early for the paper boy. Right away I missed my Colt. I looked around for a weapon, but all I could find was a steak knife. It seemed like a crummy way to greet a guest, even at that hour, but I tossed it on the counter just to have it handy. I took a deep breath and assumed my karate stance. I glided up to the door, but it wasn't locked and before I could reach for the knife, a tall man in a Stetson strode inside and extended a weathered right paw in my direction.

"Howdy, neighbor!" he said, in a friendly twang. He slapped me on the back with a force that jolted me out of my karate mode,

into a repose of extreme neighborliness. "I'm J. B. Cranston—
the wife and I live upstairs. Heard some rumblin' around, figured
we'd help you get organized down here so's we can all get some
sleep."

"Much obliged." I breathed deeply to dissolve the adrenaline
and shook my neighbor's hand. "I'm Murray Solomon."

"How the hell are ya, Murray!" Cranston replied, and didn't
wait to find out. He jerked my suitcase off the floor, hauled it
into the main bedroom, plugged in the entertainment center, and
turned up the thermostat. "We'll get your heat and hot water
goin', get your circuits all turned on; you'll be ready to hit the
slopes at the crack of dawn. You a friend of Sam and Barb's?"

Cranston stood about six feet, one-eighty; he wore a red-
checked flannel suit and blue jeans. He looked mid-fiftyish. I had
a couple of inches on him, but I couldn't get much of a read on
his strength. "I'm a third cousin," I told him. "Of Barbra's.
Never been to Sunburst. Had a little vacation, they were kind
enough to lend me the keys."

"Beautiful place, Murray. The condo, the village, the whole
damn mountain. You'll love it." Cranston wrapped his arm
around me and led me back toward the kitchen. "Smells like you
got dinner cookin'! Lemme check your fan, test the disposal.
Damn maintenance takes a week to get anything fixed around
here."

I offered Cranston a beer, then slipped into the bathroom while
he fiddled around under the sink. I had Barbra's white envelope
in my pocket and I quickly checked the list of neighbors—sure
enough, there was J.B. and Betty Cranston at the top, with J.B.'s
name circled and the words "a real peach" scrawled beside it. I
stared at the bathtub, which had a built-in bubble bath and Jacuzzi. I wondered how you got to be rated a real peach in Barbra
Kaplan's book, but I didn't think I'd find out tonight. When I
returned to the kitchen, Cranston had turned the fan on and
flipped my steak. He cranked down the heat on the beans before
they got charred and set a place for me at the dining table.

"Helluva cheap butler," he laughed, pulling me out a beer.
"Where ya hail from, Murray?"

"Chicago. Got a little retail business there—"

"Ha! Flatland, what a waste of bad weather. You just enjoy
yourself at Sunburst this week, Murray—you'll never go back."

"Fine with me, pal." I took a peek at my steak, hoping it and J.B. were both about done, but Cranston was making himself right at home. "So, J.B. You a permanent resident hereabouts?"

"You betcha! Been here eleven years." Cranston took a card from his pocket and dropped it on my steak knife. It read: "Sunburst Realty, J.B. Cranston, President."

I slipped the card in my pocket and swigged down a healthy dose of Heineken. "Just a hunch, J.B., but I bet you're seein' some prosperous times."

"Hell yes, and I ain't ashamed to say so. Twarn't nothin' but bears and moonshiners up here when I came over the hill. Damn snots over at Vail and Aspen thought we'd be nothin' but rusted cables and redneck snowmobile bars; now we got the finest resort on the whole continent. You stayin' for the World Cup, Murray?"

"World Cup? They race this mountain?"

"Hell, you didn't know about that? We got the whole danged European circuit over here next week. We got Swiss and Austrians and French and Eye-talians. The Snowburst Downhill, crown jewel of the Rocky Mountain circuit. We got the TV networks and everything. Just let me know, I'll get you a spot right at the finish line."

"Just might take you up on that. Get my Rossis runnin' smooth, maybe I'll enter myself."

"Heh, heh, heh," cackled Cranston. He scooped my steak out of the broiler, spooned the beans onto a plate, and pulled a napkin from a cabinet above the sink. "Eat 'n' enjoy, neighbor. Believe me, you're gonna fall in love with this place." He gave me a pat on the head, poured my beer into a mug, and headed for the door. "You have yourself a right fine time. Call me or the wife if you need anything. You got my number."

"Will do, J.B.—"

"Come by my office the end of the week; I gotta nice little chalet with your name on it—"

"Save me something by the bunny slope," I said, and started to slice into my steak. "Say, J.B.?" I asked casually.

"Yessir?"

I glanced at my beer mug, then plunged into the void. "I was just wondering. I gotta little cousin out here, name of Dani. Heard she'd become sort of a local nowadays. Thought I'd pop in and say hello, if I could find her."

Cranston walked back into the kitchen and leaned over the chair across the table from me. "Well ain't that sweet, Murray. Poor kid, thought Sam and Barbra'd shut her out of the barn completely."

"Third cousins find it easier to forgive."

"So do neighbors. Betty and I used to have the little gal by for dinner once in a while over the summer. Haven't seen her in about a month, though. Course, once the season starts, we all get pretty busy."

"Natch. I heard she's workin' there in the village; maybe I'll stop by on my way to the slopes."

"Well, I bet she'd get a real kick outta that!" J.B. stood straight up and headed for the hallway. "I think she's over at the Village Deli, right next to the rental place. Get yerself a nice sandwich and a beer, have a little picnic. Helluva lot cheaper than the cafeteria."

"Sounds like the ticket," I said and lunged over to shake Cranston's hand.

"Don't get up, Murray! Get that steak down, get yerself a good Rocky Mountain snooze, hit them slopes bright and early." J. B. Cranston waved goodbye and tramped out the door. "Say hello to the little girl for us if you see her."

"Will do," I said, but Cranston was already gone; a few moments later I heard him stamping around upstairs, and then all was quiet.

I sipped on my brew, contemplated my perfectly broiled T-bone, and wondered if I'd overplayed my hand. I didn't want word out around the mountain that someone was snooping after Dani Kaplan, that was for certain. But I had to start somewhere, and I figured it's better to start with a peach than a bad apple. Still, when I was all finished I made sure the front door was bolted tight.

And before I went to sleep I slipped a steak knife underneath the box spring just in case.

4

I awoke at the crack of dawn, or more accurately the thunder of cannons—I was jolted out of my sleep by three sharp blasts that echoed over the mountains and sent me scrambling onto the floor. I instinctively reached for my steak knife and crouched behind the door. I was groggy, I couldn't believe that my neighbor had alerted Dani's kidnappers already, but when danger leaves a wake-up call, you don't ask questions. Another round rattled the roofbeams. I was wide awake now, but as the boom reverberated through the valley I breathed a sigh of relief—it was only the local ski patrol at work. There'd been a foot of snow overnight and the cannons were setting off controlled avalanches on the upper slopes so we recreational skiers wouldn't get buried by real ones later on. I smiled to myself and pulled the shade open. It had been too long between ski trips, but I figured I could get used to the routine.

In an hour or so I had shaved and showered and duded myself up in my new ski outfit: burnt orange bib overalls, a silver turtleneck, the sweater from Magnin's and a white down parka with a silver streak down the side. One look outside and I could see that J. B. Cranston was right—I was already in love with the place. The storm had snowed itself out during the night. The sky was bright blue, a warm breeze blew gobs of snow off the pine trees; they thudded down on the stained wooden beams of A-frames and the covered bridges that dotted the pathways into the village.

Looking straight up the mountain, I could see acres of fresh powder and hear muffled whoops from the ski patrollers who were getting first crack at it. I considered skiing right over to the chair-lift from the back door of Barbra's condo; I tried to think if there were any urgent questions that couldn't wait until I'd taken a few runs from the top of the gondola, gliding through the powder on Liberty and Fox Hunt, then running the moguls on Dragon's Head and cruising the catwalk back to the village. But I'm just a working stiff, I had a blank check from a beautiful lady; I thought I'd get the job done before I filled in the zeros. I snapped my boots halfway up, slung my skis over my shoulder, and hiked into Sunburst Village.

As I walked by the rows of plush chalets, I couldn't help think-ing about that day fifteen years ago when we'd bused over from Aspen to ski a crusty, boulder-pocked mountainside, miles from nowhere. The village was just a cluster of shops around two chair-lifts. There was a small ski rental agency and a saloon called the Gold Dust Inn, where we whiled away the evening munching on Slim Jims, hustling girls in pickups, and shooting down whiskey and beer. A little outings office across the street offered cross-country ski trips into the back country and burro trips in the summertime; we'd all taken brochures and vowed to return some day with our backpacks. Well, here I was, finally, but the burros were gone and so were the pickups and the Slim Jims and espe-cially the cheap whiskey.

In their place were real estate offices and designer sunglasses boutiques and a half-dozen sports shops, all with major credit cards plastered on the windows, offering to dress every skier in Sunburst like me, at only double the price. Restaurants were spread all over: little bistros with outside seating and Wild West names like "Clem's Claim" and "Lodestar"; fancy places with menus in French where dinner and a bottle of vino were the rough equivalent of the Gross National Product of Lithuania. Not to mention the lift tickets, which were thirty-five dollars a pop.

The Village Deli was located between Claude's Fur Boutique and a vacant storefront undergoing renovation—the windows were soaped and a bunch of carpenters were raising a racket in-side. It looked like a perfect place for a Rocky Mountain branch of Glick Investigations; the clientele was certainly made-to-order. I could already imagine some special marketing tie-ins: free half-day lift tickets with each missing-persons case; rental coupons with every stakeout. But a small sign on the door said the place was the future home of Alfredo's Nail Salon, so I put the idea on the back burner and walked next door.

The deli was packed, which was no surprise. Behind the counter a large blackboard listed sandwiches and salads, nothing over six dollars—the line of American Planners in blue jeans and rented skis stretched halfway to the fur shop. There were three girls working the shift, they were standard Sunburst issue: Colorado tans, sun-bleached hair tied in pony tails or bobbing just below the shoulders, luscious figures hidden under overalls and Village Deli smocks. And there was that perpetual smile: not the weather-beaten Northbrook Court "Have a nice day" crinkle, but an authentic "Howdy Pardner, how can you NOT be happy at 7,000 feet on a bright beautiful day with a foot of fresh powder" grin.

"What can I get you?" asked the first available angel—she looked to be the oldest of the three, which put her barely out of college.

"Sunburst SuperSub, hold the anchovies and pepperoni." I figured that would keep her busy for a few minutes and give me a chance to wedge in some questions. I tapped my silver money clip on the counter, while she moved a turkey breast onto the cutting board. "Excuse me, Beth—" That was her name, according to the tag embroidered on her smock. "—but I couldn't help noticing that you're just about the most gorgeous lookin' critter ever wandered this side of the Continental Divide."

Beth peeked up from a mean-looking carving knife. "Did you say mustard and mayo?" I could see by the sparkle in her eyes that I was still in touch with the Youth of America.

"The works. Sure are pretty earrings you got there. Turquoise?"

"Yep. Thanks." Beth smiled through a thin layer of pink lip gloss. It was all the makeup she needed.

"Say, Beth, I was wonderin'. I met a girl here, coupla months ago, said she was an artist. Nice-lookin' gal, honey-blond hair, gave me a few sample slides—"

"Wait'll you see this sub, now there's real artistry, pardner." Beth packed in some sliced tomatoes and Swiss cheese and reached for a layer of ham.

"The name's Murray. And I'm talking photography. This gal, her name was Danielle, she showed me a few slides from her portfolio. Took 'em back to Denver about a month ago to have my people look at 'em, they were pretty dang impressed—"

"Dani left," Beth said, as she slapped some turkey and cotto salami together and added a layer of mustard. "Did you say anchovie?"

"Well ain't that a shame? Listen, my people were knocked over by her stuff. I don't suppose you know where she's hidin' out these days?"

"Anchovie?" repeated Beth, and this time she spoke firmly and the sparkle was gone. "I'm sorry, sir, I don't know what happened to Dani. She just stopped working here; maybe she got a better job. She's been gone nearly a month."

"Well, have you seen her around the village?" I started to look at the crowd around me—they were beginning to shuffle their ski boots and stare at their wallets. "This is kind of important, Beth, she could get an exhibit."

Beth gripped her carving knife in her left hand and brought it down on the sub like a guillotine. She placed the two halves in a cardboard bottom, tossed in a pickle, and wrapped the whole thing in cellophane. "Look, I'm honestly sorry. No one's seen Dani for weeks. She must have left town. Try the Art Center; she used to work there nights." She rang up the cash register. "That'll be five-fifty. Can I get you anything else?"

I smiled and gave her a ten. "Maybe a drink after work?"

"I'm busy."

"Think it over." I pulled a napkin from the container and scribbled down my phone number at the condo.

Beth sighed, rang up the ten spot, and handed me my change. "Look, it's not even nine o'clock, you've got the whole day to hit on girls all over the mountain. Why spoil the suspense so early?"

"I feel much more secure if my day's planned by breakfast."

"Make a new plan, Stan."

"Murray."

"Hurry, Murray." Beth pushed the napkin back at me, but I folded it up, placed it in her palm, and closed her hand around it.

"Years from now you'll treasure this as a memento of our first meeting. Make it eight o'clock, dinner at the Lodestar—"

"Next!" said Beth, shoving my sandwich at me and stalking to the other end of the counter.

I gave her a wave and a big, broad cowboy smile. I turned and sauntered away, oblivious to the smirks I was getting from the other skiers who assumed I was getting shot down and didn't know how to recognize the nuances from a nervous chick that only a trained detective can pick up.

I walked out of the Village Deli and looked back over my shoulder; there she was, hands on her hips. She turned quickly to another customer, but I knew her eyes had followed me out the door.

And I knew she was going to hold on to that napkin. Pretty little Beth may have been on a Rocky Mountain High, but the name of Dani Kaplan had sobered her up pretty damned quickly. For Dani's sake, I knew I'd better find out why.

5

Sooner or later I was going to have to talk to Dani's boyfriend, but discretion was still the top priority, so I opted for a reconnaissance mission first. That entailed purchasing a lift ticket, getting an edge on my Rossignols, and leaping into a foot of fresh powder—some days you just can't get a break. I tightened my boots, snapped into my bindings, and went to work.

I glided over to a roped-off area about twenty yards from the triple-chair lift, where the ski school congregated. It was a Tuesday morning, the first week of March; the resort was booked solid. A couple of hundred people flocked around the small wooden signs stuck into the snow, numbered one to ten according to skiing ability. I modestly leaned my poles against number seven, then waited for a ski instructor to herd us up the hill.

The ski staff was clustered at the base of the chairlift. They all wore powder blue parkas with yellow sunbursts fashionably dipping over their right shoulders. They were eyeing the crowd, counting the people at each sign, and reporting to a tall guy with a reddish-brown beard. He playfully poked one of the male instructors in the ribs and grabbed his stocking cap, then fluffed it over the braids of one of the girls and put his arm around her. She didn't seem to mind. His parka was open—a tight gold turtleneck rippled over a set of deltoids that could have kept the chairlift turning by themselves, although I doubted that was the kind of work that Casey Wright did.

Wright looked more like a busy executive than a ski pro. He held a clipboard in his hand and barked out some instructions to the staff, while behind him a shorter man in a heavier parka and

corduroy slacks tugged at his sleeve. The shorter man was wearing moon boots and sipping on a cup of coffee. He looked like an
accountant-type; he whispered something more to Wright and
shuffled off in the snow. Wright shook his head, scanned his clipboard for a moment, then shouted out some final assignments to
the staff. As he skied off, I noticed that the braided girl plucked
the hat off and flipped it over to its rightful owner with a disgusted
look on her face. The clubbiness of the staff melted away. The
instructors peeled off to each group, collected our tickets, and sent
us up the bunny hill on the T-bar where they would evaluate and
split us into lesson units of eight to ten.

When I got to the top I did a few quick stretches and then
pushed off, carving a series of quick, perfectly formed parallel
turns on the way down. I felt a little guilty hitting Barbra Kaplan
up for a lesson, but I figured I hadn't skied all winter and even
the best can always pick up a pointer or two. As I glided to the
bottom, one of the instructors started to wave me off to a group
of eights that was a body short, but another instructor stopped
him. She was a cute redhead with a tassled yellow cap sticking
out of her open jacket. She whispered in his ear. He said something to her and she gave him a whack on the fanny; then she
waved her pole at me and signaled me over. I could tell we were
going to have a lasting relationship.

"Murray's the name," I said, gliding right to her ski tips and
dusting her lightly with powder. "I'm a diligent student when
not totally knocked over by the grace and splendor of a beautiful
woman." Normally I'd play harder to get, but the meter was
running and it wasn't my nickel.

"Nicely put," grinned the instructor, brushing the powder
from her parka. She turned to the rest of the group. "I'm Sara.
Stick with me, folks, we'll be acing the diamond slopes by lunch.
Let's boogie!"

"I'm forever yours," I whispered, and followed her to the
chairlift. We traded small talk as Sara alternated our class into
the crowded lift line; with a bit of finagling I managed to wait till
the others were gone, so we could ride the triple-chair up to the
top by ourselves.

Sara was from Bennington, Vermont—she'd skied locally there
all through her teens. She'd even taken a shot at the U.S. Ski
Team, but wasn't quite good enough to get a sponsor and didn't
have the money to keep after it on her own. She'd moved out to

Denver after high school, much to the displeasure of her parents. She'd waited tables there for a year, established residency, and enrolled at Boulder, where she'd majored in sociology and slalom skiing—she got her degree in the former and paid for it with the latter. She taught weekends at Arapahoe and Copper Mountain; when she graduated she tucked her degree away for safekeeping and tried unsuccessfully to join the ski staffs at Vail and Aspen. She hit Sunburst right at the beginning of one of their expansions and they offered her permanent employment.

"That was this fall?" I guessed, gazing at her ageless Sunburst complexion. Her cheeks reddened as our eyes met.

"Aw, ain't you sweet? It was five years ago. I'm twenty-seven."

"You're awfully well-preserved."

Sara laughed and pulled her stocking cap on. The chairlift had ground to a halt, leaving us creaking in the wind—probably some novice at the bottom slipping as the chair swung past him. "You looked pretty slick on your practice run, Murray. What do you want to work on today?"

"Beats me. Turns, maybe find some bumps. Get a nice tour of the mountain. The group looks pretty solid."

"Wait'll they hit Cherry Bowl." The lift squeaked and jerked, started running again, then stopped. "Ever skied here before?" Sara asked, grabbing my leg for balance.

"Once, years ago. Nixon was president."

"I think I read about him in history."

"Ouch."

Sara waved at another instructor who was zipping below us. "Get this crate moving!" she shouted, then turned back to me. "This was all National Forest then, this whole side of the mountain. Wish I'd been here. You could put on a backpack and disappear for days."

"Yep. And then the Lord spread the heavens and said, 'Let there be Condos. And He smiled and it was Good.' "

The chairlift started up again. "The Lord chooses funny messengers," Sara said, pointing off toward a ridge that was covered under the new snowfall. "They're talking about adding a whole new face, three more chairs, and a second gondola. Westin's going to build a resort down there, maybe Marriott, too."

"Maybe we should open up a real estate office, get in on the ground floor."

"Too late." Sara's laugh had a sardonic edge to it. "Way too late. Sunburst Corp owns it all; they'll start work as soon as the snow melts."

"No bargains for us little guys."

"Sorry. Should be lots of room for advancement in the ski school, though." The wind died down a little as our chair swung over the last ridge and headed for the drop-off. "So what do you do for a living, Murray?"

"I'm into travel and leisure."

"Rough life. Sounds like you really needed a vacation."

"No, really. I book cruises all over the world. Acapulco, Martinique, St. Croix. How'd you like to spend next Christmas in the Caribbean."

"Sorry, I work winters. Tips up!" she said, as we hopped off the lift and joined the group at the wooden trail markers a few yards below.

Sara led us all through some calisthenics; she stretched through them easily while the rest of us groaned and tried to keep our ligaments from ending up in Utah. She had us all introduce ourselves: I was surrounded by two commodities brokers from Des Plaines, a fashion designer from Manhattan, a couple of MBAs from St. Louis who hadn't got around to cashing in the sheepskin yet, and a pair of twelve-year-old twin sisters from Bloomfield, Michigan, who I had a sinking feeling would ski circles around everyone but Sara.

After a quick summary of the plans for the day, which mainly called for us to ski until we dropped, Sara tapped one of the hog traders on the butt and said, "Follow me." We were off, snaking behind her in a scraggly line, trying to duplicate her turns and her form, or in my case just admiring it. We attacked the intermediate slopes first. Most of us wanted to head in the direction of the black diamonds, the ski symbol for expert runs, but the Rockies are a different universe from the hills most of us had been skiing in Wisconsin and Michigan. It took most of the morning to adjust. We stopped whenever someone fell or when Sara detected a turn that wasn't quite right, but all in all the group was more than competent with the exception of the hog traders, who didn't look like they were ever going to get much better. Sara just smiled, encouraged them, and tried to keep them from breaking anything important.

When everyone had their snow legs pretty much under control we traversed over to Cherry Bowl, a wide, clear-cut basin filled with deceptively tricky moguls, which are not Hollywood producers but big bumps covered with snow, although I've heard the difference is arguable. Cherry Bowl's moguls were steep and close and hidden in the new-fallen powder like icebergs—one false step and you wouldn't be heard from until spring.

It took me a few wobbly swoops to get my rhythm right, but in all modesty I acquitted myself with my usual éclat. I skied better than everyone but the Bloomfield twins, toward whom I was developing a healthy hatred. The little squirts zipped in and out of the moguls like toy slot cars; in three hours on the mountain they hadn't even ticked an edge, skiing all the time in perfect symmetry, chasing down errant hats and ski poles for the rest of us adult-types each time we took a tumble.

Finally, out of consideration for my fellow classmates whom I sensed were tiring and needed a break, I staged a glorious wipe-out, catching an edge while flying over a mogul the size of the Astrodome. I flipped, spread-eagled, and came to a rest headfirst in a soft pile of snow.

"Looks like a good spot for lunch," said Sara, drifting over to me. She was followed by the twins, who had retrieved my hat and ski poles and one ski.

The group fanned out on the hillside, cordoning off my crash zone from the other skiers in the bowl; Sara planted her skis in a big cross to make it all the more obvious. We broke out our sandwiches and fruit and bottles of pop. The commodities boys had thoughtfully brought some cabernet and a bunch of plastic cups—they ate much better than they skied. They poured Sara and me a glass, then found a nice chaise mogul a few yards off, leaving me for a few more minutes alone with Teach.

"That was a magnificent belly flop," Sara said, munching on an apple. "You should get into free-style skiing."

"I think I'd prefer something a little safer, like hang gliding or solo rock climbing."

"I could give you a private lesson." Sara clinked her little plastic glass against mine and snuggled closer. I could feel her heart pounding beneath her parka. "It's easy once you master the technique—"

"Sara!" said one of the Bloomfield twins. They were named

Trish and Annie, and they had their names stiched on their ski jackets for the benefit of the general populace. This one was Annie; she came up to Sara and whispered shyly in her ear. "Can Trish and I ski Dragon's Head while you eat lunch?"

"No you can't ski Dragon's Head while we eat lunch."

"Why not!" squeaked Trish, who had tagged along.

"This is rest period."

"We're not tired!"

"Look, if you run away and disappear inside a big mogul then I'd have to call your mother all the way in Michigan—"

"We won't disappear, I promise!" said Annie. "Just let us do Dragon's Head and Fox Hunt and then we'll take the eight lift back to the top of Cherry Bowl—"

"Sit!" pronounced Sara. She grabbed Annie's pole and pulled the little girl down into her lap; Trish fell on her as if the two were attached, which I was beginning to suspect was true. They fell into a giggling fit, then stretched out in the snow with their heads in Sara's lap and pretended they were asleep.

"Looks like the end of our private lesson," I said, putting my mittens back on. I packed a little snowball; Annie immediately stole it out of my hand and fired it at one of the hog traders. Then she closed her eyes and snuggled between me and Sara as if nothing had happened.

"We'll see what we can arrange for later," Sara said. "I might be able to squeeze in a half-day Thursday."

"Actually, if you're busy, someone gave me the name of a guy, told me I shouldn't leave without spending a morning with him." Sara looked at me, her pretty mouth fell into a pout. "According to the people I borrowed my condo from, this guy's the greatest thing since shredded wheat. Course, now that I've met you—"

"Who is he?"

"Uh . . . some guy named White, I think. Casey White—"

"Casey WRIGHT?"

"Yeah, that's the guy."

Sara shot a look at me like I'd mentioned Colonel Qaddafi.

"Friend of yours?"

"Professional acquaintance. He's head of the ski school."

"No kidding. The tall guy with the beard?"

Sara nodded.

I took the last bite out of my sub sandwich and washed it down with some wine, then crinkled up the cellophane and stuck it in the glass. "Is he as good as everyone says?"

"Sure, just ask him."

"Right. I take it you're not a great admirer of Boss Casey."

"We get along."

"A solid professional relationship?"

"Let's just say I know how he operates—Hey!" Annie had sneaked a hand over Sara's jacket and tickled her in the belly, then quickly rolled back in the snow and closed her eyes. Sara flashed me an elfin grin, then rolled toward Annie. "Who-o-o's the culprit?" she hissed. She gave Annie a suspicious look, then turned around and tickled Trish, who gave Sara a belt in the tummy. A few seconds later the three of them were immersed in a giggling fit, rolling around in the snow. "All right, troops," Sara announced, suddenly jumping to her feet. "Break's over. Let's SKI!"

I pulled myself out of my snow hammock and snapped on my Rossis. I traded a furtive glance with Sara; we both knew there was a lot more to talk about but this wasn't the time.

As for the rest of the lesson, let me just say that I skied better than even I had a right to expect—inspired no doubt by my gorgeous teacher. I reached a glorious finish on the last run of the day. It was the back of Snow Leopard, a hellish concoction of moguls laid out on a drop about the angle of the Hancock Building. My legs were tired, but I picked out a perfect line, which coincidentally was almost exactly the line that Sara had taken. But, of course, I'm taller, and my legs are longer, so it wasn't quite the same—if it was that easy the Bloomfield twins wouldn't have caught their edges on the same bump and somersaulted halfway down to the bottom of the hill. It was a tough break, but they're young and resilient. I fetched their hats.

We split up at about four. The hog traders wanted to buy everyone a drink afterwards, but I had a few more errands to run—in my line of work when you're on assignment, your day never ends. I pulled Sara aside; I only had a few seconds before the twins stole her away. "We still on for a private lesson, coach?"

"Sure. But I've got this group again tomorrow. You coming back?"

"Hard to say. I've got a tough schedule."

"More cruises to arrange?"

"It's a brutal business, you wouldn't believe it."

"Probably not."

"Look, how about dinner tomorrow night? We'll discuss all those new techniques of yours so I'll be prepared the next morning."

"Hey, Sara, let's go!" shouted one of the hog traders. He'd already gotten a head start with a bottle of Coors. "Clark's got a table at Hermit's—"

"I'll be right there," Sara shouted, then turned to me. "Okay, Murray, you're on. Tomorrow night, eight o'clock. Meet you at the clocktower."

"Where'll we eat?"

"You're the cruise director." Sara swatted me on the behind with her skis, then slung them over her shoulder. "Don't be late," she shouted as she disappeared into the crowd.

"Not a chance," I shouted back, waving goodbye. "Be good!"

I unsnapped my boots and headed for my most important errand, which happened to be a rendezvous with the Jacuzzi outside the condo. Not that I wasn't in sterling shape for a thirty-five-year-old in my profession. I just figured that I had Sara and Beth to contend with now, as well as Casey Wright and a missing teenager. It was no time for carelessness.

When you depend on your body as a deadly weapon, you'd better make sure the moving parts are all in working order.

6

Two cold hands wrapped around my throat, eight gnarled fingers pressed against the front of my neck and dug into my windpipe. I sat perfectly still, staring into the Jacuzzi jets, wondering if they'd stop in time for me to pick up a faint reflection off the water before I toppled in. When all's said and done, the only thing a detective asks is to know who killed him.

I took a deep breath, a couple of seconds was all I had—maybe time enough to test his grip or reach backwards for a quick toss. Something told me that would only make those hands tighten. I hyperventilated. I dug my hands into the side of the spa.

"Hell's bells!" I heard a voice say, as I readied my elbow for a shot to the gut. "I was wondering who was runnin' that thing all afternoon. Dang, Murray you stay in there much longer, you'll have more wrinkles'n my Aunt Bess." I turned around slowly as J. B. Cranston lowered his hands and gave me a quick neck massage. "Course that was before she up and got that surgery."

"Your Aunt Bess had cosmetic surgery?" I took another deep breath and let it out slowly, trying not to let J.B. know how close he'd come to buying the condo.

"Damn near made me drop. This Dr. Feingold fella, moves in from Los Angeles, sets up shop kitty-corner from the mink store, right there in the village."

"No kidding. I was down there today, I must have missed it."

"You musta been at the other mink store. Hell, we got three of 'em now, prob'ly be three Feingolds before too long. Anyway, he had an introductory offer and my Aunt Bess, sixty years old, never wore a lick of makeup in thirty years, decides to give it a whirl.''

"Well good for her, J.B. How'd it work out?"

"Took ten years off her face." Cranston thumped me on the back. "Now she looks fifty, helluva lotta good that'll do her. C'mon Murray, get yer ass outta there, 'fore it turns into a stewed tomato. You eat dinner yet?"

"Not exactly—"

"Great! Betty's fryin' up some chicken—we'll raid the hen-house for you."

"Don't sacrifice your poultry for me—"

"C'mon, git!"

Truth was, I'd have happily stayed in the Jacuzzi another hour and taken the chance that a fried chicken might eventually fall down from heaven, but I figured I'd better get out of there pronto before J.B. yanked me out by the gizzard.

"There you go, pardner," he said, tossing me a towel as I swung my legs back onto the deck. The cool air closed the pores and sent a chill up my spine. "Get some clothes on, meet us upstairs in twenty minutes. Don't bother knockin', just walk right in!"

I hopped along the shovelled path that led to the back steps of the condo, let myself in, and took a quick shower. I considered sampling Barbra's Scotch before plunging into dinner with J.B. and Betty, but I figured he'd have plenty to offer. Besides, I had a few things to discuss with him before I got too sloshed.

The Cranstons' condo was laid out exactly like Barbra's, the appliances and light fixtures appeared to have all come from the same warehouse. The motif, though, was distinctly Western. J.B. was a cowboy art connoisseur. There was a collection of bronze Remington sculptures scattered around: broncos and Indian warriors flanked the fireplace, a cowboy roping a steer was mounted on a pedestal in the middle of the living room—I'd seen one like it on exhibit at the mall for $3,500. There was an oil painting over the mantel; I didn't even want to speculate what that was worth.

Betty Cranston made a brief appearance when I came in; she was a tall, handsome woman with a slim frame and graying blond hair. She wore jeans and a checkered blouse with an apron over it. She was shaking up a fried-chicken recipe—I could see the various ingredients laid out on the counter along with two fryers cut up and spread out on some paper towels. She said hello and flashed me a coy smile, then returned to the kitchenette while J.B. and I sunk into a leather sofa and worked on lowering the sea level of a bottle of Jack Daniel's.

"So you're out hustlin' them ski gals already," chortled J.B. after I told him about my afternoon with Sara. "Damn, Murray, you may HAVE to stay here."

"Easy, J.B. Just an innocent flirtation."

"That's what they all say. That's what Barbie said when your little cousin started foolin' around with that ski teacher of hers."

"Murray," shouted Betty from over a bowl of bread crumbs, "did you see our Dani? We haven't heard from that girl in weeks."

" 'Fraid not, Betty. I went down to the deli and they told me she split town a month ago."

"Dani left town?" Betty walked over and rested her arms on J.B.'s shoulders. "Well that's news. What about that feller of hers?"

"I do believe she left him behind."

"Smartest thing she ever did," snorted J.B. "Not that I wouldn't mind seein' him clear his butt off the mountain, too. I tell ya, I don't much care for the way Sam handled things, but that boy was no good from the gitgo."

"He's head of the ski school," I said. "Seems to be making his way in the world."

"Hell, I don't give a damn if he's the goddamn King of Egypt. You know what he saw in your cousin Dani, don't ya?"

"She's kinda cute—"

"Cute? There's cute gals poppin' outta every gopher hole on this mountain and Casey Wright knows half of 'em. Hell, Murray, you ain't been here twenty-four hours, already you got 'em lined up."

"It's just one date." I looked up at Betty, who winked at me and refilled my whiskey glass, then excused herself and went back to her chicken batter. "So what did Casey Wright see in my darling cousin—"

"Dollar signs, boy! Her daddy's vice-president of Kozlo Realty, they own half of Chicago."

I sunk back in the sofa and took a snort of Uncle Jack. Sam's profession was hardly a scoop. Barbra had told me he worked for Kozlo and I knew their realty management signs were plastered all over the Loop, not to mention apartment buildings on the Near North and condo villages from Northbrook to Schaumburg. But Kozlo was local, their talons didn't extend much past Milwaukee and Rockford. I couldn't figure out what potential a ski instructor from Sunburst saw in a mid-level veep who spent most of his time shuttling between the North Shore and LaSalle Street.

"Hell, Murray," J.B. explained, reaching over to a leather ice bucket and dropping a few ice cubes in his whiskey glass, "this whole mountain's one big hustle. They got plans to build a brand new ski area on the other side of the hill—construction's s'posed to start this June. Whattaya think they're financing it with, Israel bonds?"

"I thought Sunburst Corp owned the whole thing."

"Sure they do. But they needed investors. Now the Kaplans've had this condo three years, you think Sam doesn't know what's cookin' out here, and they don't know Sam?"

I emptied down my whiskey and set the glass on the coffee table. "All right. So Sam was point man for a potential Kozlo buy-in?"

"They sure hoped so. You gotta understand, Murray, it's a small town. Casey Wright's a risin' young employee of the Sunburst Ski School, he hangs out at the same waterin' holes as his bosses. He figures Dani Kaplan might be his ticket to an executive position on the other side of the hill—" J.B. stopped and let out a wild cough. He got up and opened the patio door a crack, then walked over to the kitchen and dipped his finger in the batter. "Mmm, mm. Perfect, honey."

" 'Bout ready to fry," Betty announced. "Murray, would you like another drink?"

I was getting a little punchy, but it was a short walk home. I held out my glass and let J.B. fill it up, then leaned back into the sofa. "So Sam didn't cotton to the idea of Casey Wright as a future son-in-law?"

"Bet yer sweet ass he didn't. Tried to scream some sense into his girl—you can imagine how much good that did. Hell, we got two daughters of our own; we're experts on that, ain't we, Betty? One word from us, they do whatever the hell they want." J.B. pulled out his wallet and showed me a picture of a baby being

held by its mother. "Our Bobbi sure did us proud, though. Loo-
kee here, Murray, that's my grandson, three years old next week!
Future president of Sunburst Corp."

Betty cringed in the kitchen as she smacked a couple of chicken
legs onto a skillet.

"What? I'm a great judge of talent. Just look at those eyes!
Wouldn't you trust your escrow money to those eyes?"

"Let me know when he starts work," I said. "Maybe I'll be
ready for that chalet." I grabbed a handful of cashews from a
bowl on the coffee table. "Anyway, J.B., I take it Casey Wright
wasn't always destined to be head of the ski school?"

J.B. put the baby picture back in his wallet. "Hardly. That
happened after Dani moved out here to live with him. Sunburst
figured he was bound for greatness, might as well move him up
the ladder. Damned if he wasn't buckin' for the front office before
the first snowflake hit the ground."

"But they couldn't have been getting any encouragement from
Sam Kaplan—"

"None at all. Sam called 'em up, made things clear about
that."

"So why didn't Sunburst just bust him down to buck private,
tell him to lose Dani or else?"

J.B. stood up and stretched his arms; he walked back to the
kitchen and helped Betty spoon out some salad. "Naw, Murray,
you got it all wrong. See, Casey Wright's a smooth talker. And
them cowboys on the board kinda admire a mountain boy who'll
take on the city folks. Casey says, 'Relax fellas! Sam's daughter
is in love with yours truly—they'll get used to me by and by.
They ain't gonna cut off their little girl forever.' "

I nodded silently. Maybe Wright was a shameless weasel, but
at least he was scientific about it. "So Casey settles in for a war
of attrition. He sets up his love nest with Dani and starts trying
to work his way from the slopes to the boardroom."

"Damn snake's been callin' my office twice a week. He's tryin'
to get his hand in some of the lots we got slated for development."

"You've talked to him, then?"

"Hell no!" coughed J.B. "I told my secretary to get rid of
him. He may be able to bullshit them Brooks Brothers cowboys,
but he ain't settin' a foot inside Sunburst Corp, not even a baby
toe." J.B. swallowed his whiskey and slapped the glass down with

a force that nearly shattered it. "Now that our Dani's done run off on him, maybe he'll stick to his ski lessons—he'll be lucky if they still let him do that."

"Oh, the boy'll probably just go off and find himself another rich girlfriend," said Betty, finishing up the fried chicken. "Murray, did Dani go back home?"

"I don't rightly know where she went," I answered; this Western-speak was getting contagious. "Far as I can see, she didn't leave word with anybody."

"Well I'm sure she'll be fine. She's a sweet girl, everyone should be allowed to go off the deep end once or twice a lifetime."

"Amen to that," I said. I wasn't sure, but I thought I heard my telephone ringing downstairs. I tried to concentrate through the crackle of frying chicken and the whiskey haze; sure enough, it was the phone, it rang five times and then stopped.

"Must be your sweetie pie," said J.B., reading my mind. "That's okay, just let it ring. Make her think you're out for the evening. Makes her that much more eager to see you the next time."

"J.B., you're as bad as that Casey fella," Betty said, loading the fried chicken up on a platter.

"Now that ain't true, Betty. Your family didn't have a red cent when we met. I married you purely out of love and beauty and that magic fryin' pan of yours."

"Brains and devotion had nothin' to do with it?"

"One helluva bonus, sweetheart. Turns out I was a lucky fella."

"I'll say." Betty turned her back to him and drained off a batch of cottage fries. They continued their banter as Betty set dinner in front of us, but I artfully avoided taking sides. Still, I couldn't help wondering if Cranston and Casey Wright didn't have a lot more in common than J.B. let on. They were both making a living off the mountain; maybe the only thing separating them was opportunity.

No, I decided, after a moment's reflection, that wasn't all. There was a sense of honor, which I assumed J.B. had and Casey never knew he missed. My gut instinct told me that if I was picking sides, I wanted to be on J.B.'s.

If there was any doubt, it disappeared after tasting his wife's fried chicken—it was so mouth-watering it'd make the Colonel toss in his herbs and spices and open up a tofu stand in Santa Barbara. The muffins were exquisite, the cottage fries deliciously crisp. How could a kidnapper possibly be married to such a wonderful cook?

Maybe that was a rush to judgment. Call it a hunch, call me old fashioned. But after eight years in the business, you learn to pick up certain signals of honesty and integrity. Sometimes a hot meal and a tender smile can tell even the toughest detective all he needs to know.

And sometimes not.

7

I didn't realize the Kaplans had an answering machine until the next morning. I was stumbling bleary-eyed around the kitchen, searching for some tomato juice to pollinate my vodka with when I saw the little red light blinking at me. I thought it might be some type of electronic hangover detector, picking up ions generated by too much whiskey, beer, and fried chicken, then automatically dispensing coffee and Bufferin. It turned out to be a Panasonic filled with dial tones and a brief message from Beth, telling me in a tentative, vulnerable near-whisper to meet her at the Sunburst Art Center at five o'clock to discuss the latest trends in photography.

I found the tomato juice and pushed some rye bread into the toaster. I wondered if Beth had suddenly found Dani's forwarding address stuck at the bottom of a desk drawer—or maybe she was just feeling lonely on a Tuesday night. In any case, I had a dinner date with Sara at eight o'clock. Beth had played hard to get; she'd have to wait her turn.

When I'd finished my toast, coffee, and OJ, I popped down an extra dose of vitamin C; I could tell it was going to be a busy day. I was hoping that the bloody Mary and a cold shower would kill off the hangover—I'd heard J. B. Cranston roaring off to work an hour ago, so obviously it wasn't terminal. Still, in the interest of personal maintenance and professional responsibility, I decided to limit myself to a half-day's skiing. The lift ticket began at twelve-thirty; that gave me three hours to unlimber my legs, unfog my brain, and buttonhole a slick, young, upwardly mobile ski operator named Casey Wright.

I figured Wright would be prowling around his office by ten o'clock. He'd have dispatched his ski instructors and would be busy trying to impress his superiors that he was executive fast-track material. Fortunately, I had enough working brain cells by then to form a caucus. I pulled on my cowboy boots, grabbed my portable cassette recorder, and tramped over to the village.

The ski school headquarters was located on the bottom floor of the Clocktower, across from the gondola. Most of the administrative work was handled in a large office separated into cubicles by a maze of dividers. The walls were light blue with the Sunburst logo peeking through. Ski posters were hanging behind almost every desk, illuminated by bright mountain light that streamed through the windows. The place was nearly empty—most of the instructors were off leading classes—but a small reservations staff was taking calls for group and private lessons.

When I asked for Casey Wright, I was pointed to a closed door at the back of the room. There was a secretary outside. She looked distinctly older than the ski-bunny crowd—she must have been at least thirty. Her blond hair was cut short, in a page-boy style. She wore pale red lipstick and was dressed smartly in a turtleneck sweater and slacks. She looked perfectly capable of running the ski school while Casey concentrated on getting his picture in the annual report.

I pulled out a cigar, stuck it in my mouth unlit, and slid into my office-crashing routine, a staple in the Glick method-acting school of detection. Hair slightly astray, shirt loose just a tad at the belt, clutching a cup of coffee and glancing at the clock on the wall, I came to a rolling stop at her desk. I announced I was Murray Sanders, from *American Southwest* magazine, here for the interview.

"Excuse me?" The secretary referred to an appointment book, but I kept walking toward the door. "Sir, wait—I don't have anything here, let me at least buzz Mr. Wright."

I paused and slurped on my coffee. "I phoned in yesterday. Look, I gotta be in Steamboat for dinner, I gotta whole series on ski areas, no time to hang around—"

"Steamboat?" Almost as if on cue, she broke into a broad chamber of commerce smile. "Forget Steamboat, Mr. Sanders, we've got everything you need right here. Mr. Wright," she said into her intercom, "there's a Mr. Sanders here to see you. He's here for the magazine article . . ." She winked at me. "On the various Colorado ski areas . . ." The door swung open. Casey Wright stood there in his ski bib, one suspender flopped over his shoulder, a harried look on his face.

"Casey, pleased t'meet ya," I said, slapping him on the back and ambling into his office. "Murray Sanders, *American Southwest.*" I slammed the door behind me. The office was plastered with photographs, most of them of Casey Wright in his ski getup, posing with people I vaguely recognized from old covers of *People* magazine. "Pretty fancy place ya got here, Case. Ski instructor to the stars!" I noticed a few politicians sprinkled in; I thought I saw Kathleen Turner peeking from behind a pair of goggles. "Maybe I should hang around for a while, pick up a few of your loose starlets."

"I'm afraid I haven't had much time for the ladies these days," Wright said, straightening his suspender. "We're expanding; not enough hours in the day—"

"True dedication, Case, I don't find much of that in today's business world. And I've covered every angle from the Divide on out—"

Wright aimed a sharp glance my way and showed me to a seat beside his desk. He rubbed his beard and did his best to look corporate, but what I saw was a twenty-eight-year-old kid with a false air of self-assurance. "Where did you say you came from, Mr. . . ."

"Sanders. Murray Sanders, *American Southwest.* Business and financial, we're THE book for entrepreneurs in the Southwest. Gotta cover story on Jack Webber over at Taos next month; Jack says we oughtta be talkin' to you boys—stole the World Cup right out of his pocket."

"We didn't steal it," Wright said with a trace of indignation. "We have the most attractive setup on the tour. The best course in North America, the finest accommodations, same-day network coverage, corporate sponsorship."

"Well by God, Casey, you really put together a helluva package. I sure would like to hear all about it." I turned on my cassette recorder and leaned back in the chair. "Now, I understand you're coordinating this entire event?"

Casey cleared his throat. "Uh, technically, no." He leaned over the desk. "I'm head of the ski school. Technically. But I'm running the whole thing, de facto."

I raised my eyebrows. "Is that right?"

"Look, Dave Rydell's got the title, but he's not a ski person, understand? He's a bean counter."

"Of course. Pays the bills, makes sure the trams run on time. But someone's got to run the show."

"Exactly. Honestly, Murray, I've been working twenty hours a day, trying to keep the ski school functioning. Seeing that the race is set up right, getting the TV people set. Camera positions, gate settings, seedings."

I looked at Casey's eyes; they were bloodshot. Strain can do that to you, among other things. "All left up to you?"

"I do it gladly, Murray. I volunteered. I wouldn't LET anyone else do it." Wright got up and moved behind me. He wrapped an arm around my shoulder, I could feel the strength rippling through his shirt. "And you know why, Murray?"

"I can guess, but I'd prefer you tell me in your own words."

"Because I love this damned mountain. I grew up on this hill, Murray. I skied it when it was just a run-down, two-chair mudslide—we had to BEG people to ski here."

I hunched forward, searching Casey's face for some sign that would dispel his finely honed image of sincerity; I couldn't find any. "Casey, my publishers marvel at what you've done here in just a few short years—"

"You don't even know the half of it. Take a look." Wright led me over to a large relief map of the mountain. It detailed the myriad of ski runs and the village below, as well as the west side of Sunburst, with several dotted lines indicating where the expansion was going to take place. "Here it is: Sunburst Mountain, 1992—" The phone rang and Wright picked it up, barking some orders into it as I walked over and looked at the map. The proposed runs on the west side of the mountain would nearly double the size of the resort; in fact, it would really be two resorts, according to what J. B. Cranston had told me last night, with separate lift tickets and a whole new village.

"Listen, Murray," Casey said, placing the phone down hard on the receiver. "I don't mean to be rude. I've got producers from CBS here in twenty minutes. I don't get over there, Dave Rydell'll have 'em airlifting cameras to the back bowls, probably have 'em spending a hundred grand on deer and chipmunks."

"I understand, Case. Just a few more minutes—" .

"You want a story, this is it: two years from now, Sunburst'll be THE premier resort in North America. It'll make Aspen look like a state fair. Here . . ." He gave me a pocket-sized map of the proposed expansion. "Take a look at this." He lowered his voice. "Just do me a favor. People get a little sensitive—I'm head of the ski school, that's all. Hopefully, by the time you print your story, things'll change. For now, deep background—I'm a spokesman, got it?"

"Absolutely, Casey." I stood up and paced around the room, trying to think of some reason to extend my stay. A young girl was missing, days were slipping by. And Casey Wright had to know something. "Hey, is that Penny Mallory?" I asked, looking at a group picture in the corner. "I saw her movie, the one where she's on the run in Mexico—"

"Yeah, yeah. And that's her husband, right next to her. Bigshot producer, used to do her hair. Gave 'em lessons in December."

"Any good?"

"She is. He's a total clod."

"Figures. Who's the babe with you? That her sister?"

"No such luck. Just one of the local girls, wanted to meet a movie star." Wright looked slightly aggravated. "Don't know how she got in that one," he mumbled.

"Jeez, Casey, bet ya got so many ya don't know what to do with 'em—"

"Not by a long shot." Wright stroked his beard again and showed me to the door. "Now I really do have to run. It was nice talking to you, Mr. Sanders—"

"Course, now that you're a risin' young honcho, you might have to grab one of 'em and settle down."

"Fat chance." Casey led me out of the office. "Good-bye, Mr. Sanders. I'll look for your article."

"Been a pleasure, Mr. Wright."

Casey grinned, I could tell he liked being addressed as Mr. Wright. He closed the door halfway behind me and walked back to grab a parka from his closet. I waved goodbye and winked at the secretary; she was busy stacking up a pile of brochures, but she saw me and waved her long red nails my way. I strolled over to flirt for a moment—my dance card was full, but nature does take its course, and who am I to fight it? We were discussing the wine list at the Italian bistro next door when I noticed Casey, on his way out, walk back to his wall of pictures. He took a deep breath and lifted one photograph from the wall. He stuck it in his desk drawer, then headed out the door.

I didn't have to go back and look to tell which picture had been banished from the gallery. It was the one of Penny Mallory and her husband, the klutzy producer. And Casey Wright. And Dani Kaplan.

8

That afternoon I skied off alone, trying to find a few untrammeled patches of yesterday's magic. The temperature had risen into the forties; the powder had been skied over, groomed by snowcats, or just thawed and refrozen into corn snow. I picked a few runs at the outer reaches of the ski area and glided among the fir trees, making neat turns around stumps and boulders. A ski patroller watched me as I skirted the boundaries, but I stayed out of un-charted—and uninsured—territory, so he left me alone.

It occurred to me that in only a couple of days I had spread myself dangerously thin, with only a few vague conclusions to show for it: Beth from the deli and Casey Wright both had a bug up their ass about Dani Kaplan; Sara and J. B. Cranston had a mutual distaste for Casey Wright. Worse, I was losing track of my various identities—in a burg like this it was only a matter of time before one of them came back and bit me.

I skied off into a little meadow on the back side of a run called Honey Bear; it rose to a ridge that overlooked the west side of the mountain. Across the ridge were acres and acres of firs, a lush green canopy frosted with snow, framed by a deep blue sky. I looked back at Sunburst Mountain and tried to superimpose the machine-groomed slopes, multiple chairlifts, and hordes of skiers onto the western ridge. It was going to be one hell of an under-taking, but I had problems of my own to consider.

Specifically, I needed someone to help me with my legwork—someone who had an official function at the mountain and would have access to Sunburst officials, particularly Casey Wright. I knew who that someone was, and I knew he wasn't going to like it, but what the hell—what are friends for?

CBS was covering the World Cup Race and my buddy Andy Sussman was one of their top play-by-play men. Andy was a basketball junkie at the height of his season. It had taken him two years to get the game-of-the-week assignment and it wasn't going to be easy pulling him away from the Boston Garden to cover a ski race—his idea of winter recreation was a fireplace and a back-rub.

But he owed me: I'd bailed him out twice. It was only a year ago that I'd solved the Dr. Double-X wrestling caper, otherwise he'd be back doing "Celebrity Schlock Sweepstakes" on Sunday mornings. Hell, I'd even stood up at his wedding, a ceremony I've gone to some trouble to avoid over the years. And I happened to know that his lovely wife, Susie, who goes to incredible lengths to hide her deep-seated affection for me, is an ace skier who'd be happy to get away from New York for a week, especially a week in Sunburst, even if it meant staying under the same roof with yours truly.

I resolved to call Andy as soon as I got off the hill—or better yet later on in the evening when it would be, say, midnight on the East Coast and he could better appreciate the urgency of the situation. In the meantime, the shadows were starting to crawl over the mountain. A chill was beginning to set in. It was four o'clock, which left me just enough time to take a dashing run down Honey Bear, change into my après-ski togs, and prepare for an artistic rendezvous with Beth.

9

Andy Sussman listened to the phone ring once, twice, three times. No, it can't be, he thought. Good timing had always been one of Murray's strengths, but telepathy was surely beyond him—in real life, anyway. On the fourth ring the answering machine took over. Andy sipped on his Irish coffee, listened to his pre-recorded voice warding off whoever was on the other end, then waited to see if it was anything urgent.

"Andy! Get out of the rack, will you? It's important."

"Whups." It was Susie. Sussman stumbled out of his easy chair and picked up the phone. "Hiya, babe. I just got in."

"I'll bet. Out there shoveling the driveway?"

"Umm . . ." Sussman glanced out the window. It was still snowing. With any luck, the kid next door would come by after school and do the job before his wife got home. "Well, no. I was reading, actually."

"Good for you! Did you finally start *Love in the Time of Cholera?* Our group's discussing it next Tuesday."

"Nope." Sussman didn't want to lie about that one either, because if he claimed to have read the book, he might actually have to go to the discussion group. He had been to three of them already this winter; it was sort of like being in school again, except that it was difficult to fall asleep or read the sports section in someone else's living room. "It's, umm . . . one of those mystery novels."

Andy thought he heard a disgusted sigh on the other end. "Oh. Well, Professor Bonner keeps telling us there's a few of them around worth reading. Who's it by? P. D. James? Hillerman?"

"Some new guy. You've never heard of him."

"Is it any good?"

"Well, I'd say it's somewhat autobiographical—which you'd expect for a first novel. The author's definitely, um . . . full of himself. Perhaps slightly overdependent on the use of metaphor. But he seems to have found his voice after the first few chapters."

"Boy oh boy. Wait'll I tell Professor Bonner he's turning my husband into a literary critic."

"I'm sure he'd be proud. Hey, it's about skiing, you'd probably like it." Sussman regretted saying that almost instantly.

"Good! I can't wait to read it. Listen, about the contract: CBS wants a two-year no-jump clause with the other networks."

Sussman groaned.

"Well, since NBC has pro basketball next year, they naturally figure there'd be some temptation for you to go over there."

"They're right."

"Andy, this is a solid offer. You're guaranteed the NCAA tournament: play-by-play through the regionals, and one semifinal. Plus the back-up game on major league baseball. And—listen to this—you'll be anchoring an event at the Winter Olympics in Albertville. Three nights of prime time—"

"Did I get ice hockey?"

"Sorry. I think they mentioned something about bobsledding."

"Wonderful."

"C'mon! It's a great package, NBC couldn't match it if they wanted to."

"The numbers are okay?"

"Haven't changed. Andy, it's too good a deal to pass up."

Sussman finished his coffee. He had been trying not to think about the fact that his pro-basketball assignment was in its last few months. It was his first love, and the idea of switching networks had been in the back of his mind since the NBA's new deal had been announced. But life for Andy was different now. He was married. There was a mortgage. Hopefully a child, somewhere along the way. And who knew if NBC was even interested in him?

"Take it, Suse."

"Good. I'll try and close this afternoon. Why don't you stop over at Friesen's and get a couple of tenderloins; we can have a nice celebration tonight."

"Do they deliver?"

"Do they DELIVER? They're a butcher shop."

"Well, it's snowing." There was a long silence at the other end of the line, which Sussman interpreted as a complete lack of sympathy. "It's just that I'm so engrossed in my book, Susan. Now that I have this literary background, I read much more carefully."

"Fine. I'll bring home a pizza."

"Great. I've got some carefully aged bottles of Heineken's. It'll be nice and cozy."

"I'm sure. Oh, and don't forget to call the travel agent, Andy. Make sure they got the tickets for going to see Carol—"

"Will do. Hey, Suse?"

"What?"

"Did I get any, um . . . phone calls while I was in LA?"

"No . . . unless you want to count my mother. Who were you expecting?"

"Well . . . possibly an old friend, trying to get in touch. What about the week before, in Denver?"

"Sorry. Wouldn't they know you were doing the game?"

"Right. Of course."

"Go back to your novel."

"Thank you. So long, sweetheart."

"G'bye. I love you."

"I love you too, darling."

Andy hung up the phone. He walked into the kitchen and poured himself a fresh cup of coffee, then returned to the den and picked up the second part of the manuscript. There were only sixty pages left—it didn't seem long enough for Murray to solve much of anything.

Why hadn't he called? Andy wondered. And why had this Cranston guy sent him the manuscript?

Sussman started to pour a few more drops of Jack Daniel's in his coffee, but he held back. He was starting to feel woozy. He couldn't remember which babe Murray had been chasing before the interruption. Not that he ever could.

He capped the whiskey. He settled back in his easy chair and returned to the manuscript. He had a nasty feeling that he was going to have to start paying closer attention.

10

I found her standing at the back of the gallery, the edges of her sandy-brown hair illuminated like a nimbus by the track lights. She was staring at a Galen Rowell photograph of Half Dome, bathed in the soft Sierra twilight—she stood so still she seemed part of the exhibit. The entire rear wall was devoted to Rowell. The rest of the gallery consisted of oils and watercolors, most of them with naturalist themes. There was a stairway leading to a basement, where there were more paintings and an exhibit of Hopi tapestries and jewelry.

"Rowell does have a touch with light and shadow," I said, surprising Beth as I sidled next to her. She jumped backwards for an instant, then turned around and brushed her hair away from her eyes. "Where did you come from?"

"I crept up on little cat's feet."

"You're pretty good at that," she said, her pink lips moist and quivering.

"Just a habit I picked up, spending so much time in galleries." I took a brief look at the Rowell collection. The photographs were all of the High Sierra: El Capitan, Tuolumne Meadows, the Alabama Hills. "We have a collection of his Himalayan work lined up for next August—he's supposed to give a lecture at the opening."

"Actually, I prefer black and white." Beth walked toward the oil paintings. "I like the texture, the drama. You can inject more of your personality into a black-and-white image."

"I used to think that," I said. "Given the chance, I'd show Ansel Adams prints all year long."

"Or Edward Weston. Or Stieglitz."

"But, as an exhibitor, I've got to say that color has a broader appeal."

"And what exactly does that mean?" Beth rested her hands on the pockets of her denim skirt. She wore a bright yellow V-necked sweater over a peach knit Polo shirt. Her face was tan; I thought she was a great argument for colors.

"Visitor appeal. Patron appeal."

"I thought we were talking about art."

"We are. But art's defined by those willing to support it. Far be it from me to tell young photographers what medium to use; but if you want to be pragmatic, if you want to get published—"

"Well we CERTAINLY want to be pragmatic—that's why we get involved with art in the first place, isn't it?" Beth drew her pretty lips into a pout and lowered her eyebrows.

"Some of us have to consider those things. Those of us who make a living at it."

"Dani Kaplan wasn't making a living at it."

Two elderly ladies walked over to us and started chatting about the paintings, a series of birches and birds set against an icy stream. I put my arm around Beth's waist. I could feel the suppleness of her hips, I could sense the ferocity of a friendship between two young girls. I pulled her back toward the photographs. "Beth, we happen to think Dani has potential."

"She'll be very pleased to hear that."

"I'd be very pleased to tell her." Beth turned away from me and wandered toward the stairway. She walked downstairs, toward the tapestries, and I followed her. "I'm just having this gosh-darned awful time setting up a meeting."

"Artists have that mysterious air about them."

"Especially this one." I grabbed Beth by the hand. "Why the black veil? Her phone's disconnected. Her friends tell me they don't know where she went. The guy she lived with pretends he never heard of her."

"You talked to Casey Wright?"

"He gave me thirty seconds of his time."

"More than he's worth."

"Look, Beth . . ." I turned around to see whether anyone else was around. There were a few stragglers looking at the jewelry,

wandering toward us. I took Beth's arm again and led her to the
far end of the room. "Sweetheart, I'm just trying to talk to her.
I've seen samples of her work. I like it. I want to see more."

"She's never heard of you."

"Maybe she forgot—"

"She didn't."

"Beth, it's possible there's been a misunder—"

"There's been no misunderstanding. She's never heard of any
Murray Solomon. She never sent any samples to anyone in Denver."

I took a deep breath. For the first time since I'd been here, I
knew that Dani Kaplan was alive; but if I didn't play my cards
right, my only contact with her was going to walk out of my life.
"Beth, listen to me—"

"Dani's out of the art business," Beth said, firmly taking my
hand and shoving it away. "And she most certainly does NOT
want to see anyone sent here by her father—"

"Her father? That's ridiculous—"

"Who is staying at her father's condominium, using her father's phone number."

I could have protested at that point. I could have slapped my
forehead and explained what a remarkable coincidence it was that
a gallery representative from Denver, in town to locate Dani Kaplan, would rent a condo that just happened to belong to her parents. But judging from the look on Beth's face, it would have
been a waste of a wonderful piece of fiction. "Beth," I said, "I
think you and I need some more time together."

"We most certainly don't."

"How about drinks and dancing tomorrow night at Hermit's?
It'll put us both in a better frame of mind." I slid my arm around
her shoulder. "You know, darling, I watched you put together
that tasty sub yesterday. Don't think I didn't notice the smile.
The wink. The extra layer of ham—"

"Fuck OFF," Beth whispered.

"You're cute when you're feisty." I held Beth by both arms.
Her face was turning flush red, but her gaze was fixed on my
crinkled smile and steely blue eyes; all she could muster was a
trenchant sigh.

"Murray, will you please let go of me?" she said, her hands
clinging to my waist, her breath hot against my neck.

"Look at me, Beth. Do I look like a nasty person?"

"I know who sent you."

"Sorry to disappoint. I don't work for Dani's father."

"I don't care who you work for." Beth sniffled back a nervous cry. "Look, Murray—or whoever you are. I don't believe a single damn thing you say."

"Not a thing? Not even if I told you I was madly in love with you and want to run off to Tahiti with you this weekend?"

"Cut it out." Beth was blushing. "How stupid do you think I am?"

"Oh, I think you're a smashing, sensuous genius." I glanced at my watch. "Trouble is, I've got to run—would you believe I've got a date for dinner?"

"That I'd believe."

"It's only because you play so hard to get."

"I'm sure."

"I'll be thinking of you, Beth. I'll be craving for you."

"Take a cold shower."

"How about a Jacuzzi? With a bubble bath?"

Beth threw her arms down and started to slap me, but it was a soft slap. She shook the bangs from her eyes and stared at me; I knew she was at that thin line between whacking me one and leaping into my arms.

"Well, I've got to go," I said, pushing her away. "I'll be here all week; maybe we can have dinner. Let's see . . . Friday's out, maybe Saturday."

Beth stared at me, her arms folded.

"Maybe I'll stop by the deli—you can make me a sandwich."

"I'll start looking for the arsenic first thing in the morning."

"I'd die a happy man." I smiled and kissed her gently on the cheek. "Bye, now. Oh, and one more thing." I held her by the shoulders and whispered in her ear. "This is God's honest truth, Beth. I'm here to help Dani. I'm a friend, got that?"

Beth didn't move a millimeter.

"F-R-I-E-N-D. Murray the Good."

Beth closed her eyes and turned away from me.

"Just think about that, Beth. Because I've got a hunch Dani Kaplan's in trouble. Deep trouble."

"I'll ponder it," Beth said, turning her attention to one of the tapestries.

"Ponder hard, sweetheart." I let go of her and started to walk away. "Because if you know where she is—and I'm betting you do—then you could be in big trouble, too."

11

Sara Felder met me underneath the clocktower at eight, her full-length pink down coat unzipped from the waist up, revealing the top of a black satin dress that clung to her body like static electricity. Her red hair fell back over her shoulders in soft curls, a pearl necklace dipped tantalizingly toward her cleavage. For a moment I felt underdressed; fortunately I'm the kind of guy who can make a pair of Levi's and a cable-knit sweater look like they came straight from Armani. I took her hand and planted a kiss on it, then waltzed her over to Lorenzo's Loft, a chichi French dinner club a block away.

I felt relaxed with Sara; for once I wasn't reaching backwards or forwards across generations. Eight years age difference didn't seem like much, compared to the company I'd been keeping. There were a few things she'd missed out on, like Vietnam and Woodstock, and a few things I'd done without, like U2, networking parties, and an MBA. Still, we had plenty in common. An appreciation for '86 Bordeaux. Coq au vin. Beethoven's "Moonlight Sonata." Well, maybe I faked the Beethoven.

Sara was curious about my business. After a couple of bottles of wine I found it much easier to blurt out the truth, or part of it, anyway. "Mystery cruises?" she asked, with that cute giggle she had stolen from the Bloomfield twins.

"Very much in vogue these days. I've got a waiting list, over a hundred names."

"What kind of mysteries?"

"Murders are my specialty. We leave port in, say, Miami. We announce that a famous zillionaire passenger's been done away with in a most dastardly manner. Members of the crew and a few planted passengers are suspects, everybody's got a motive and an alibi.''

"And the paying guests have to figure it out?''

"Exactly. A tenacious bunch, too. Bugging me all hours of the night. They come up with the most bizarre scenarios: stabbed to death with an icicle, choked by seaweed. You wouldn't believe all the devious minds out there.''

Sara giggled again and sipped on her wine. We were on the main course by now: Chateaubriand, medium rare, with mussels and fresh green beans and a hot loaf of French bread. I hoped Mrs. Kaplan knew how much I appreciated it. "Is there some sort of a prize for solving the murder?''

"Absolutely. Free dinner for two at our port of call. Plus a silver dagger, personally inscribed. And a free gift certificate from a famous detective agency in Chicago.''

"A GIFT CERTIFICATE?'' Sara thought that was the most hysterical thing she'd ever heard. "What do they use it for, to check up on their hubbies? See what kind of dress their sister-in-law's wearing to the Rotary Club?''

"Sorry, that's confidential.''

"How would you know?''

"Why would you ask?''

"I just wanted to hear you invent something.'' She gave my hand a soft caress. "Do you write the plots yourself?''

"Yep. Each one based on an actual case.''

"Whose case?''

"The, uh, world-famous detective.''

"Close personal friend of yours?''

"Right. You know how it is with the cruise business. You meet all these exotic types.'' A waiter came by and offered us another bottle of Bordeaux, but we were pretty well sloshed and I wanted to give myself some recovery time for later in the evening. "Here's a little mystery I've been working on,'' I said, finishing off my beef. "See if you can help. I get rave reviews about a ski teacher—turns out to be head of the Sunburst ski school. Bucking for an executive position on the mountain, from what I hear. Only problem is, everybody hates his guts.''

"So what's the mystery?''

"Why such loathing?''

"He's a self-centered, manipulating prick."

"I see. So how did he get to such an exalted position?"

"Same as above."

I pushed my plate away and helped myself to one last chunk of French bread. "I can see what I missed by not going to business school."

"Maybe you can take one of those 'mini-MBA' programs."

"I'm a little pressed for time," I said. "I don't suppose you've had any personal experiences with the gentleman in question?"

"What possible significance could that be to Murray's Mystery Cruises?"

"It's that grain of truth I'm seeking, from which springs a pearl of a plot. My customers can sense that; it's why I'm the best in the business."

"I'll bet it is." Sara waved to the waiter and ordered some cappuccino, plus a look at the dessert cart. "How do you fit a ski mystery onto a cruise?"

"Oh, I'll just add a few twists here and there. Pretend there's an Olympic champion on board—these folks have a great imagination."

Sara emptied her wine glass just as the waiter brought over a cart of eclairs, tarts, and Napoleon slices. "You know, Murray, I really do believe you run these mystery cruises."

"I'm touched. Why shouldn't you believe me?"

"Because everything else you've been telling me is a bucket of fertilizer." She looked up at the waiter. "Too rich, Monty. Just the coffee."

Monty nodded and walked off, without consulting me. "Fertilizer?"

"Not that it bothers me—you're kinda cute. And I'm not surprised you're snooping around after Casey. As far as I'm concerned, he's a felony waiting to happen."

"Maybe he's already happened." I pulled out a cigar and tamped down the end.

"Don't even think of lighting that. I'm a working athlete." I put the cigar away. "And tell me who's paying for all this. I'd order another bottle of champagne, only I don't think it's you."

I took a deep breath. I could see it was going to be little use carrying on this charade—I could only hope that Sara was a kindred spirit. "All right, kiddo, you got me pegged. Truth is, somebody hired me. They're looking for their daughter."

Sara rolled her eyes. "Murray, you're the type of person parents pay to stay AWAY from their daughters. No offense."

"None taken." I sipped on my cappuccino and gathered a few crumbs from the bread; it was all the waiter had left us. "So happens, this particular girl was last seen sharing a love nest with Casey Wright."

"Aha, the plot thickens. This wouldn't be the darling little waif from Northwestern?"

"The very one."

"Gave dear Casey the heave-ho and disappeared into the woods?"

"Part of what I'm trying to establish. Your assistance would be much appreciated."

"And here I thought I was in for a romantic evening."

I touched Sara on the cheek. "You most certainly are—as soon as we dispense with the bookkeeping."

Sara glanced around—for the first time she seemed to notice that there were other diners in the restaurant. She looked at her watch, then signaled the waiter for a check. "I detect a few members of the Sunburst politburo in the area. Perhaps this discussion should be continued in another venue."

"Perfectly acceptable. Any suggestions?"

"I've got a roommate. She likes to sit home all night and watch TV."

"My place it is."

We left Lorenzo's Loft and walked through the village. The weather had chilled back into the twenties, freezing the slush that had melted during the day into a slippery carpet. "So what was the story with you and Casey?" I said, holding Sara tightly by the waist.

"Still none of your business."

"Just happens it is my business. I'm relying on your testimony; I want to make sure it's not biased."

"Murray, if I wasn't so crazy about you I'd give you a kick right in the jewels."

"But since we both know you ARE crazy about me, I'm afraid I'm going to have to proceed ruthlessly." I pulled her close to me and gave her a hard kiss on the lips.

"Mm," Sara shuddered. "I'll talk, I'll talk." She kissed me gently, then started walking again. "It was short and not too sweet. Maybe a month or two. When I first came here, I actually felt sorry for the guy. He worked so hard, he didn't have a lot of friends. He seemed so vulnerable.''

We were out of the village now, walking among the chalets, about a half-mile from the condo. ''So you took him under your wing?''

''Innocent me. He was such a dreamer. We'd sit in his crummy little apartment outside of town, drinking Coors and schnapps. He'd go on about how he was going to be running the ski school by the time he was thirty.''

''He was right.''

''So true. What's more, he was sharing his dreams with two other women the whole time.'' Sara squeezed my hand. ''One of whom was married to the executive treasurer of Sunburst Corp.''

''Ah, a vile character indeed. And how did that come to your attention?''

''It's a small town. I had her son in my ski class. Fifteen-year-old kid, tried to make a move on me during a private lesson. Gave me that tidbit of information when I resisted, just to make me feel bad.''

''Were you crushed?''

Sara flashed a sly grin. ''The pipsqueak, he was lucky he didn't get impaled on my ski pole.''

''Admirable restraint. I take it Casey escaped a similar fate?''

''Just barely. He handled himself quite professionally. He hinted it was the kind of thing I should consider keeping to myself, if I wanted a permanent career at Sunburst. Or even a temporary one.'' She stopped and held me as I led her into the cul-de-sac. ''I hope that helps you with your case, Mr. World-Famous Detective.''

''It helps to know your quarry.'' I led her toward the condo. ''If he is the quarry.''

''If I can be of any more assistance in stringing him up by the balls—''

''Wait—'' I stopped about thirty yards away. There was a light on inside the condo.

''What?''

''We've got visitors.''

''The world-famous detective in peril?''

''Shh.'' I turned back to the street, where I'd parked the rented Land Cruiser. I walked Sara over to it, unlocked the passenger side, and helped her in. ''Stay put, babe. I'll be right back.''

"Hey! It's cold out here—"

I tossed her the keys. "Turn on the heater. And keep quiet."

I crept back along the walk, toward the window where the light was shining. I didn't want to risk the front door—whoever had broken in wasn't being too discreet; I figured it was the type of guy who would just as soon put a bullet through your gut as say hello. I slogged through the snow, past the small firs and bushes that were growing by the side of the condo. I crept underneath the window—the shade was pulled, it wasn't quite down all the way. I heard water running in the bathroom. I bent underneath the sill and peeked in. I saw a long, smooth leg. I followed it up to a towel that didn't quite cover a generous chassis, and then all the way up to those baby-blue peepers and wavy eyelashes.

I shook the snow out of my boots and walked back to the Land Cruiser, where Sara was stretched out in the backseat. The heater was up full blast. "What's the story?" she asked.

"Hang tight, kid. I'm going inside."

"Murray, be careful. I'll help—"

"No way. Stay right where you are, my lovely."

Sara zipped her long down coat tight and shook some snow out of her hair. "For how long?"

"Um . . ." I took a quick look back at the light in the window. "About an hour. If I'm not back by then, call the ski patrol."

Sara stared at me, she pushed me away and settled back against the far door. I blew her a kiss and headed for the condo. I didn't look back.

I crept up slowly to the front entrance. I tramped up the walkway, into the foyer, and unlocked the front door. The hall lights were on—so were the bedroom lamps. I took a peek inside; it was empty. I took a deep breath. Chanel No. 5 filled my lungs. I walked toward the bathroom and heard the water stop. I stepped inside. I found Barbra Kaplan lying in the bathtub, lathering bubbles onto her naked body.

"Close the door," she said, blowing a bubble my way. "I'm getting a draft."

"You're the boss," I said, and did as I was told.

Barbra sat up in the tub and rinsed some soap off her breasts; they were round and firm—small beads of water dripped off them into the bubbles. "How's my daughter?"

"Compared to what?"

Barbra licked her lips and gave me a soft, sweet sigh. "Murray, Murray. I do hope you're making progress. I came here for a personal inspection."

The bathroom was getting hot and steamy. I took off my parka and sweater and folded them over the towel rack. "Truth is, I was about to do some investigative work. I just dropped by to change clothes." I glanced quickly behind me, I took nothing for granted. I tried to keep my muscles ready, but I knew all the action was right in front of me.

"Investigating? At ten o'clock on a cold March night?" Barbra reached out and placed her hand on my knee.

"That's how we detectives work. Breaking into offices, peeking into bedrooms. Skulking around under the cover of darkness."

"It sounds dangerous." Barbra pulled me closer and slid her hand up my leg. "I'm very excited."

I felt her wet fingertips on the inside of my thigh. "Right. Well, Mrs. Kaplan, I'm afraid so far it's just been lots of tedious interviews. Following up leads, putting the pieces together." I felt Barbra's long, elegant fingers searching for something to grab onto. "Now, uh . . . what I've discovered so far is that your daughter definitely jilted this Casey fellow—"

"Aren't you hot?" said Barbra, leaning over; she trickled some water on me.

"And he's pretty darned hacked off over it, because he was figuring Dani as a pipeline to Kozlo Realty, which would put him—"

"Murray, why don't you take that shirt off?"

"Mrs. Kaplan, the truth is, I've had a little chill—must be something in the air."

"Then warm up." Barbra Kaplan lunged out of the bathtub and slid her soap-bubbled body on top of mine. "And get wet," she said, pulling me toward the bathtub.

"Mrs. Kaplan—" I slid helplessly toward the bubble bath, my mind whirling, my jeans and turtleneck and three-hundred-dollar cowboy boots caking up with suds. I had only a fraction of a second to sort things out—in this business that's all you get. I thought about professional ethics. I thought about Sara, waiting in the Land Cruiser. I thought about Barbra Kaplan and me humping like sea turtles until dawn.

"Are you going to take those damned boots off?" Barbra said, biting at my earlobe. She rolled around and pushed herself on top of me. "They could get waterlogged and we'd both drown."

"Barbra," I said, squirming away, "I'm afraid I'm pressed for time."

"Press harder." Barbra squeezed the suds out of my turtleneck, I thought I was going to drown while she pulled it over my neck. She ripped off my undershirt. She was clawing at my boxer shorts when what was left of my professional instincts finally kicked in. I flipped over and broke loose. I pulled Barbra's hands off me and pinned her against the side of the bathtub. "Oh, Murray!" she shrieked. "My darling sea creature, let me feel your tentacles!"

"Mrs. Kaplan," I said, leaping sidesaddle over the edge of the tub, "I'm afraid duty calls."

"Tie me to the faucets!"

"I've got work to do. Crucial evidence that'll lead me to your daughter."

"I'll wait right here for you."

"I won't be back till dawn."

"I'll take a long bath."

"You'll catch pneumonia."

Barbra sat up in the bathtub. Her wet hair glistened, the steam rose over her body and dripped off in little beads of sweat. "So," she whispered, her eyes flashing. "My detective has work to do."

"You're catching on."

"Such dedication. You're a dying breed."

"I hope not."

"Me too." Barbra turned the water on in the tub; the bubbles began to build up again around her breasts.

"Mrs. Kaplan," I said, edging toward the hallway, "I want you to know I'm flattered. Honest." She stared at me. I thought I detected a tear in her eye, barely distinguishable from the suds and the sweat. "Barbra, you're a sensuous woman. You deserve more than a seedy gumshoe, dropping in between gigs on a Wednesday night."

"I know what I deserve."

"You hired me to find your daughter. I think she's in trouble—until I find her it's a twenty-four-hour-a-day job." Barbra turned off the water. "Assuming you still want me to do it."

"Toss me a towel."

I tossed her a towel. She reached into the tub and pulled the plug out.

"You better get going, if Dani's in all this danger."

"Right. I'll just change my clothes." I grabbed my sweater and parka and headed for the bedroom. "I can find a nice hotel," I shouted. "If you're staying long."

"I'll just be a day or two,"Barbra answered. "There's no need to run away. Come back when you get your work done."

"Absolutely."

"We'll discuss the status of the case. I'll expect a full report."

"Sure thing. Sleep tight, Mrs. Kaplan. See you tomorrow." I headed for the foyer, just as Barbra stepped out of the bathroom. The single towel was wrapped around her hair.

"Au revoir, Monsieur Glick. Dress warmly."

"I will."

"Don't forget to brush your teeth."

"I won't."

Barbra walked back into the bathroom and closed the door. A few seconds later, I was slogging back out in the snow, wondering if you could get an Oedipal complex from someone else's mother. I climbed back into the Land Cruiser, where Sara was stretched out in the backseat, listening to James Taylor on the radio.

"Murray, are you all right?" she said, leaping for me as I opened the door.

"It was a close call."

"You're wet," she said, feeling my hair.

"I was ambushed. It was a tough fight—"

"And you smell." Sara pulled me close and sniffed at my chest. "You smell like soap or perfume or something." I detected a slight lowering of her concern for my personal well-being.

"Well, I got kind of sweaty and beat-up, so I thought I'd freshen up."

Sara pushed me away and ran her fingers over my clean shirt, sweater, and jeans. "That was an amazing feat. You snuck in, fought off a trained killer, showered, changed clothes, and here you are."

"Your humble servant." I kissed her on the lips. I held her close.

"Wait, Murray. Not here—"

"Sara, darling, Land Cruisers bring out the beast in me—"

"It's uncomfortable. Can't we go inside?"

"We'll spoil the moment—"

"Murray, we're not teenagers!" Sara held me at arm's distance. "Damn it, Murray, I want a bed and a bath and big fluffy blankets."

"Let's find a hotel. I'll order up champagne from room service—"

"What's wrong with your condo?"

"We can't go back there; we just had a disturbance inside."

Sara pushed me against the seat. "What kind of disturbance?"

"A disturbance with another person."

"Is this other person hurt?"

"I'm afraid so."

"Dead?"

"I'm afraid not."

Sara took another whiff and held me by the collar. "Murray, is this person of the female variety, by some chance?"

"I don't know, Sara. It was dark. We scuffled; whoever it was had a mean karate chop."

"Whoever it was wears expensive perfume."

"Darling," I said, giving her shoulder a soft massage, "this is an expensive resort. We only get thugs of the highest social standing—"

Sara sat up straight. "She's still there, isn't she?"

"If it's a she."

"And you're not kicking her out?"

"Sara . . ." I stammered for a moment. I began to consider that the truth, in one form or another, might work as well as anything else. "See, Sara, the woman has this crazy idea that it's her condo. She got hold of a key somehow, and it's late at night and I can't afford to call the police and make a scene—"

"Take me home."

"Sara, this woman attacked me—"

"Take me HOME."

I stared longingly at Sara. I hadn't tried my hand at virtue too often over the years; I could see that I didn't have the technique down quite right. I climbed out of the backseat and got behind the wheel. "You could at least sit in front with me."

"I live over at the Powderhorn Apartments, right outside the village."

"Get in front."

"Get moving."

I sat still. I turned the radio off and stared straight ahead.

About a minute went by, then I heard the rear door open and close. The front door opened and Sara climbed in beside me.

"I should have called a cab."

"Sara, trust me—"

"Who was she?"

"Dani's mother."

"Gimme a break."

"It WAS, Sara—that's God's honest truth."

Sara sighed; she shook her head. "Turn left here," she said, as we got back to the fringe of Sunburst Village.

"My offer still stands. There's suites available at the Four Seasons."

"I don't think so," Sara whispered. I thought she was starting to waver. "It's the third building on the right. Murray, listen."

I listened. I listened for almost a full minute, but all I heard was the humming of the Land Cruiser and the howling of a dog somewhere in the night.

"Look," she said finally, "maybe we can try dinner again. Saturday night, okay?"

"It's a long time to wait."

"It's three days."

"I'm in a dangerous business. It could end for me any time."

"I've got great confidence in your instinct for survival. Oh, and by the way," Sara said, as I pulled up to her apartment building, "there was one other thing I meant to tell you—it might even keep you busy for three days."

I stopped the car and pulled her close to me. "You DO want to go to a hotel—"

"Forget it, Murray. Listen: when your friend's daughter jilted Casey Wright, there was someone else involved."

"He had another girl?"

"She had another guy."

I raised my eyebrows and let out a soft whistle. "No shit. Who was he?"

"Name of Rick Allanson. He worked for the Forest Service."

"A ranger?"

"Yep. Spent some time in Utah and Minnesota, ended up here. We're in the middle of the Rocky Mountain National Forest; they have a bunch of offices—one in the village, one just outside the ski area."

"Did Casey know about this?"

"Probably not at the time. I think he knows now."

"How did you find out?"

Sara shrugged. "Ski school gossip. Somebody saw them cross-country skiing together outside of town. Don't quote me." She edged toward the door.

"So. This guy and Dani, are they still an item? Did they run off together?"

"Nope."

"Does he still work for the Forest Service? Can I talk to him somewhere?"

"Sorry." Sara kissed me on the cheek and slid over toward the door. "Goodnight, Murray. Thanks for dinner."

"Sara—" I pulled her back close to me. "Sara, I'm absolutely wild for you. I don't think I can live three days without you."

"I've got lessons all day tomorrow and I promised the Bloomfield twins I'd take them out for dinner. Go skiing, have a great time. Work on your mystery."

I kissed Sara long and hard. I held her close to me, then watched helplessly as she slipped out the door. "Goodnight, beautiful. I'll dream about you."

"Sweet dreams, then."

I grabbed her arm and pulled her back toward me. "Now, will you please tell me where I can talk to this Ranger Rick?"

"You can't talk to Ranger Rick," Sara said, getting out of the Land Cruiser.

I held onto her by the coat sleeve, but she pulled away from me and hopped down into the snow. "Why not?" I shouted.

Sara walked back to my window. "Because," she whispered as I rolled the window down, "Ranger Rick is dead."

And with that she turned around and ran back to her apartment.

12

I woke up at six-fifteen the next morning, just as the first rays of sunlight spilled through the windshield of the Land Cruiser. I'd spent the night at the far end of the parking lot behind the gondola, ignoring the ominous NO OVERNIGHT PARKING signs scattered about, with their threats of deportation and confiscation of wealth. It was safer than returning to the condo, and I didn't need to spend two hundred bucks just to lie alone in a hotel room. By the time I'd pulled in, after several fruitless hours camped outside Sara's window, the Sunburst Police Force had put away their motor scooters and gone home for the evening.

Outside, the snowcats were already on the mountain, grooming the hill. We hadn't had any new powder since my first night. The runs were becoming hard-packed and icy—a few more days and they might have to start making snow, especially with the World Cup coming to town next week. I made a mental note to call Andy Sussman and give him his marching orders—the closer we got to the race, the more help he'd be to me. I was going to have to construct some type of emergency scenario to get him transferred this late in the game, but I decided I could put it off at least a few hours—a growling stomach had first dibs on my time.

The cafeteria was open, mostly for the lift operators and snow groomers. I slipped in, scored some donuts and coffee, and took them back to the Land Cruiser; by now it was a quarter to seven. I took my binoculars from the glove compartment and focused on the clocktower. At seven o'clock, I saw Casey Wright pull into the parking lot in a red Trans Am with black racing stripes. A pair of long racers' skis were clamped to the roof. He parked about fifty yards from me and strode toward his office, the skis slung over his shoulder. He stopped outside and chatted briefly with a man in a parka and slacks; it looked like the same accountant-type I'd seen him with two days before. After a few minutes the smaller man walked off toward the cafeteria; Wright locked his skis in a rack near the door and went into his office.

I gave Casey points for diligence; if it was money and power he was after, he was at least willing to wake up early in the morning to get it. How that connected to a missing girl and a dead forest ranger I wasn't sure. I guessed that Casey knew, but standing around staring at his window wasn't going to get me any further than staring at Sara's window had the night before. I revved up the 4 × 4 and pulled out of the parking lot; it was time for an encounter with Smokey the Bear.

The Sunburst Ranger Station was a mile east of the airport, in a brown building with stained wooden siding and a sign in front of it that welcomed me to the Rocky Mountain National Forest. The door was locked but the lights were on; I figured this was a fine opportunity for a breakfast chat. I even began to consider that there might be some merit to this early rising business, although I wasn't ready for a lengthy experiment.

I knocked on the door. Through the window, I could see a single man inside. He pointed to the clock but I knocked again and he walked over, looking very put-out. "We open at eight-thirty," he said.

"Sorry 'bout that, friend. I gotta hit the road. I needed to talk to someone for a second—"

"There's another station in Eagle. If you're leaving, there's not much we can do for you—"

"No, no. I wanted to talk to someone here. About a buddy of mine, used to work for you fellas. Name of Rick Allanson."

The ranger took a long gulp of coffee. He opened the door all the way and motioned for me to come inside. "Shoulda said so." He straightened his tie; it was brown to match his Forest Service uniform. "Thought I might hear from someone eventually. You know, I take it?"

"Sort of. I heard he died, that's all."

The ranger led me to a counter at the back of the room. Behind it was his desk and an entrance to an inner office. "Rick was a buddy of mine, too. Coffee?"

"Sure. Name's Murray Wilcox."

"Brian Ellsworth." Ellsworth walked behind the counter, over to a Mr. Coffee, and drew me a cup. "Where'd you know Rick from?"

"Utah. Worked one summer up at a ranch near Heber; he was headquartered up in the Wasatch." I sipped on the coffee and tried to remember a few details about Utah from a ski trip too many years ago. "We used to shoot a few beers over in Park City."

"No wonder you and Rick hit it off," Ellsworth laughed. He was a tall kid with rust-brown hair. His features were sharp, he didn't have much of a tan; it looked like he'd spent too much time in the office. "You been in town long?"

"Just passin' through. Came out from Salt Lake, got a gig in Denver. My uncle raises horses out there." I sipped on my coffee. "I couldn't believe it when I heard about Rick. How'd it happen?"

Ellsworth leaned on the counter; it was covered with a large topo map of his sector of the National Forest. I saw weather forecasts scattered about, road reports, some Xerox copies of cross-country trails. He walked back toward a file and cleared his throat. "Rick was buried in an avalanche."

I felt a sour swirl in my stomach. "That's awful. Christ, Brian, where was he, on a rescue?"

"We never knew exactly." Ellsworth spoke slowly and deliberately, as if he were gauging my reaction to every word, as if he didn't exactly buy my act. "It was early in the morning. We'd had a foot and a half the day before. He was supposedly out cross-country skiing, out by the ski area boundary."

"Supposedly?"

"He was wearing cross-country skis when they found him."

"Who found him?"

"The ski patrol."

"When?"

"The next day."

"Had he told anyone he was going skiing? On the morning after a blizzard, you'd think he'd leave word somewhere."

"You'd think that."

I stared at Ellsworth. I had the unmistakable feeling that Rick Allanson's death was no accident. I figured Ellsworth knew it, but he didn't need to know that I knew it, too. "I don't mean to be nosy, Brian, but if he just took off and didn't tell anyone, and this avalanche catches him early in the morning, how was it that the Sunburst Ski Patrol just stumbled on him the next afternoon, buried under a ton of snow?"

Ellsworth straightened out the weather reports. "He didn't show up for work. His car was found up on County HH, up near the trailhead where he would have skied in. Plus he had his beeper."

"Beeper?"

Ellsworth reached into his desk drawer and pulled out what looked like a small Sony Walkman. "These. They'll send out a signal if you get buried. They're mandatory out in the bush. When the ski patrol picked him up, he'd been buried over thirty hours; that's what the doctors estimated."

"How precise are they about that type of thing?"

"Well, now, that's an interesting question." Ellsworth took out a bandana and blew his nose. "I suppose, bein' his good buddy and all, you're more than a little curious."

"Damn straight." I picked out a reflection of myself in the glass countertop. I hadn't shaved; spending the night in the Land Cruiser had done wonders for my latest alias. "Rick was no fool. I can't see him goin' out and gettin' himself killed that easily. That much snow, he'd know if there was avalanche danger."

Ellsworth walked back to the file cabinet, opened a drawer, and pulled out a battered manila folder. "Yeah, that's what we figured."

I sipped on my coffee and leaned over the counter, trying to find the spot on the map where Allanson had parked his car. "What about that girlfriend of his? Did you ask her?"

"Girlfriend?"

"Yeah. you never met her?"

"Hell, he never told me anything, the little weasel—"

"He wrote me a letter, couple of months ago. Said he'd been seein' some cute chickie named Dani something. Said he was meetin' her on the sly; she was really a hot number."

"No shit." Ellsworth furrowed his brow. "Well, that's news. I never set eyes on her—unless it was that girl came over here the day the congressman stopped by—damn Rick, almost got us all fired right on the spot.''

"That sure sounds like Rick,'' I chuckled, taking a shot in the dark. "Who'd he piss off this time?''

"Oh, just the chairman of the House Agriculture Committee, his wife, and ten of the richest men in Colorado. Course, he only had an hour.''

"What'd he do?''

Ellsworth opened up his folder. He pulled out several folders, some newspaper clippings, and a frayed bumper sticker that said "EARTH NOW!'' in big capital letters. "Just an informational file, of course.''

"Yours?''

"Rick's. You know that Sunburst has an expansion planned later this year.''

"I'm not much into real estate.''

Ellsworth pointed over at his map. "That sector where Rick got buried, that's the edge of the ski area. By this time next year it'll be smack in the middle of their resort. They want the whole west ridge of the mountain for ski slopes, hotels, condos. Right now it all belongs to Uncle Sam.''

"More specifically, the Rocky Mountain National Forest.''

"Administered by the U.S. Department of Agriculture, payer of my biweekly stipend.'' Ellsworth browsed through his notes. He pulled out a couple of reports and tossed them on the counter. "Course, there's a lot of people here in the Forest Service aren't too crazy about all that.''

I took a look at the reports. They were outlines of Environmental Impact Statements that had been drawn out. I skimmed over them; there were sections outlining the damage to wildlife and water drainage, there were smaller segments about air and noise pollution. "Look's as if someone thinks that West Sunburst ain't such a hot idea. Did Rick write this up?''

"I did. Rick's version never would have gotten past the censors.''

"Hmm.'' I flipped through a few more pages of the report. "All this is true? Not just some tree-hugger's manifesto?''

"Of course it's true. Listen, this is our livelihood—someone chooses to spend their whole life in a forest, they better damn well love trees.'' Ellsworth grabbed the reports from me, glanced at them for a moment, then stuck them back in the folder. "We commissioned wildlife biologists, geologists, water people. We've got golden eagles out here, black bears, cutthroat trout. All of it's endangered if they tear up this side of the hill. And they're talking about re-routing Blackrock Creek to make room for their condos—" Brian pointed to a section on the map, just below the proposed new area. "That affects the whole watershed below there. It would drastically dry out the Nugget Lake chain, wipe out a native population of cuts."

"So what happened to your Impact Statement?"

"Never got published. They got some Ag lifer in Denver to do it. Made the whole thing into a fog, didn't sound nearly as damaging."

"And that, I take it, is what pissed Rick off so royally?"

"Oh, it helped. And when Congressman Farrell and his wife and the pinstripe cowboys from Sunburst came by for a quick tour of the facilities, Rick really lost it. He threw my reports at them. He accused them of being fascists. Greedy, corrupt, environmental rapists. Said it was the biggest swindle since Teapot Dome."

"Was it?"

"Oh, maybe top ten," Ellsworth said with a smirk. "God knows it's hard to keep track."

I sipped on my coffee. "I take it Rick didn't exactly extend his circle of friends with that outburst?"

"Well now, the representative took it all in good stride. Gave him a nice, patronizing speech about how Congress appreciated the fine work of the U.S. Forest Service. Went on about seeing the big picture; how the proceeds from the lease of the land and the increased tax revenue would not only allow more people to enjoy our beautiful national bounty, but also help pay for the maintenance of the rest of our desperately underfunded forests in this time of rising national debt."

"I take it that didn't soothe Rick's savage breast?"

"He called them a bunch of lying faggots and stomped out."

"And ended up dead under a ton of snow a few weeks later."

Brian took my coffee cup and drew me a refill. "The timing was funny, but I don't know—I can't see the Ag Department taking out one of their own, just 'cause he got his nose out of joint. And anyway, I'M the one that wrote the report."

"Did they know that?"

"Sure. I sent a signed copy to Senator Parker from California—we're old acquaintances, from my days up at Mammoth Lakes. Turns out he's on the wrong committee or something. He sent it over to another senator; it got bottled up in Interior, which is the wrong place to begin with since we're under Agriculture."

"Never to be heard from again?"

"You got it." Ellsworth put the file away. "Just like its author." He pulled out a memo. "I'm getting transferred to Superior National Forest in Wisconsin, effective May first."

"Geez, Brian, I'm sorry to hear that."

"All part of the game. I was due for a rotation—just came a little early. I'm lucky they didn't ship me off to Samoa."

"Do they have National Forests in Samoa?"

"They could make one." Brian tossed away his coffee cup and looked up at the wall clock. It was a quarter past eight. He began straightening up the maps and flyers and writing out the day's weather report on the chalkboard behind him. "Anyway, they had to send me somewhere. This office is closing; the entire district becomes part of Sunburst Mountain."

"A fait accompli?"

"Almost. There's a few congressmen trying to block the Special Use Permit, but it's a lost cause. It's attached to the National Forests appropriations bill, contracts are already drawn out. Tell you the truth, I'll be happy to go to Wisconsin. Find a nice lake up there, stock myself up with cold beer, frozen pizza, and walleyes. Become a hermit."

I tried to imagine Brian Ellsworth after three years as a hermit on his little lake in Northern Wisconsin: roly-poly and red-faced, whiskers down to his belt, giving sage advice to wandering fisherman and drunk snowmobilers. Somehow he just didn't seem the type. "Tell me about the girl, Brian."

"Why? You conducting some type of special investigation before workin' on your uncle's ranch in Denver?"

"Hell no, just curious—he was so impressed by her. C'mon, what was she? Blond, brunette?"

"I didn't say it was his girl. It was just this kid, couldn't have been more then twenty. Light blond hair. She came with one of the Sunburst fellas."

"One of the board members?"

"Naw. He was ski patrol—no, ski school, that was it. He was yakkin' at all the pinstripes about how he was going to make the west ridge ski school world famous; they were kinda pushin' him away, like a puppy."

"But you think this was the girl Rick took up with?"

"I didn't, until you brought it up. She seemed kinda disturbed when Rick blew his gasket. Afterwards, when the congressman was talking to me and my boss, she walked outside and found Rick off on the back porch, staring into the woods. They had themselves a nice talk; her boyfriend had to damn near drag her away. I could see him lecturing her when they got back in his car."

"And that was the last time you ever saw her?"

"Yep."

"And Rick never mentioned her?"

"Not once. Listen, we're about ready to open for business. You're welcome to browse around if you want, but I'll have customers to take care of."

I looked out the door. A few scraggly cross-country skiers were huddled up, awaiting the day's snow conditions and trail information. "Well, I'm outta here, Brian. Thanks for filling me in. Incidentally, was there ever a police investigation about Rick?"

"Nah. They did an autopsy. Died of suffocation."

"Did anyone ASK for one?"

Ellsworth looked around. The skiers were pushing at the door. He lowered his voice. "I did. But not very loudly. The local police weren't interested." He walked over to the door and unlocked it. "Howdy folks," he said to the group as they pushed inside. They were mostly college kids, but there was an older couple too, dressed in Nordic pants and jackets.

"So long, Brian," I yelled, walking out the door. "Good luck."

Brian waved at me as he led the skiers back to the counter. "Have a safe trip, now!"

I headed toward the Land Cruiser, taking one last look at the ranger station. A year from now it would be gone—or maybe it would be converted into a trendy restaurant with entrees like "Smokie's Stew" and "Avalanche Burgers." Or maybe it would just be a mink salon, or a Sunburst West office for Dr. Feingold.

One thing for sure: there wouldn't be much room for golden eagles, or black bears, or cutthroat trout.

Or, I thought, as I pulled out onto the road and back toward Sunburst Village, for Brian Ellsworth. Or Rick Allanson. Or Dani Kaplan.

13

I drove back to Sunburst Village and found a pay phone in the bar over at Clem's Claim. I didn't figure anybody important was going to see me there at ten in the morning, but I slid into a dimly lit corner anyway. I punched in my credit-card number and dialed Andy Sussman—I needed him here now. I had a feeling the Sunburst Corporation had some bones rattling around in their ski bins. They'd never talk to me, but they'd roll out the red carpet for a network sports reporter during World Cup week.

I reached Andy's office in New York, but he wasn't there and his secretary wasn't too keen on divulging his whereabouts; it was probably easier getting a message through to the Chief Justice than reaching a network jock on assignment. I did manage to get the location of the game-of-the-week. It was in Denver, fortunately; the Nuggets were playing Detroit. I called the CBS affiliate in town, but he hadn't checked in yet. I didn't leave a message. I figured I'd try again tonight—I could always get his hotel from Susie. If I couldn't track him down by tomorrow night, I'd fly over and find him at the game.

Back outside it was a dazzling bright day. A light spring breeze tickled my neck, I could hear the *swish swish swish* of skiers gliding down the bottom runs. I thought about checking in for another ski lesson. I figured I could get Sara for a private half-day if she wasn't tied up with a group, but she'd already caused me to spend one night baying at the moon. I figured I'd give us both a few days to cool down. I decided instead to pop into the Village Deli and have Beth fix me another Super Sub. I wondered how much she knew about Ranger Rick. I figured I'd hit her with the facts between the salami and the lettuce and see how she reacted.

Only Beth wasn't there. I assumed she'd gone out for coffee or lunch. I waited by the cooler, comparing Cokes, Dr Peppers, and New York Seltzers for about fifteen minutes, but she still didn't show. I was beginning to get hungry, so I walked up to the counter and ordered a sub from the first sweet young lass who came my way. She was a cute blond with freckles and a pony tail. She looked at me nervously, but I put her at ease with a wink and a grin. I complimented her on her earrings; they were frizzy little white snowballs. I gave her a few tips on packing in the lettuce so it wouldn't fall out the sides; we were getting along just fine. But when I asked her when Beth might be coming in, all I got was a puzzled glance.

"Who?"

"Beth. She's a friend of mine." Another blank look. "About your size, short brown hair—"

"Oh, that Beth. She quit."

"Quit?"

"Uh-huh. Yesterday was her last day. We were supposed to have a party for her last night, but she said she was leaving right after dinner."

"Leaving for where?"

"I don't know." The girl cut the sandwich in half; she was efficient but she seemed preoccupied. "Do you want coleslaw with this?"

"No, thanks. Look, was Beth splitting town? Does anyone know where she went?"

"I sure don't. You could ask the manager, but he doesn't come in till noon. I only started last week, I hardly knew her." She wrapped the sandwich in cellophane. "That'll be five-fifty."

"She's a cousin of mine," I mumbled, pulling out a twenty. "I thought she was acting a little strange—"

"She WAS a little strange," said the girl; the tag on her smock said "Julie." "I mean, she was nice enough when she had to be, but she didn't talk to anyone much. I heard she had boyfriend problems." She handed me my change.

"Who's her boyfriend?"

"I have no idea. She's your cousin."

"Right. Well, I'll check with your boss when he comes in. Her folks'll be worried."

"I hope she's okay," said Julie, without really meaning it. I thought about asking her out for a drink, but she'd already shifted her attention to the next customer; I gave her a last fleeting glance and headed back outside.

So I'd missed Sussman and I'd missed Beth. I decided I'd try the police next—there had to be someone home there. I hopped into the Land Cruiser and drove a few miles outside of town. The Sunburst police headquarters was a shiny new two-story building with a circular driveway; a couple of squad cars and a police van were parked there.

I've always felt uncomfortable around police stations, particularly in small towns. It's not a big city bias; cops everywhere do a hell of a job. But let's face it: if they always got their man, I'd be out of business. Naturally, when I walk into a precinct station and show them my license, it's a pretty strong hint that I think they've fucked up. So I make my appearances brief. If possible I make a few friends on the force. I try to keep informed on department politics—maybe a cop's been passed over for promotion or a case has been buried for one reason or another. Sometimes I can get help from the inside.

But I didn't know anybody on the Sunburst Police Department, and I didn't have a whole lot of time to make new friends. I had a suspicion a man had been murdered. My guess was that somebody didn't want it investigated, probably someone with clout in the sheriff's office. I also knew that the only thing cops hate worse than a PI from out of town is a PI who hides his ticket, and mine was nowhere in sight. It was a chance I had to take.

The squad room was quiet, the desk sergeant was friendly. He had me pegged for a tourist. He asked me why I wasn't out on the slopes; it was where *HE'D* be soon as he got a day off. Behind him there were four or five uniforms milling around without any particular sense of urgency. There was plenty of snow and plenty of skiers—life was easy for everyone. Not that Sunburst wouldn't have their share of problems. Drugs, maybe a few burglaries from their chichi clientele—but even those would be hard to pull off with eighty inches of snow on the ground. All in all, being a cop at Sunburst in the wintertime beat the hell out of Division Street in Chicago.

I gave the desk sergeant the same Utah story I'd given the ranger; it was my most recent one and easiest to remember. He escorted me to the back of the office and introduced me to a sergeant who handled ski accidents and emergencies. I didn't hear anything about homicide.

Craig Gustafson was a big, brawny fellow with reddish-brown hair and a mustache. He had thick hands and spoke quietly; he'd be tough in a fight, but I didn't think he got in many. Mounted at the back of his cubicle was a portrait of a rainbow trout leaping out of a stream; a hunting magazine was tossed on the top of his file cabinet. There was a small vise on the back of the desk, and behind it a box of feathers—apparently those thick hands were skilled in the art of fly-tying.

Gustafson put away his paperwork and offered me some coffee. He seemed an easy-going sort, but when I mentioned my interest in Rick Allanson he let out a deep breath and drew his mouth into a scowl. "You from the insurance company?"

"No, no. An old friend of Rick's." I walked back toward his picture. "Pretty rainbow. I do a little flyfishing myself, up in the Wasatch—"

"Damn insurance people were in three times. Freaking nuisance." He showed me over to a chair, then pulled a file out of his desk, and spread it out on the table. "National Life and Casualty. I'm glad I'm not with *THEM.*" Gustafson tossed me a sugar cube to go with the coffee. "Wasn't even a big policy. Five grand to his parents—cost 'em more to investigate."

I leaned over toward Gustafson's file. "Look, Sergeant, I'm just an old buddy of Rick's. It's probably none of my business— it's just that we were tight, and some things struck me as odd. I only got a few questions, then I'll be on my way."

Gustafson picked up the file and skimmed through it. "We get maybe a half-dozen avalanche deaths in a season. That's assuming there's no major disaster. Mostly it's hotshot skiers, out where they don't belong. They see fresh powder and start heading off the trails early in the morning."

"Rick was a forest ranger. He knew where he belonged."

"That's what I thought at first. But I talked to his boss, said he was an independent sort. Didn't have a lot of friends. Liked to go off alone, didn't always tell folks where he was headin'."

"His boss said that? John, uh . . . ?" I stuttered around, trying to fake a name, until Gustafson looked at his report.

"Jack Carvell, District head."

"Yeah, that's right. Rick mentioned him. I don't think he was crazy about the guy." I let a hint of resentment edge into my voice. "He told you Rick just walked into it?"

"Carvell was upset, believe me. He was the one called him in missing, gave us the license plates on his car. He helped us all he could."

"But no one asked you to investigate any further? Not even his family?"

"No—well, yes, one of the rangers did. Asked us to check the coroner's report, see if there was anything that would lead us to believe he died some way other than being suffocated under the snow." Gustafson skimmed over the report. "Ellsworth, another ranger. Friend of his. S'pose I'd a done the same thing, it was my buddy."

"So you did check?"

"Yep. No evidence. Like I say, we do a fair number of these types of fatalities. Not very pleasant, but we know what they look like."

I tapped my fingers on Gustafson's desk. I tried to read the sergeant's eyes. He didn't seem to be hiding anything; he was at least trying to give me enough information so that I'd go away. "Sergeant," I said, "I'm not stickin' around long. It's just that I wanted to satisfy myself about Rick before I go. And I keep thinkin'—a highly trained forest ranger goes cross-country skiing by himself, early in the morning, after a foot-and-a-half snow-fall—"

"An eccentric ranger, according to his boss—"

"But not according to his friend Ellsworth. And not according to me. Sergeant, did you do any checking on Rick's work here? Was there any reason to believe that someone might have wanted him dead?"

Gustafson's face began to turn red, his stubby fingers clenched the file. I was glad that I wasn't a deer or a trout. "Mister, let me assure you. Nothing and no one suggested this death was anything but an accident. Not the medical reports. Not the circumstances. Not the people who knew him. Now, if you're suggesting that your friend was the victim of some type of foul play, we'd naturally like to know what your evidence is." Gustafson folded his hands on the table. "Otherwise, I've got work to do." He leaned over at me and waited for an answer.

I sat still for a moment. I saw little use in drawing out deductions that were based on hearsay and hunches. Maybe I trusted Gustafson, but I didn't know who he reported to. And the truth was, either he'd failed to do his job or someone had 86ed an investigation into what I was reasonably sure was a murder. "I don't have any evidence, Sergeant."

"Well then. I appreciate your interest in our work. You can leave your name if you want. Anything else comes up I'll be sure and let you know."

"Thanks," I said, getting up. "But I won't be local. And you won't be looking." Gustafson didn't much care for that, but he shook my hand anyway and showed me out of the office.

I headed for the Land Cruiser. It was parked in the lot about fifty yards away, I could see the top of it over a pair of squad cars. As I approached it, I heard a door slam and an engine start. I sensed danger in the air, but it wasn't immediate; who would assault me in a police department parking lot?

I stood still. I was twenty yards from the car, looking at my wallet as if I was inspecting my own license. A pickup truck pulled away; it was a blue Dodge Dakota. I couldn't make out the license number, but it had a dent the size of a basketball on the left fender. It rolled out of the lot and onto the street, then screeched away in the direction of the village.

I walked over to the Land Cruiser and got in on the passenger side. It wasn't locked. I checked the wiring under the dash. I went out front and opened the hood; everything was in order. I started the engine. I'd only gotten a few feet when the glove compartment popped open. I could have sworn I'd locked it, but it didn't exactly take Houdini to break into that. I reached for my binoculars; they were Nikons but they hadn't interested whoever had been inside. What HAD interested them was my car-rental agreement.

I picked up the folder. I'd rented the Cruiser under the name of Murray Solomon—whoever was following me wasn't going to track me down that easily. Still, they had a MasterCard number—I couldn't rent the Land Cruiser without one. It wasn't a lot to go on. But if they were anywhere near as smart as me, they'd have a place to start.

And I figured they were.

I kicked myself for being careless, but the truth was I didn't have a safe port anymore. I'd resolved to rent a motel room, but

I was going to have to go back to the condo sooner or later. I needed a change of underwear, not to mention a shower. I wanted my skis back. I was tired, my back was sore. I was being tailed by murderers and kidnappers. A naked woman in a bubble bath didn't seem like such a frightening prospect.

I drove the Land Cruiser back to the rental place at the airport and turned it in. I didn't want to rent another car there; whoever my tail was would be onto me in a flash. Instead, I went inside the terminal and purchased an airline ticket to Denver. I charged it to the Murray Solomon card. Then I took a shuttle bus to the village and hiked back to the condo.

Outside, the bright blue sky had turned ashen. The wind had picked up, a storm was blowing in. The temperature must have dropped ten degrees by the time I got to the condo. The front door was locked, the lights were off. I slipped my key in the latch and edged inside. It was early afternoon, but the shades were drawn; the place was dark and empty. And it was perfectly clean. The bedroom was made up, my belongings were carefully folded and put away. The bathroom was sparkling, my sweater had been hung out to dry over the shower panel. A small, scented note was pinned to the sweater. It read: "Another time, another place. Find Dani. B."

I took the note and crushed it into a little ball. I walked back into the living room; the place was mine again. I opened the refrigerator and grabbed a beer. I chugged it down in about thirty seconds, then dragged my butt into the bathroom and treated myself to a long, hot shower.

As I was drying myself off, I thought I heard the door bell ring. I turned off the fan. I opened the bathroom door. This time I was sure I heard it. There was a knock and a loud voice shouted, "Murray! Hey, pal! It's J.B.!"

"Hang on!" I shouted. I toweled off, tossed on a pair of jeans, and ran to the door, but by the time I got there J.B. was gone. I was about to run upstairs when I saw a letter taped to the door. Scrawled on the side were the words, "THIS CAME FOR YOU—J.B."

I took the envelope inside. I held it to the light. I could see a message inside. I opened it up and pulled out a single, typewritten page. It was only two lines: "Meet me tomorrow morning. 6 A.M. Base of the gondola." It was unsigned.

I took the note and put it in my pocket. There was no stamp

on the envelope. I walked upstairs, still dressed in my bathrobe. The wind was gusting now, kicking the snow around. I shivered as I knocked on J.B.'s door. I thought he might know who had delivered it, but no one was home.

I went back into my kitchen and poured myself another beer. I pondered the note. Who could have written it: Beth? Sara? Ellsworth? the cop?

Who the hell knows?

I stretched out on the couch. The long night and early morning were beginning to take their toll. So were the beers. I kicked off my shoes, drew the curtains and turned out the lights. I stuck the message under a pillow and gave myself until dinner to catch a few Zs and think things over.

Outside, it had turned completely dark. It was snowing. I figured it would be a long time before I saw the sun again.

PART TWO

14

"This is absolutely the worst drivel I have ever read."

"Oh, come on now," Andy Sussman said, massaging his wife behind the neck. "What about Stan Birnbaum's fifty pages on computer game copyrights in the *Chicago Law Journal?* You complained about that for weeks."

"That was different. I had to read that, he was my boss." Susie Sussman took the last dog-eared pages of the manuscript and shoved them back in the envelope, then stuffed the envelope into the pouch attached to the airplane seat in front of her. "World-famous detective, discreet-is-my-middle-name. The man has no shame. Buy me a drink."

"I think it was just that part about you having the secret crush on him," Andy said, flagging down a flight attendant and ordering two bloody Marys.

"The Sultan of Slime. And don't tell me we're going to chase off to Colorado for the rest of the story. If we're lucky, his typewriter fell into the bubble bath."

"Now, now." Andy stroked his wife on the back of the neck. He was glad he'd waited until they'd got on the plane to show her the manuscript; in a less public place she might have torn it up and stuffed it down the garbage disposal. "The NCAA tournament starts Saturday; I don't have any NBA games for three weeks."

"You've got the Western Regional Finals—it's in the new contract."

"So, that gives me two weeks. Anyway, Merle Summers has been bugging me to get a little variety—especially in winter sports.

If I don't volunteer for something pretty soon he's going to ship me off to Nome for the dogsled races.''

The pilot interrupted them with the information that they were starting their descent into Chicago, where it was thirty-eight degrees and raining. "Sheez," mumbled Sussman. "Why couldn't your parents have gotten married in the summer like everybody else?''

"My mom figured if they had anniversaries in March, it'd be a good excuse to fly off somewhere exotic every spring.''

"What happened this spring?''

"A delayed reaction from last year—Dad took her to Palm Beach and played golf for a week. Mom figures he owes her a night at Le Français for that one. Plus, Carol's eight months pregnant.''

The stewardess handed them their drinks; Andy opened the tiny vodka bottle and split it between his and Susie's tomato juice. "Well, at least while we're in town we can drop by Murray's office, see how his morning rendezvous worked out.''

"Andrew, that is perfectly crazy." Susie shoved the manuscript deeper into the pouch. "Look, if he actually needed you— which I don't believe for a second—he surely would have called.''

"Maybe something happened to him.''

"Oh, please.''

"It could have been a setup—''

"Did you try his office?''

"I got his service. Peggy was home with the flu.''

"What about the guy that sent you this?''

Sussman pulled the envelope out a few inches and stared at the return address. "I called J. B. Cranston. Nobody answered. I tried his office—his secretary said he was out of town, visiting grandchildren, I think. I passed a message on, but I haven't heard back from him." Andy poured the last few drops of vodka into Susie's glass. "Anyway, Suse, you're the skier. I called last night, Sunburst's got a ninety-inch base, a foot of fresh powder. Think it over. We'll get a bird's-eye view of the World Cup. You'll meet Tomba and Zirbriggen—hell, maybe you can get a new client out of it.''

"I've got all the clients I need." Susie caressed Andy and pulled him close to her.

"Glad to see the honeymoon isn't over yet.''

"Don't push it." Susie tried her best to conjure up a snarl, but it quickly collapsed into a giggle. The best she could do was tickle Andy in the navel as the landing gear rumbled below them and the 747 glided toward O'Hare.

It was nearly five o'clock, the traffic at Northbrook Court had slowed to a trickle. Andy Sussman wandered through the mall, peeking in Brooks Brothers and the Athlete's Foot, taking a quick walk through a furniture store that was new since he'd been there last. Susie had stayed home with her sister Carol, who lived in Northbrook with her husband Bob, a building contractor. Carol was expecting her first child in April, and Susie had planned this trip to visit her as much as Pat and Charley. The two girls were putting together some type of anniversary gift and accompanying song, which would be delivered to their parents right before dessert tonight at Le Français, a ritzy French restaurant in suburban Wheeling.

The anniversary party would be the first big social affair with the in-laws since the wedding last September. Sussman had no particular dread of Pat and Charley Ettenger. Charley was a big basketball fan; they could happily discuss the approaching NBA playoffs all night. Pat had been slightly slower to respond to his innate warmth and charm; Sussman guessed it had something to do with his getting shnockered at the wedding reception and bribing the band to play "Louie Louie" sixteen times. But she'd had six months to get over that; Sussman had, in fact, detected a genuine warmth in Pat's telephone voice the last several weeks. He had a suspicion it related to the grandchild question, which he expected to be raised sometime during the evening, probably about ten seconds after they walked through the door.

Andy climbed the stairs to the mall's second level and headed straight for Glick Investigations. All was quiet. A few strollers dropped inside to look at Murray's rate sheet, which was posted on the front window like a Chinese menu: surprise birthday gifts, $100 per item; fashion scouting, $25 an hour. March was Missing-Person's Month: "Track down an old friend or relative, $18 an hour plus expenses." And, of course, there were Murray's Mystery Cruises. Posters were splashed all over the office; there were still a few openings on the Caribbean Easter Extravaganza. Sussman tinkered with the idea of surprising Susie, but on second thought he decided he'd like his marriage to last at least until April.

"Hi, Mr. Sussman!" shouted Peggy. She had just stumbled back from the Food Mart with a large Orange Julius and a salad. She looked slightly disheveled—her red hair fell over her eyes, and she was sniffling. "Boy, am I glad to see you. It's getting lonely around here." She slurped down some of her orange drink. "I'm trying to load up on Vitamin C and get rid of this darn flu bug."

"Relax, Peggy," said Andy, helping clear away her desk to make room for the salad. He had never paid much attention to Peggy before. She was friendly and efficient, but now that he thought about it, she wasn't quite as tall or vivacious as Murray had written in his manuscript. Of course, the flu could do that to anyone. "I think what you need is a week in Barbados, Peg. When was the last time Murray gave you a vacation?"

"Vacation?" Peggy snuffled. "What's a vacation? I'm lucky if I get Sundays off. I had to hire a temporary to come in last week; I may have to do the same tomorrow. You haven't talked to him lately, have you?"

"Not exactly. I, uh, got a letter. From Sunburst, Colorado."

"The ski place? God, what a sleaze! I thought he was on a case." Peggy munched on her salad.

"I was sort of hoping you might be able to fill me in there. He needed help with something, but I haven't been able to reach him."

Peggy shrugged and spread some dressing on her salad. "I haven't heard a word."

Sussman scratched his head. "I thought he shares every shred of evidence with you."

"He never tells me anything."

"You don't know where he is twenty-four hours a day?"

"I haven't heard boo from him in three weeks. I thought you might know something. He missed a paycheck, you know. He's never done that before."

Sussman walked back toward Murray's office. The door was locked. "Peggy, do you remember anything about a lady named Barbra Kaplan? Fortyish suburban, came in right before Murray left? She was trying to find her daughter."

"Kaplan, Kaplan . . ." Peggy pushed away her salad, opened

a file drawer, and started flipping through it. "A lot of those women come in when Murray's around. They all have sunglasses and a shawl . . . I think that last day he signed one up for a cruise. Here—" She pulled out a file. "Hey, you're right. Kaplan. Filled out the form and everything."

Sussman pulled out Murray's standard contract. It wasn't much, legally speaking; it was mainly designed so the client would have a souvenir from hiring a detective, plus a few loopholes for tax purposes. But it gave Sussman an address for the Kaplans; they lived on Strawberry Hill Road in Glencoe. There was a notation that Murray was indeed looking for a missing person. "You don't remember the lady at all?"

"God, I'm trying to think. I might have been at lunch. Do you think Murray's in any trouble?"

"Hard to say. Peggy, are you sure you haven't heard anything from him since he left? Messages? Mail?"

"Not a thing. I've been getting a lot of crank calls, though. Some lady asks for Murray, I say he's not in, she hangs up. Sometimes she asks when he'll be back. I tell her I don't know."

"Always a she?"

"Yeah. Never leaves a name. Here . . ." Peggy reached into her in-basket. "Maybe you can use these." She handed Sussman a stack of MasterCard bills. "I can't pay 'em anyway, not till he puts some money in the account."

Sussman took the bills—there were three of them. One was addressed to Murray Glick, another to Glick Investigations, another to Murray Solomon. He opened Murray Solomon's and read through the charges. He saw the bill for the Hertz outlet in Sunburst. There was a dinner at Lorenzo's Loft. There was a charge for a hardware store and a sport shop and an airline ticket. "What about his phone bill, Peg? Do you have that?"

Peggy searched through her in-basket. "Here's Illinois Bell, and here's Sprint."

Sussman stuck them in his pocket.

"Wait, I've got to keep a copy of those." Peggy took the bills back and photocopied them, then gave Sussman a large envelope to put everything in. "There you go. I've been watching your basketball games, by the way. Greg absolutely hates the Lakers. I wish you'd put someone else on, just so he wouldn't cuss so much—"

"Greg?"

"My husband."

"You're married?"

"Of course I'm married!" Peggy flashed Sussman her wedding band. "Three years in July! Remember, I introduced you to Greg at the Flames game two years ago—"

"Right, right. Geez, I'm sorry, Peggy, I forgot."

"Sure," Peggy said, smiling. "Big network star now. Forgets all his friends."

"Nothing of the sort. That's why I'm here, all the way from New Yawk." Sussman looked at his watch. "Look, Peg, I gotta run. My sister-in-law's eight months pregnant, I barely said hello. You've got my office number in New York, right?"

Peggy tapped her Rolodex.

"You hear ANYTHING from Murray, let me know."

"All right, Mr. Sussman. Hey, you're not really worried about him, are you?"

"Nah. Probably just another one of his practical jokes."

"Tell him to get some money in the bank, before we get evicted and I have to get a job doing nails."

"Will do. In fact, if you're really short, call me. I'll make sure you stay afloat."

"Hey, thanks, Mr. Sussman!" Peggy sniffled again and slurped down the rest of her Orange Julius. "Have fun skiing! Tell the boss I'm alive and starving."

"You bet." Sussman waved goodbye to Peggy and walked back into the mall. It did indeed look like there was a ski trip in his future. He just had to arrange things with Merle Summers, his producer, and figure out some way to mollify his wife— hopefully another foot of powder at Sunburst and the chance that Murray Glick would be underneath it would do the trick. In the meantime, there were phone bills and MasterCard bills to go over, and an anniversary dinner to attend.

And, Sussman feared, a long night ahead trying to separate fact from fiction.

15

Andy Sussman hadn't had much of a chance to get to know his brother and sister-in-law, Bob and Carol Silver. When he had first started dating Susie they had been living in Minneapolis, where Bob taught real estate at the University of Minnesota and did some consulting work on the side. But Bob had come back to Chicago a month before the wedding to go into the contracting business with his cousin, no doubt inspired by the incipient arrival of their first child. That had made everybody happy, especially Pat and Charley.

"I figured you'd start getting interested in real estate sooner or later," Bob said. They were splitting a beer in his basement while Carol and Susie, upstairs, were wrapping the anniversary gifts. "Hell, in Manhattan, even the taxi drivers can figure out mortgage balloon payments. I had a guy once, took me in from JFK, actually had a license. Tried to sell me a walk-up on the Lower East Side. Three hundred grand, a real steal."

"Tell me about it. We paid nearly that much for a sardine can in the Village before we finally gave up and moved to Connecticut."

"Affordable, at least. I bet the drive's a real bitch."

"Don't ask." Sussman munched on a pretzel and steered the conversation back to Chicago, specifically to the subject of Kozlo Realty and Sam Kaplan.

"I only know Kaplan in passing," Bob said. "We're mostly residential, north and west suburban. But we did do some work on a commercial building in Deerfield. He was Kozlo's point man. What was it you wanted to know about him?"

"I'm not sure. What kind of guy is he?"

Bob shrugged and sipped on his beer. "Direct. Knows where the bottom line is. Makes sure everybody else does, too."

"Difficult to deal with?"

"Not really. As long as you don't fuck up. What's your interest?"

"A friend of mine has to do some business with him. Somebody I saw in Denver last week. You wouldn't know anything about Kozlo Realty getting involved in Colorado real estate, would you?"

"Out of my turf. I could have you meet him, though, if you want. Maybe a drink after work. He doesn't bullshit around."

"Maybe in a few days. I'll wait on it for now."

"Suit yourself."

Later, as Sussman got dressed for the anniversary dinner, he wondered if he ought to take Bob up on his offer. He could try for some quick answers from Sam Kaplan, clear this thing up in an afternoon, and spare himself a wild-goose chase in the Rockies. But something told him that Sam should be kept at a distance. There was already one murder to deal with (if Murray's manuscript could be trusted) and a missing daughter whom Sam might not know was missing. Sussman decided that it made more sense to have a chat with Barbra Kaplan first. And he was going to need Susie for that.

"Surely thou jest," was Susie's icy response. They were upstairs in the guest bedroom, where they would be staying through the weekend. Andy realized he had just committed a cardinal sin—starting an argument while his wife was getting dressed. She glared at him, her dress half unzipped in the back. He pulled her toward him and gently rubbed her back.

"Darling, would I jest about such a delicate assignment?"

"Andrew, I am NOT, under ANY circumstances, going to pass myself off as Murray Glick's partner. N.O. Period." Susie broke loose and sat down on the edge of the bed.

"Well I certainly can't do it."

"Why not?"

"Someone could recognize me. I'm on network television now, Suse. Even if she's not a basketball fan—"

"Wear a disguise. Look, can't Murray do his own home-work?"

"Murray's not available."

"I'll bet. He's probably in Lorenzo's Loft trying to pick up barmaids. Andy, he just wants you to do his dirty work for him—he said as much in the manuscript."

"That was before its abrupt ending." Sussman started buttoning his dress shirt; they were supposed to pick up the Ettengers in half an hour. "C'mon, Suse, it's a simple job. You call her up, tell her you're Murray's assistant, you need to meet with her for a few minutes. She lives right in Glencoe. All you need to do is corroborate Murray's story, just so we know he didn't invent all this."

"And try to find out if Sam Kaplan ever got involved with Sunburst real estate."

"You'll be home in fifteen minutes."

"It'll take two hours at least, which I planned to spend with my loving parents and my pregnant sister."

"We'll be here all weekend. Besides, Susan Sussman, this simple assignment could get you an all-expenses-paid, two-weeks' vacation in beautiful Sunburst, Colorado, home of the World Cup, not to mention a ninety-inch base—"

"It'll get me two weeks with Murray Glick."

Andy took his wife's hand and pulled her up from the bed. "Darling, think of it this way: you might be saving the life of a fellow human being. Two fellow human beings. I think Dani Kaplan's in trouble."

"If she really exists. She's probably a pet collie or something. In which case we're down to zero fellow human beings."

Sussman let go of Susie, who plopped back down on the bed. He walked over to a mirror and put on his necktie; working for the network had made him fairly proficient in getting a Windsor knot right on the first try. "Sweetheart, we do owe Murray a favor somewhere along the line. He's got me out of trouble twice, in case you forgot."

"I'm trying." Susie stood up and turned around, presenting the back of her dress to Andy. "It's getting late. Zip me up, could you please?"

Andy zipped up the dress. "And, Suse, the way I figure, if we must do Murray a favor, why not do it at the world's finest ski resort, with accommodations completely paid for by CBS?"

"Can you help me with this necklace?" Susie handed a string of pearls to Sussman.

"Certainly." He placed the pearls around her neck and kissed her gently. "Am I getting close to persuading you?"

"Maybe. I need time to formulate my official bribe. You can't get out of this scot-free, you know."

"Do your worst. Start out with the week of skiing."

"Doesn't count. It's got to be totally separate." Susie turned around. "How about ten days of total and complete luxury in the bustling, cosmopolitan world capital of New York City?"

"Your wish is my command. It will be my privilege to serve your every whim in a manner that befits your lovely, sensational self."

"That sounds encouraging," Susie admitted. "Breakfast in bed? Fresh roses every morning?"

"You don't even have to ask."

"And there're a few plays I want to see."

"Orchestra seats."

"The Metropolitan Opera."

"You're too easy."

"And I want to be chauffeured to work. By you. Every morning for ten working days."

"Aack!" choked Sussman. "Driven? Susan, we live in Connecticut now, remember? What's wrong with the train?"

"It's dirty and late and I'm tired of getting hit on every morning by lecherous accountants."

"I'll hire a limo."

"Nope. I want to be driven by you personally, every morning, to the front door of the Equitable Building. I want to share your wonderful conversation and sprightly sense of humor in private those extra three hours every day."

"It takes three hours to get to work?"

"One and a half up, one and a half back."

Sussman slumped onto the bed. "Susan, that's sheer misery."

"Then it's an even deal." Susie tightened Andy's tie and kissed him on the cheek. "C'mon, dear—"

"What if I ride with you on the train?"

"No deal."

"I'll charter a helicopter."

"It'll ruin my hair." Susie grabbed her purse, pulled Andy off the bed, and pointed him toward the door. "Let's get going." She held up his suitcoat and guided his arms through it, then gave his tie one last jerk, and pointed him toward the door. "We'll be late for dinner."

16

Susie Sussman was not exactly pleased with herself. It wasn't that the rewards promised for this little mission weren't pleasant enough. She couldn't remember the last real ski vacation she'd taken; it was sometime before she'd entered law school. She hadn't had a solid week off the whole three years she'd worked at Chavous and Birnbaum. Then she'd met Andy, who was busy with basketball games most of the winter. Occasionally they could manage a day at Vail or Snowbird after a broadcast assignment, but CBS rarely scheduled games from Denver or Salt Lake City, and Andy was the last person to argue against the continued hegemony of the Celtics and Lakers.

Then there was her pampered week in New York to look forward to—she had absolutely no guilty feelings about that. She was the one who'd made the career sacrifice by moving there— she'd done it gladly. She knew what the stakes were for Andy and she certainly didn't want him to have to go back to Chicago and be a local radio announcer again. But life was more difficult for her in New York. It wasn't just the traffic and the crime and the pollution, different from Chicago only by degree. She'd had to re-establish herself at a new law firm, where the inference was that Chicago was some provincial hogtown that couldn't possibly have yielded any meaningful experience, and where the unmistakable impression from her peers was that she'd gotten her job only because she represented her husband. She kept these feelings to herself, but personally Susie Sussman didn't think any of her new confreres would last twenty minutes in Chicago. She'd like to drop a couple of them in the soybean pits for a few days and see if they escaped with anything except their ninety-dollar Calvin Klein skivvies.

Still, she was looking forward to the shows and restaurants and chauffeur service when she got home. She'd happily accept the princess treatment for a week—it was the least she deserved for carrying out this masquerade. And she couldn't help thinking that even the skiing and the roses and the opera and the constant companionship of her darling husband were not reward enough for helping out the insufferable Murray Glick.

Susie hoped she was not turning into some type of harpy on that subject. She knew that men—even loving, selfless boons to humankind like Andy—sometimes had these inexplicable male bondings with people that only marginally belonged to the same species. She was even willing to admit that Murray was fairly proficient at what he did and had helped rescue Andy twice from delicate situations, and had only once gratuitously taken all the credit for himself and made an obnoxious ass of himself all over the media. Mostly, though, Murray represented every male that had ever told her she couldn't get through law school or succeed as a lawyer and, even with all her achievements, had regarded her mainly as a test of their great barristorial and persuasive talents for getting her into bed.

She hoped that evaluation didn't sound too shrill. She was one hell of a wife, she thought. And she WAS helping Murray, after all. But when she did find him, that manuscript was damned well going to get some editing.

Susie drove to the Kaplans' home in west Glencoe; it was eleven in the morning on a brisk, cloudy day. A few snowflakes were falling, although the snow seemed dry; it stung a little when it touched her neck. The Kaplans lived in a split-level house with a sloping lawn and a wide driveway. There was a basketball hoop set up over the garage and a red Jaguar parked outside. Susie parked her sister's Cutlass behind it and walked up to the front door.

A woman answered. She was smallish, with short brown hair that was cut smartly. She wore a yellow turtleneck sweater, gray slacks, and jogging shoes. She looked fortyish; pretty but not glamorous, and not trying to be. She hardly wore any makeup, just a thin layer of matte rose lipstick. She didn't look like she took a lot of bubble baths with strange men. "Mrs. Kaplan?"

"Who were you expecting?" the woman replied rather sharply.

"No one—it was just that from your, uh . . . voice on the phone, I had a different picture."

Mrs. Kaplan squinted; she seemed more than a little on edge. "Come in, Ms. Anthony."

"Call me Susan, please." Susie, doing business as Susan B. Anthony, walked inside and followed Barbra Kaplan into the living room. It was sunk a half-level below the foyer, with plush white carpeting on the floors and a series of French countryside oil paintings on the walls, illuminated by track lighting. The furniture was all upholstered in white, with the exception of a chrome and glass coffee table; everything was spotless, not a pillow was out of place. Susie sat down on the couch and glanced at the coffee table. There were several magazines spread neatly over it. She noticed that the one on top, a February *Art World,* was addressed to Mrs. Barbara Kaplan, not spelled like Striesand. Nice touch, Murray, she thought.

"Mr. Glick never mentioned anything about a partner." Mrs. Kaplan spoke with a slight nasal accent that suggested there was some New York in her history. "In fact, I don't recall hearing about another office."

"Mr. Glick has several offices. And our employees are kept confidential, Mrs. Kaplan. Now, I'd like to review a few aspects of the case—"

"Listen," said Mrs. Kaplan, "in the first place, I'd like to know what happened to your boss. He's on retainer, you know. I'm paying a hundred dollars a day plus expenses—"

"Which I'm sure you'll agree is an investment well worth it when he finds your daughter—"

"I haven't heard a word out of him in nearly a month!" Barbara Kaplan's voice pitched upwards, her small right hand clenched into a fist and banged against her knee.

"Mrs. Kaplan, let me assure you that Mr. Glick is hard at work. It's only the extreme confidentiality of the case that keeps him from staying in constant touch with you." Susie sat up primly and pulled her skirt over her knees. "Incidentally, Mrs. Kaplan, have you made any attempt to contact him?"

"I've called his office a hundred times—"

"But you didn't leave a message."

"He told me specifically never to leave a message. Ms. Anthony, I haven't heard one word from him since he took me on."

"Not at all?"

Mrs. Kaplan frowned, her eyes flashed in irritation.

"You didn't, uh, go to Sunburst?"

"Go to Sunburst? For God's sake, if I wanted to chase all the way out there I wouldn't have hired a detective! How could I go to Sunburst? My husband wouldn't LET me go. If he found out, he'd probably sell the damn condominium before the plane landed."

"I see . . ." Susie wished that this woman would offer her some coffee or something; she needed a few seconds to get reorganized. "Mrs. Kaplan, I just want to review the situation, so I can make sure there haven't been any new developments on your side. To begin with, does your husband know anything yet about Dani's disappearance?"

"No." Susie waited for some amplification, but Mrs. Kaplan had nothing to add.

"So as far as Mr. Kaplan is concerned, Dani is still living in Sunburst with Casey Wright?"

"As far as Mr. Kaplan is concerned, Dani doesn't exist."

Susie took a deep breath. "Well then. Is it safe to assume that Mr. Kaplan has no interest in further investments in Sunburst, either individually or through his employers at Kozlo Realty?"

Barbara Kaplan's tight little mouth gaped open, she sat forward on her chair. "Good Lord, my husband would no more do business with Sunburst than he would with Noriega. I had to beg him not to sell our condo when Dani moved out there. What on earth makes you think Sam would even consider doing business with that place?"

Susie folded her arms, she was tiptoeing through a minefield. She was glad that Sam was still furious; at least Murray had told the truth about that. She had a hunch that most of Murray's narrative was dependable, with the exception of one particular subject. "Mrs. Kaplan, we have the strong suspicion that Dani's disappearance may be somehow connected to real estate in Sunburst."

Barbara Kaplan rolled her eyes toward the ceiling. She sighed and sunk back in her chair.

"And we've learned that your daughter had another boyfriend. He worked for the Forest Service."

"What in the world . . ."

"The boyfriend was adamantly opposed to the expansion of the ski area onto the west ridge of Sunburst Mountain. He wanted the forest service to cancel the deal. He ended up buried in an avalanche."

Barbara Kaplan's eyes snapped to life. "Dead?"

"The police said it was an accident, case closed. We don't think so. And Dani disappeared at about the same time."

Barbara Kaplan edged up from the chair. "I . . . I think I'd like a cup of coffee, Susan. Would you like some, too?"

"Very much so." Susie looked heavenward and thanked God for the small favor. She got up and followed Mrs. Kaplan into the kitchen. It was sparkling clean, like the rest of the house; an open window over the sink let in some of the chilly March air. Susie scanned the room; she would have liked to meet the Kaplans' decorator. There were beautiful bronze pans hanging over the oven, there was a spice rack with a hundred varieties, most of them imported.

The coffeemaker was on a wooden counter next to the range; Mrs. Kaplan nervously replaced a filter and started to brew a new pot. "Susan, has anyone seen my daughter since this other boyfriend of hers, uh . . ."

"We think someone has." Susie was dealing now with one of Murray's less dependable subjects. "We have every reason to believe she's alive and well. But she may be in some danger, and we think this real estate angle may be important."

"I told you Sam wasn't involved."

"Mrs. Kaplan, we know that Sunburst Corporation tried to get Kozlo Realty to invest in their expansion."

"I know that, Susan. My husband told them that as long as Casey Wright was employed at Sunburst they'd never get a penny from him or Kozlo. He told them he wouldn't buy a goddamn lift ticket—he won't even lease the condo; he doesn't want to generate any profits for them."

Susie gazed around the kitchen. She walked over to the refrigerator and looked at the tiny animal magnets that clung to the door. A couple of recipes were tacked up, along with a luncheon invitation. "Mrs. Kaplan, does your husband talk much to you about business?"

"No, but he talked to me about that." The coffee machine light flashed on. Mrs. Kaplan poured two cups and gave one to Susie. "Cream or sugar?"

"Cream."

Mrs. Kaplan fumbled for a cream pitcher that was sitting on a counter by the refrigerator and handed it to Susie. "It's the only way he acknowledges that Dani's alive. I don't know how you could suspect that he's involved out there."

"We don't have any evidence. But we do know that Dani jilted Casey Wright. Now IF Casey was involved in the death of the forest ranger, and IF Dani knew it and was afraid of Casey, why would she hide from her parents?"

"Who says she's hiding from her parents?" Barbara Kaplan spoke sharply, the lines on her forehead creased. "You don't know anything about her, you don't know anything about us—" The coffee cup trembled in her hand. "What if your boyfriend was murdered? What if your father wasn't speaking to you? You'd be shocked, upset—who's to say what you'd do, where you'd run?"

"I don't know what I'd do, Mrs. Kaplan. But it's been over a month now, and if she was afraid of Casey it seems logical that she'd contact you, or even your husband—"

"What are you suggesting? That Sam actually got involved there? That he was doing business with Casey Wright?" Barbara Kaplan's eyes danced in anger. "That he may have been mixed up in a MURDER?"

Susie stared into her coffee cup, wondering if she had gone too far. She knew nothing about this woman. She was taking it as an article of blind faith that Barbara Kaplan was herself innocent of any wrongdoing. Why had she told her anything about Murray's investigation? On the other hand, that was Murray's problem— Susie reminded herself that she was doing him one gigantic favor; she wasn't responsible for the consequences.

"Ms. Anthony," said Mrs. Kaplan, "let me tell you something about my husband. He can be an irascible, angry, overbearing son of a bitch. He can be unforgiving. But he's also loyal and honest and he's worked damned hard for every penny he's ever got."

"I'm sure he has, Mrs. Kaplan—"

"No, you're not. But listen to me: I don't know why Dani ran off. I don't know why she's hiding, if that's what she's doing.

But it's not because she's afraid of her parents. It's not because she's afraid of her father. Now if you've got any other theories, I'd like to hear them.''

Susie didn't, and she could see that this interview wasn't going to last much longer than the cup of coffee. "At this point, Mrs. Kaplan, that's all we have to go on. Of course, since the police aren't investigating the death of the forest ranger, we may have to look into it ourselves.''

"What about this person that might have seen Dani?''

"We're trying to follow that up.''

"Was it a man or a woman? Give me a name and telephone number.''

"Mrs. Kaplan, you're just going to have to let us do the detective work,'' Susie said. She had given this woman about all the information she was going to get. "If you want to help us, try and keep your ear to the ground about your husband's real estate investments. Call Mr. Glick's office if you hear anything. You can leave a message with his secretary; her name is Peggy.'' Susie pushed away the coffee cup and slung her purse over her shoulder. "I think that's all for now, Mrs. Kaplan. I've got work to do.''

Barbara Kaplan didn't protest. She calmly escorted Susie to the front hallway. "You'll keep me informed from now on, Ms. Anthony. I don't expect to wait another three weeks for a progress report.''

"Of course.''

"Find my daughter.'' Mrs. Kaplan showed Susie out the door. "I'm running out of patience.''

"You're not the only one.'' Susie walked stiffly down the front walk and hurried back to the Cutlass. She roared out of the driveway, nearly clipping a Volvo wagon that was cruising down Strawberry Hill with three kids in the backseat. There was something inside Susie that wanted to turn back and plow Mrs. Kaplan's Jaguar halfway to Milwaukee, but that would only be an expensive waste of energy that could be better aimed in other directions.

Susie had a better idea. She drove straight to Northbrook Court, and not to make a report to the "home office." If she was going to ski at a posh resort like Sunburst, after all, she needed a new sweater and a new down overcoat and some new après-ski boots. New earrings wouldn't hurt either. And she'd seen some fur-lined mittens that she absolutely HAD to have, although she might have to save something for the ski village. One thing was certain: she was going to be treated like royalty for carrying out this charade.

She had a feeling it still wouldn't be enough.

17

Persuading Merle Summers to assign him to the World Cup race
in Sunburst proved slightly more difficult than Andy Sussman
had anticipated; he was beginning to build up a debt load of
favors that would bankrupt a small monarchy. Merle was the
producer at CBS Sports who had worked closest with Andy since
he had joined the sports department—it was his lobbying that
had secured Sussman's eventual assignment to the NBA Game
of the Week. But Merle's first love was "Adventure!", a weekly
anthology that sent semi-celebrities into deep dark jungles and
uncharted wilds in search of God knows what nearly extinct tribe
or mammal or natural wonder that was about ready to explode,
erupt, or flood the nearby countryside into oblivion. Andy had
assiduously avoided an "Adventure!" assignment for two years;
fortunately there was nearly always a basketball game or horse
race or golf tournament to pre-empt him, or if all else failed a
Jewish holiday or a grave illness somewhere in the continental
United States that required his presence.

"Andy, it IS awfully short notice," Merle said over the telephone from his office in Manhattan. "Fred Ortiz already has his
bags packed, he's been watching videotapes of the European
tour—"

"Fred hates skiing, Merle. He hates winter, he's from Miami.
Send him to Orlando; there's a women's tennis tournament there
next week."

"ESPN has the tennis tournament—"

"Let him do golf, then. Give him Daytona, he won't know
how to thank me—"

"Not so easy, Andy. Think of the paperwork. Changing press accreditations, hotel reservations. Plus you've never even been to a ski race. I'll have to send you all the tapes, you haven't even met our ski guy—"

"I'm a quick study."

"Besides, there has to be a hidden motive for this, which I'm dying to find out. Since when do you even own a pair of skis, Sussman?"

"Merle, Merle," Andy replied. "I hope you're not implying that I'm making this request for any reason other than to expand my journalistic horizons."

"It's Susie, right? She a skier, I saw those K2s in your garage."

"She is, but that has nothing—"

"Jeez, Andy. Not even married six months, she's already calling the shots. What's it gonna be next, play-by-play of women's field hockey in New Delhi?"

"I won't even dignify that with a response."

Sussman heard a lecherous chortle on the other end of the line and waited for what he assumed would be the latest price for doing business with friends and loved ones. "So," Merle said, "you want me to sign you up for a week in Sunburst—"

"Two weeks, actually. I need the preparation time."

"Two weeks. To expand your journalistic horizons. Accommodations for two, I take it?"

"It's all double occupancy anyway."

"You could share a room with one of the technicians."

"Read my contract."

There was a long pause from Manhattan, then a slight clearing of the throat. "Andy," said Merle Summers, "have you ever been to French Guiana?"

"No I haven't, Merle. But I heard McDonald's bought the entire country last week; they're turning it into a Ronald McDonald's theme park—"

"Andy, there's a rare species of giant anaconda that lives in the jungles of French Guiana. They feed exclusively on an equally rare species of tropical three-horned toad. You can only find it by paddling up the Grand Inini River in a dugout canoe—"

"I flunked canoeing at camp, Merle. I rammed a hole into a sailboat, I was grounded the whole summer."

"All you have to do is sit in the bow. We have a crack guide; we used him last year when we went up the Amazon in the pirogues—"

"Merle, a cameraman nearly died on that trip."

"It was just a mild case of dysentery. You'll be fine, Andy, as long as you take your pills. I'll be there myself—we'll have a great time. It'll be two weeks in September; you don't have any conflicts."

"Of course I do. It's the High Holidays."

"They come late this year."

"There's my anniversary—"

"You'll be back in time."

"Merle, please don't do this to me."

"Do what to you?" Merle said with total innocence. "It's strictly a programming decision, Andy. Everybody gets a crack at 'Adventure!' Fred went to Peru, Al Simmons went to Auckland. Think of it as a mission, like the Mormons do—only it's just two weeks instead of a year, we all get rip-roaring drunk at the end, and you don't even have to convert anybody."

Andy clenched the telephone and stared at it; he would have hurled it into Lake Michigan if he thought it would drag Merle Summers along with it. "Merle, I want first-class accommodations at Sunburst. None of this network economy stuff."

"We always go first class."

"Unlimited dining, private ski lessons."

"We want you to feel completely at home with your assignment, Andy."

"And I swear to God, Merle, if I get strangled by some crazed snake that hasn't been seen since Noah's Ark I'm going to personally see that 'Adventure!' gets booted off the air and replaced by 'Great Moments In Suburban Zoning Ordinances.' "

"Glad to have you aboard, pal."

Sussman slammed the phone down and flopped onto his bed, just as Susie walked in. She was juggling three boxes from Neiman Marcus and wearing a full-length down overcoat with the sales slip still attached to the collar. She kissed him, gave him a hug, and deposited the boxes in his arms. "Like it, darling?"

Sussman mumbled something under his breath and inspected the pricetag on the coat. "I don't suppose you were their millionth customer or anything?"

"Andy, dear, we're going to be hobnobbing with the crown princes of Europe; we do want to look our best."

Sussman put the boxes down. He didn't open them—he couldn't begin to imagine what the bill would be. He figured he might as well wait until Susie wore whatever she'd bought, at least he'd have the pleasure of seeing how scintillating she looked in it. Besides, she might as well spend all their money—by the end of the year he'd no doubt be dead of some rare tropical disease found only in the jungles of French Guiana. "How did the interview with Barbra Kaplan go?"

"Want to see my earrings?" Susie pulled a small jewelry box out of her purse. "Sterling silver."

"That bad, huh?" Sussman opened the case. He had to admit the earrings were gorgeous; each one had two small, elegant silver stars dangling from a crescent. He unclipped the costume hoops that Susie had been wearing and replaced them with the new ones. "Very pretty, sweetheart."

"Thank you." She kissed Andy on the cheek.

"So. No word on Murray or the girl?"

"Zilcho. And Sam still won't have anything to do with Sunburst."

"So Murray speaks the truth, after all?"

"Selectively. His romantic interludes with Barb-a-ra Kaplan may have been slightly exaggerated."

"How slightly?"

"Oh, about 2,000 miles." Susie stacked her boxes on the end of the bed, took off her coat and slung it over a chair. "Andy, I was wondering. Whatever happened to that girl Murray used to go out with?"

"You want to narrow it down to time zones?"

"You know, the one he took to our wedding. He met her right before he helped you with that wrestling thing in L.A."

"Let's see, that was, uh . . ."

Susie folded her arms and smirked. "Gather your memory cells. The four of us? Drinks at McMahons, dancing at Thrills? Breakfast at the Oak Tree, 5 A.M.?"

"Right, right . . . Terry." Sussman smiled sheepishly. It had been a long, drunken night on Rush Street a few days before the wedding. As Andy recalled, it wasn't his dancing with Terry that had irked Susie so—it wasn't his fault they changed to a slow dance right after he cut in. It was just that the exchange left his bride-to-be in Murray's paws for almost an entire five seconds, before she twirled into the ladies room and disappeared nearly long enough for him to call back the invitations. "Gee, I kind of liked that girl, Suse. She actually had Murray talking to himself for a while."

"As I recall, you were considerably more optimistic than I was."

"Well, it was our wedding week."

"How long did it last?"

"About three months. She broke it off, I think. He was semi-devastated."

"That's what he gets for finally dating a girl more intelligent than your average tree."

Andy shrugged. "He claimed he wasn't ready to be domesticated. His cruise business was hot, she was feeling a little uneasy about him traipsing off to the Caribbean four or five times a winter. That's how she met him; she knew how he operated. According to Murray, they still see each other now and then. Why do you ask?"

"I just thought he might have called her. If they were still close, and he needed help. Maybe she knows something."

"It wasn't in the manuscript."

"Fictional sleuths with babes lined up left and right don't call up old girlfriends who've just given them the boot. I'd look into it."

Sussman walked over to their night table, opened the drawer, and took out the Sprint long-distance bill that Peggy had given him. He recognized the calls to his office in New York and the CBS affiliate in Denver. He saw another call to Chicago. It was at 7:45 A.M., local time. It was only one minute long. "Hmm. She worked at the Rehab Center, didn't she?"

"I think she was some type of therapist."

"Let's see." Sussman picked up the phone and dialed the number on the bill. A secretary answered, it was indeed the Rehabilitation Institute of Chicago; Sussman had reached the physical therapy department. After a slight delay, he managed to track down Terry Tollison. She had been in a staff meeting, but she didn't seem upset by the interruption—Sussman guessed that staff meetings were the same, no matter what the profession.

"Well hi, Andy!" Terry sounded bright and cheery—the memories were coming back. She was a tallish blond, on the slim side, her hair about shoulder length; like all of Murray's women she was a real looker. But she had a sharp, jabbing sense of humor; she didn't let Murray get away with much, particularly when it came to his alleged life of danger and intrigue. Murray took it all gracefully; for a few weeks, Andy actually thought he'd met his match. He was genuinely surprised and a little disappointed when Murray told him about the breakup.

But if Terry was harboring any resentments, she wasn't showing it. She was open and friendly; she wanted to know how Andy's career was going at CBS. There was no mention of a certain detective. Sussman danced around the issue of the phone call; after about five minutes of banter he casually asked if she'd talked to Murray Glick recently.

"Oh, sure. He called me from some ski resort in Colorado, the lucky dog. All summer he complains about being stuck inside that mall, then presto—he disappears for the cruise season and shows up three months later at some Glitzville luxury condo in the Rockies. I hung up on him after thirty seconds."

"Oh." Sussman's mind went blank for a moment, then he heard laughter on the other end.

"Hey, I had a patient—Murray's not in the 'drop everything' category anymore. I called him back later."

"Oh, good. So you two are still, uh . . ."

"Friends? Soulmates? Speaking to each other?"

"Any of the above."

"We talk. I told him that one day he'd wake up in the middle of the night and realize that his glamour gumshoe bit wasn't as much fun as it used to be. The old knees are starting to creak a little, the cutesy tastettes are holding at twenty-three while his bronze mug starts to wrinkle. Some day."

"I hope we both live to see it." Sussman looked over at Susie, who seemed to be picking up the gist of the conversation. "I don't suppose that was on his mind when he called you from Sunburst?"

There was a pause at the other end of the line.

"I don't mean to get personal—"

"Andy," Terry said softly, "is Murray in some kind of trouble?"

"I'm not sure. He wanted me to come out to Sunburst a couple of weeks ago, but we missed connections and now I can't seem to get hold of him. I have this feeling he's just trying to lure me out there to help him do something he'd rather not do himself." Sussman thought he detected a giggle at the other end of the line.

"Sounds familiar. When are you leaving?"

"Uh . . ." Sussman glanced at his wife. "Oh, probably Thursday."

"That's one of the things I especially admire about Murray," Terry laughed. "You can see right through him, but it doesn't really matter, does it?"

"I'm afraid not. Anyway, if it's not too private, I was wondering if his call had anything to do with a case."

"It might have. He wanted to know about hypothermia."

"Hypothermia?"

"It's what happens when you get real cold real fast. Like falling through the ice on a frozen lake, or being abandoned in your car on a freezing cold night."

"Or being buried under a ton of snow," Sussman said. "Did he mention why he was so interested?"

"Not exactly. You know Murray, complaining about how cold it was on the mountain, how the wind was blowing on the chairlift and he was turning into an icicle. Then he mumbled something about hydrothermia or hyperthermia like he didn't know what it was, but I'm sure that's why he called in the first place."

"Why do you say that?"

"He started asking about how quickly body temperature fell, and how long a male about his size and build could last, and what kind of clothes it was best to wear to protect yourself—in a mountain environment, by the way. Not in a frozen lake or a stalled car."

"Was that the extent of the conversation?"

"That was the part you'd be interested in."

"But there was no mention of a case?"

"Nope. I asked, I got the usual 'you don't want to know about my dangerous work' routine."

"And you haven't heard from him since?"

"No. Hang on." There was a muffled sound, which Sussman assumed was Terry holding her hand over the phone and shouting something at someone. "Andy," she said, "I've got to get back to this meeting. Listen, I wouldn't worry about Murray. He can take care of himself."

"I'm sure he can. But look, if there's anything else you can remember—"

"That's it, believe me. Be good, Andy. Have a great time in Colorado."

"Hey, the snow's supposed to be great there, Terry. You ought to take a week off and join us."

"Wrong. But hit Murray with a snowball for me when you see him."

"Absolutely."

"Bye, Andy."

"So long, Terry."

Sussman hung up the phone and turned to his wife. Susie smiled seductively and shook her soft brown bangs over her forehead. "Detective work over for the day?" She grabbed his arm and pulled him toward the bed. Andy sat down beside her, next to the clothes boxes and the phone bills. He pulled a pillow from beneath the bedspread and fluffed it under her head. "If it means anything," she said, "I think you're totally crazy."

"Only about you, babe." Sussman pulled her toward the pillow. His mind drifted back to when he had first asked Susie Ettenger out for a date. From the moment she had agreed to have dinner with him, he had sworn to himself that he wasn't going to let this girl slip away. And he hadn't.

Sussman ran his hand through Susie's hair. He wondered about his friend Murray. What had gone through Glick's mind when he had first seen Terry Tollison? Did he think to himself, this is it? Did he vow, I won't let this woman escape me?

Did it even cross his mind?

"A penny for your thoughts," Susie said, kissing Andy on the cheek.

Sussman smiled. He guessed that Murray had given it a fleeting consideration. But ultimately, he had let the opportunity pass. That was why Murray Glick was off in Colorado somewhere, chasing after women from six to sixty, real or imagined. And, Sussman thought, that was why he and Susie were about to go chasing off to Sunburst in search of Murray. Andy snuggled next to his wife and turned off the lights.

"Two cents," Susie said. "Final offer."

"Sorry, babe, no sale."

This was what Andy Sussman was thinking: for a world-class detective with an international clientele, nerves of steel, and a mind like a steel trap, it might not hurt Murray Glick to use a little better judgment once in a while.

18

Andy Sussman stood teetering at the top of the Sunburst downhill course, a portable camera strapped to his chest. He pulled the goggles over his eyes; his knees brushed against the aluminum trip wire that would signal the start of his run.

"Hyperventilate," shouted Kevin Cumberland, the CBS ski expert, who was standing just outside the starter's shack. "Remember: weight, unweight on the turns. Don't fall back into the hill. Don't worry about speed, we'll make you look good."

Sussman waved his left hand at Cumberland and stared down the mountain, at a two-and-a-half mile course that appeared to have the vertical drop of Niagara Falls. He had tried briefly to convince Kevin to take the demonstration run himself, but the skier, a former Olympian who ran helicopter ski tours in between network assignments, had insisted that it was the lead announcer's traditional duty. "You need to get a feel for the course, Andy. Speed, bumps, turns. Believe me, you'll have a much better sense of the race after you do this."

Sussman had pointed out that he'd have a much better sense of a suicide if he jumped off the Empire State Building, but none of his journalism teachers had ever recommended it. He hadn't pushed the issue, though. He had requested this assignment; it would look pretty wimpy if he refused to put on a pair of skis.

"Beep, beep!" honked Cumberland, emulating the mechanical signal that started the racers. "You're holding up the works."

Sussman gritted his teeth. To give himself that extra edge of determination, he dug his poles into the snow and tried to imagine that Murray Glick was underneath them. The Murray Situation was pervading his thoughts, rattling his nerves, disturbing his marital bliss. Where the hell was the guy? They'd been at Sunburst two nights; they'd had zero luck in tracking him down. He'd been unable to locate J. B. Cranston either, at home or at his office. J.B.'s absence was beginning to take on sinister overtones.

The truth was, Andy had assumed Murray would contact him as soon as he got there. He guessed his friend would be waiting for him at the condo, or outside the production set, or at a bar somewhere, with his good-natured leer and some unpleasant task that Sussman couldn't refuse now that he was here.

But there was no Murray. And Sussman, despite his prevailing instinct that this was all one typical Glick setup, was getting increasingly concerned with each passing day.

"Roll tape!" shouted Cumberland. "Let's haul ass, Jean-Claude. It's almost lunchtime."

Sussman turned on the camera and broke through the gate. He headed downhill at a steep angle, keeping one eye glued to Cumberland, who was skiing alongside just out of camera range, waving and mugging—he could have done this blindfolded.

"Weight over the skis! Don't lean back!"

Sussman tried to concentrate on the mechanical responses to weight and rhythm that Cumberland had been drilling into him all morning. He caromed off a mogul and swallowed hard. After fifty yards he was still on his feet.

"Edges in, poles out!"

Once Sussman got through the first three gates, he started to get a better sense of his skis underneath him. He could control his speed better; he was beginning to glide. He actually began to notice the fir trees that filled out the mountain scene, the fluffy clouds gathering over the village, the ski patrollers that flanked the run with their first-aid sleds.

"Piece of cake!" shouted Cumberland. "Wait'll we get you in training, you'll be ready for Albertville."

The terrain started to flatten out just a bit and Sussman smiled for the first time. He let his skis push him over a small bump and sucked in some air; he only flew a few feet before touching the mountain again, but he felt the exhilaration—for just a nanosecond he could identify with Killy and Zubriggen and Tomba. He was certain now that the run was a good idea after all, provided he reached the finish line with the same number of appendages with which he began.

"Last gates," Cumberland exhorted. "Don't fall now!"

Sussman didn't; he schussed through the imaginary tape, greeted by a screaming throng of two technicians, a ski patroller, and a tall man with a beard and stocking cap, wearing the official Sunburst Ski School jacket. A patch on the right arm read "Sunburst Downhill."

"Hey, Cumbersome," shouted the man, "What the fuck, I thought you were the pro."

"Gone to stud," Kevin Cumberland replied, forcing a laugh. He was about six foot three with a shock of blond hair. His outfit consisted of faded jeans and a light blue sweater with a jaguar knitted into the arm, a symbol of the line of skiwear he promoted on a part-time basis, when he wasn't busy leading wilderness ski treks into the Canadian Rockies or doing guest shots for CBS.

"Well for Chrissakes, dress like a skier," the bearded man chided. "You're on television. What do you want people to think—we're some pissant weekend hill for the locals?"

Sussman could barely hear this exchange. He stood a few yards past the finish line, bent over slightly, trying to catch his breath. He unstrapped the ski-cam and handed it to a technician. He assumed Cumberland and the bearded ski instructor were old friends engaging in friendly banter. But as he regained his wind, he had the distinct impression that Kevin was getting steamed.

"It's a freakin' ski race, Casey, not a black tie dinner." Cumberland speared his pole into the snow and raised his goggles over his forehead. "Be nice to us ski bums—the public's not paying to see a bunch of damn bean counters."

Sussman straightened up and stared at the ski instructor, taking in the beard and the muscular torso. Murray Glick had made at least one accurate description. "Now there's a man who knows how to present himself," the instructor said, as Sussman skied over. Casey slapped him on the back of his black and yellow CBS parka. "I'm Casey Wright, head of the ski school. Welcome to Sunburst."

"Andy Sussman, CBS Sports." Andy looked back up at the treacherous course. "Happy to be here."

"Helluva ride there, Andy. I was about to call the race officials; thought it was an unauthorized practice run."

"Har, har." Sussman knocked some snow off his boots with his pole. "I made it down in one piece, anyway—"

"Modesty doesn't become you. C'mon, ace, I'll buy you and your hobo friend a drink."

Cumberland grimaced and started to look at his watch. He mumbled something about lunch with his girlfriend, but Andy ignored him and accepted the invitation. They agreed to meet at Clem's Claim, back at the bottom of the mountain.

"Sorry to screw up your lunch plans," Sussman said to Cumberland, when Casey was safely out of earshot. They were riding the number eight chairlift back to the top of Fox Hunt, an intermediate run which would lead them over the east side of the hill and back to the village. "We'll just grab a couple of drinks, then I want to see the tape. I was shaking so much, it'll probably look like an earthquake."

"Nah, you were fine. Listen, Andy, I'm not real thirsty. Maybe I'll run the tape back to HQ now—"

"Stick around, Kev. I just want to get a little background on their operation. I didn't realize Casey's not your favorite guy."

Kevin scowled and looked over his shoulder; Wright was on the chair behind them, waving. "Arrogant prick. We trained together a long time ago. He never could cut it."

"So here he is, dedicating his life to the instruction of our youth."

"He couldn't teach a fish to swim."

"Nonetheless, he seems to have prospered."

"So he has," sighed Cumberland, as the chair creaked and groaned its way to the top of the lift. He pulled the safety latch over them and gave Sussman a brief and pointed description of Casey Wright's road to success. It jibed pretty much with the accounts that Murray had related, with a few additions; mainly, a liaison with the wife of the president of a mortgage lending bank in New York who owned a condo in Sunburst and invested heavily in the corporation. Sussman wondered if that was just another version of the wife of the treasurer in Murray's story. Perhaps they were both apocryphal. In any case, the personality sketch came through.

A few minutes later, after running Fox Hunt and taking an easy jaunt down the catwalk, the three of them were sitting at Clem's Claim, a burger and beer joint in the village. The inside was decorated in early Western saloon, complete with swinging double doors and portraits of Wild West legends: Jesse James, Annie Oakley, Billy the Kid. The bar was dark and musty; at Casey's suggestion they sat outside on the porch, their skis stuck in the snow in front of them. It was barely forty degrees but the sun was warm; within a few minutes Sussman had his jacket open and his stocking cap off. A waitress delivered them a round of Coors on tap. They sipped their beers while Casey delivered a prospectus on Sunburst's future that would have drawn a standing ovation had it been presented at a meeting of its stockholders.

"Sounds sensational," Andy said, crunching a pretzel. "Maybe CBS should buy a condo for its employees on assignment. I'll call Merle, see if we can scrape up a down payment. What do you think, Kev?"

"We could score a network first," Kevin said with a smirk. "A real estate deal closed on live TV. Maybe we could do it between runs of the downhill."

"You'd be damn lucky if you did," Casey replied, in all seriousness. "Lots for Sunburst West are on sale right now. You can still get in at the base of the new gondola for under seven figures, but I wouldn't wait long."

"I'll call my banker." Sussman leaned back in his chair. "Speaking of Sunburst West, Casey, didn't I hear something about development problems over there? A protest or something?"

"I wasn't aware of any problems. Maybe you mean out at Vail, they've been expanding. They get a lot more publicity—"

"No, no, I'm sure I heard something about this place. Maybe it was a news bite I picked up hanging around the studio—no, wait." Sussman sat up straight. "I read about it on the airplane. Some magazine, I think it was called *American Southwest.*" Andy took a swig of beer. He looked through the mug at Casey; he thought he saw his eyebrows twitch. "According to the article, they were waiting for an Environmental Impact Statement. There was a protest group—"

Casey cleared his throat and looked around the bar, then lowered his voice. "It's possible, Andy, but I'm not the right guy to ask. I'm just a ski instructor. You'd have to go through the corporation, or maybe the Forest Service—"

"The funny thing is, Case, I could have sworn he'd inter-

viewed you. I read it on the plane, coming in from Denver."
Sussman took another draw of Coors. "I was a little tired. Is
there another Casey around here?"

"I doubt it." Wright broke into a half-smile. "Look, Andy, I
see a lot of people. Come to think about it, some guy did talk to
me a couple of weeks ago, but he, uh—I don't recall any discussion about environmental problems. I didn't know he'd even filed
the story. Anyway, nothing much came of it—we're breaking
ground in June."

"Just the same, I think it's something we might want to mention. Just to be fair and accurate, especially if we're going to
spend some of our time talking about your operation."

Wright pushed his beer aside. He stood between Sussman and
Cumberland, draping an arm around each one's shoulder.
"Enough politicking, gentlemen. Let's keep our minds on skiing;
that's what we're here for. Why don't we take an expanded tour
of the hill? I'll get you into the back bowls—"

"Love to, Casey, but we've got production meetings all afternoon," Sussman said. "Maybe tomorrow morning, first thing."

"Terrific! I'd say a fifteen-minute feature would be perfect. In
fact, maybe I'll give you a lesson; it'll all be part of the show."

Cumberland responded with a dour frown. "Make sure your
medical insurance is paid up," he said to Sussman, backing his
chair from the table. "No offense, Mr. Sunburst."

"Hey, gang, I'd be happy to assign one of our lovely instructors." Casey grinned and signaled the waitress for the bill. "The
point is, Andy, I think you should get a feeling for the entire
mountain. This is the finest ski area in the world." He paused
for a moment while Kevin Cumberland choked on his Coors.
"Not counting certain areas that can only be reached by Sherpas
or amphibious aircraft."

"Let's hope we can keep 'em that way." Cumberland got up
and pulled Sussman's chair back, allowing Andy to struggle back
up in his ski boots. "You'll take care of this, Instructor Wright?"

"It's on the mountain," said Casey, as the waitress handed
him the bill. "See you tomorrow, boys. Eight o'clock; get that
morning sun for the TV cameras."

Sussman and Cumberland waved their assent. They picked up
their skis and marched off toward the parking lot. "What's all
this environmental business?" Kevin asked. "We're not doing a
'Sixty Minutes' number, are we?"

"Hardly. But there's been a few stories floating around; if they expect us to do a ninety-minute promotion for the Sunburst Corporation, it wouldn't hurt to know how they conduct their business. Just to protect our own integrity."

"Natch." They reached the end of the snow trail and started clomping on concrete. "You think old Casey's in some hot shit?"

Sussman paused. He noted the mischievous grin on Cumberland's face and decided that his partner could be trusted. He might even have some details about the area that could be helpful. "There's a rumor going around, Kev, that certain employees of the Forest Service were very much in opposition to the expansion of Sunburst mountain."

"I can understand that. I used to backpack up here and ski down the east side—years ago, before it was developed."

"And before you could afford helicopters."

"The struggling days of my youth. Spectacular terrain, though. I'm sure when they bought the west ridge someone kicked up a little dust."

"So I've heard. There's another rumor that a certain Forest Service employee met an untimely end about the time the land deal went through. Accidental, of course. Avalanche."

Cumberland found his car, a black Porsche with a ski rack on top. "I detect a sliver of doubt."

Sussman nodded.

"Well, we can find out easy enough. I got a buddy over at police headquarters; we go trout fishing in the summertime. Good guy, just a little harried."

"Keeping up with the crime wave in Sunburst?"

"Cuts into his fly-tying time. I'll talk to him, if you want."

"Please do. Quietly, of course."

"Not for the public airwaves?"

"Not at this time. Maybe never." Sussman set his skis in the car rack. "At least it'll keep the Sunburst PR guys off our backs for a while. Leave us a little time to ski the mountain."

"You betcha." Kevin Cumberland cast a last glance toward the village, then unlocked the passenger door to his car. "Let's get that tape edited. We might even have an hour to get to the back bowls before the lifts close."

"You're the boss." Sussman got in. Cumberland started the engine, and the two of them roared off to production headquarters.

19

Susie Sussman looked at the tattered Sierra Club card that had been resting in the back of her pocketbook for the ten months since she'd renewed her membership. She'd joined the club in 1970, the year of the first Earth Day; it had seemed the in-thing to do at the time. She hadn't exactly been an active member, socially or politically. There were not a whole lot of mountains and forests around Chicago, unless you counted the Skokie Lagoons, a series of polluted ponds full of carp and a few deceased mafiosi. Most of her outdoor recreation consisted of skiing and horseback riding and a raft trip once in college, not the type of thing that environmentalists tended to embrace. But she kept renewing each year anyway; she figured eighteen dollars was not so much to spend to ensure that the air remained breathable and the ozone didn't deplete too much and the Hudson River didn't catch fire. She even read the magazine once in a while; the pictures were pretty, even though the articles tended to be depressingly legalistic.

Now, after all these years, her membership was coming in handy. Against her better judgment she had promised Andy to try and extract a few guarded verities from the Forest Service. She tried to avoid thinking about who would benefit from this mission. She rationalized that the sooner these errands were accomplished, the more time she would have to enjoy Sunburst with her husband.

Susie drove their rented Toyota Camry over to the Forest Service building and parked it in the lot, which was nearly empty. Most of the cross-country skiers stopped by early in the morning;

it was close to eleven now and there were just a few stragglers
hanging around, trying to figure where they might take a short
tour or making plans for tomorrow. Susie walked into the building and browsed through the nature displays, reading the flyers
about bears and poison oak. A young woman in a brown ranger's
uniform, standing behind a counter, asked if she needed any assistance.

"I sure do," Susie said, extending her right hand. "Hi, I'm
Susan Ettenger." She didn't hesitate to give her maiden name;
she still used it for business purposes. Besides, she didn't want to
be linked with Andy, whose presence in town would be known
before too long. "I'm a free-lance writer. I'm working on a feature for *Sierra* magazine."

"I'm Carol Bevins," said the woman. She was a little taller
than Susie, with drab brown hair tied in a pony tail and horn-
rimmed glasses. "I'm one of your loyal members. How can I
help you?"

"Well actually, I was looking for Brian Ellsworth. He's a
ranger here; he wrote us a couple of months ago."

"Brian got reassigned. I think he's off in Wisconsin somewhere."

"You wouldn't know where?"

"I could check. He left before I started." Bevins looked back
into the office behind her, but she seemed reluctant to go inside.
"I, uh . . . is there anything else I could help you with?"

"I'm not sure. I'm doing an article on the expansion of the
ski resort into the National Forest area. Mr. Ellsworth had indicated that the transfer of the land didn't exactly go according to
Hoyle. I wanted to talk to him, or to someone who might have
been involved. Is your supervisor in?"

Bevins again peered over her shoulder at the closed office door,
then opened it and stuck her head inside. Susie could hear a loud
discussion going on, but it broke off abruptly when the door
opened. After a moment's hesitation, Bevins walked in and closed
the door behind her. A few seconds later she returned, along with
a man whom Susie assumed to be her boss.

"G'morning, I'm Jack Carvall. What can I do for you?" Carvall stood about five-ten; he was strong and lean, there wasn't an
ounce of fat on him. He had a rich, outdoorsman's complexion.
He wore black slacks and a blue and white checked flannel shirt.

His dark hair was perfectly combed. Susie didn't know what a Forest Service supervisor was supposed to look like, but this guy sure wasn't it.

"I'm Susan Ettenger, I'm a free-lance writer on assignment for *Sierra* magazine. We're doing a report on the annexation of the west ridge of Sunburst mountain by the ski corporation."

"I see." Carvall stepped backwards and closed the door to the inner office. "Well, I'm afraid there's not much to say about it that hasn't already been reported, Miss Ettenger. The Sunburst Corporation obtained a Special Use Permit; they'll begin construction of the new ski area in a few months. In the short run it might appear to be a loss to the forest, but if you read our literature, you'll understand how the whole system benefits—"

"I've read the literature," Susie lied, although she understood the arguments from Murray's manuscript. "Mr. Carvall, let me get to the point. We've had reports that the leasing of the land was facilitated by a considerable cutting of corners, particularly in respect to the Environmental Impact Statements required by law."

"I'm afraid that just isn't true, Ms. Ettenger." Carvall spoke calmly and confidently; he didn't appear shaken or surprised by the questions. "We have everything on file, it was all done in strict accordance with EPA procedures."

"There's some doubts about that, Mr. Carvall. We have a letter from a ranger who used to work here, named Brian Ellsworth. He told us that the original Impact Statements were censored before they got to the Ag Department or to Congress. He said the program should never have been approved."

"That's just not so. Unfortunately, Brian's been reassigned, but I'd be happy to contact him and discuss the letter point by point."

"Mr. Carvall," said Susie, assuming the barristorial demeanor that had become second nature to her after five years as a practicing attorney, "does it strike you as a little odd that Brian Ellsworth would be reassigned immediately after he protested this lease agreement?"

"No it doesn't. We're closing the station in a couple of months. He was supposed to be transferred to the Superior National Forest in May, but they had an illness on staff and needed him right away. Carol, here, will also be transferred in a few months. So will I."

"And will you be going to northern Wisconsin, too?"

Carvall drew his lips. "That hasn't been determined yet. Listen, I do have work to do this morning—"

"The files," said Susie.

"Pardon me?"

"I'd like to see the files."

Carvall stood behind the counter, his hands on his hips.

"Mr. Carvall, I'm entitled to see them under the Freedom of Information Act, unless this is a national security issue, which I somehow doubt. Save us both a lot of trouble and fetch them up for me."

Carvall smiled and nodded his head; there was a certain grace to his acquiescence. "I'll dig them up." He turned around and walked back into his office.

While Carvall was inside, Susie and Carol Bevins stood fidgeting nervously, trying not to stare at each other. "Nice-looking man," Susie said, after an eternally long thirty seconds. "For a supervisor."

Carol shrugged. "Yeah, he's kinda cute. Most of 'em are a little older, more bureaucratic. I've only known Jack a few weeks."

"You get along okay?"

"Oh, fine. I don't think he's used to being crossed."

Susie picked up a small map of the area and gave it a cursory glance. The hiking and cross-country ski trails were highlighted in red, the little numbers and isobars signified changes in elevation. The mountain rose rapidly from six to nine thousand feet; the skier inside her had to admit that it would be one hell of a ski resort. "Carol, do you know what's going to happen to Jack after they close down this district?"

Bevins shrugged. "He never mentioned it. But they usually have their assignments a month or so in advance when something like this happens. I know I'm being sent up to Oregon, but that was in the works before they assigned me here. They just needed a fill-in for a few weeks when Ellsworth left."

Carvall came back out with a folder and opened it on the counter. "Here. This is a copy of the Environmental Impact Statement, and of the report authorizing the transfer. I think everything's self-explanatory. Now if you'll excuse me—"

"I just had one or two additional questions, Mr. Carvall." Carvall let out an exasperated sigh, but he made no attempt to leave. "There was a ranger who worked here several months ago, by the name of Rick Allanson. Do you remember him?"

"Yes, I do." Carvall closed his eyes for a moment, his face drooped just a bit. "We lost him in January, as I assume you know."

"I heard. He died accidentally, in an avalanche?"

"It was a terrible tragedy. Honestly, I still can't account for it. He was an experienced ranger; he knew better than to tramp into the bush the morning after a snowfall."

"That was exactly the feeling I had, Mr. Carvall. This was a person who'd spent most of his life in wilderness terrain."

Carvall nodded in agreement.

"I've also been told that Rick Allanson was vigorously in opposition to the acquisition by Sunburst."

Carvall placed his hand on top of Susie's. "Miss Ettenger—or Mrs. Ettenger, I should say—" he had noticed her wedding band, "you represent a widely read magazine, and a prestigious organization. I wouldn't want you launching recklessly into some type of conspiracy that doesn't exist." Susie pulled her hand back and Carvall tightened his into a fist. "Nobody likes to lose an unspoiled forest area. I don't. The Department of Agriculture doesn't. Most particularly, our field personnel, who have dedicated their lives to protecting our resources, don't. Rick Allanson was upset about the transfer. Brian Ellsworth, to be perfectly candid, was even more upset. Given the circumstances, he's better off away from the area for a while." Carvall opened the counter and walked through it, over to a series of black-and-white photographs of the surrounding woods. "People's emotions work in strange ways, Mrs. Ettenger. I've given this a good deal of thought. This happened on my watch; it haunted me for weeks. Rick Allanson was an intense person, a strong individual. I wonder if he woke up one morning, saw the fresh snow on the mountain and thought, this is the last time I'll be able to ski in this wilderness alone. This is the last time I'll be able to enjoy a new snowfall."

"Despite the risk of avalanche?"

"Sometimes, if you work long enough at this job, the risks become more routine. Perhaps he even wanted to take the risk. Maybe he wanted to experience that feeling of being alone in the wild. It's a strong draw, Susan."

"He certainly got his wish." Susie stared at Carvall; he didn't blink. She heard a slight creak. She looked back at the office door—it had opened for an instant, then closed. There was one more question she wanted to ask, but she didn't quite know how to phrase it without turning her *Sierra* magazine story into a murder investigation. "In any case, Mr. Carvall, we'll probably mention a few words about Rick's passing. Apart from any conspiracy. Just a short inset profile."

"I'm sure that would be appropriate. He was a fine young man."

Susie paused; she cleared her throat. "Did he have any friends around here that might have something to share with us?"

"I think Ellsworth was closest to him. I'll give you his address."

"No relatives?"

"Nope. Parents were in Washington state."

"Girlfriend?"

Carvall laughed. "I don't think Rick ever discovered the opposite sex. I mean, he knew it existed, with bears and deer, anyway. But he'd never actually investigated the human side of things, if you know what I mean."

Susie smiled. "Maybe he had a secret girlfriend that lived in the woods."

"If he did, it sure fooled the hell out of me. Now if that's all, I do have work to do."

"I think that'll do it."

Carvall shook Susie's hand. "If you have questions, call me any time. Read the reports. I admit there's a trade-off, as far as the annexation's concerned. It's painful for a lot of people. But look over at Sunburst, Mrs. Ettenger, and try to imagine the value of the west ridge to them. Think how this arrangement benefits a National Forest system that's underfunded by millions of dollars, not to mention understaffed. The sacrifices we made will make for a much stronger program for everyone."

"That's not for me to judge," Susie said. "But I'll make sure the argument gets due representation."

"I trust you will." Carvall went back inside his office and shut the door.

Susie took the reports and stuffed them in her handbag. She lingered inside the ranger station for a few minutes, casting furtive glances at the office door. She collected some maps and fliers detailing trail hazards and snowmobile regulations. A few potential hikers had straggled in, but after short discussions with Carol Bevins they gave up and left.

"Anything more I can help you with?" Carol asked.

"Oh, no, I just wanted to get all the information I could. I'm only in town for a few days—" Susie heard a door shut; it had come from the back end of the building. It hadn't occurred to her that there was an outer door to the office. She waved goodbye to Bevins and walked outside, just as the door slammed on a blue Dodge Dakota pickup.

Susie stood on the front steps of the building, hands on her hips, staring at the truck. There was something vaguely recognizable about it. The engine started, the truck pulled out of the driveway and swung onto the road. She jogged a few feet onto the driveway and squinted into the noonday sun. She didn't get a good look at the driver, but she noticed a large dent on the left fender. It was about the size of a basketball.

Susie walked over to her Camry. She checked the locks and was satisfied that they hadn't been tampered with. She slid into the passenger seat and started the engine.

Murray, she thought to herself as she pulled out of the driveway: for a lying, obnoxious, conceited scoundrel, you have a fine eye for detail.

20

"I don't suppose you could have just asked her," said Andy Sussman.

"Oh, sure!" Susie swatted her husband in the midsection with a small couch pillow. "That would be a dead tip-off, Andy. I was supposed to be an environmental reporter."

"You were curious. The girl sounded friendly—you could have told her you saw this person, the face looked familiar."

"I didn't even know if it was a man or a woman!" Susie snapped a potato chip in half and popped the small part in her mouth; it was a lame effort toward watching her weight. They were sitting in the living room of their ski condo, drinking gin and tonics. It was a few minutes before six o'clock. "Look, Sherlock, I got us some evidence, which is more than you did."

"Hey, I had an in-depth interview with Casey Wright," protested Andy, in a slightly injured tone. "Plus Kevin's got an in at the police department; I'm supposed to talk to his guy tomorrow."

"Andy, pay attention: we're talking bona fide clue here." Susie poured some more gin into her highball glass, then stopped and laughed; her dark brown bangs fell across her eyebrows. "For God's sake, will you listen to us? We're like the kids who painted Tom Sawyer's fence."

"Murray does have his Twain-like qualities."

"Try Stephen King."

"Now, now." Sussman dropped a lime twist into his wife's drink. "So you're telling me that the Dodge Dakota you saw pulling out of the ranger station is the same truck that Murray saw when he left the police station?"

"Exactly."

"The day before he disappeared."

Susie choked on her potato chip.

"No need to get alarmed, sweetheart. There wasn't any evidence that your car had been broken into, was there?"

"No," Susie whispered. "But I'm almost certain whoever drove the Dakota had been inside Carvall's office the whole time I was there."

"Which implicates Jack Carvall?"

"Maybe. There's lots of possibilities. Dakota-person collaborates with Carvall. Dakota-person blackmails Carvall. Dakota-person has some type of personal relationship with Carvall that's separate from the whole affair."

"In any case, Dakota-person knows something about Ranger Rick," Andy said. "Probably Dani Kaplan, too."

"Not to mention a certain detective-person." Susie glanced up at the clock above the fireplace. "And Carvall must know, too. Andy, what time did the Cranstons say?"

"Seven o'clock. I don't think they're the punctual type."

"Are we supposed to bring anything? A bottle of wine, some cheese?"

"I took care of it. I got a twelve-pack of Heineken's."

Susie raised an eyebrow. "He sounded like an American beer kind of guy to me."

Sussman shrugged. J. B. Cranston didn't seem like the type of fellow who cared too much what type of beer you brought him, as long as it was cold. J.B. had finally returned Sussman's numerous calls late that afternoon at the production set. "Welcome to Sunburst!" he'd boomed over the telephone in his deep baritone. "Any pal of Murray's is a pal of mine!" He'd just gotten back from Seattle; it was his grandkid's birthday, they'd decided to make a week of it. He was curious as hell about the package he'd mailed off and sounded surprised when Sussman didn't know where Murray was. Andy couldn't tell over the phone whether it was one big fake or not, but he was more than happy to accept a dinner date, even if it did seem a bit sudden.

"Are they walking distance from here?" Susie asked.

"Other side of the village."

"Well, do you think maybe we should consider exchanging rental cars?"

"Did Dakota-person know the Camry was yours?"

"There were only a couple cars in the lot. I assumed they were Carol's and Carvall's. It was a quick exit, though. I don't think D.P got much of a look."

"I'll exchange it tomorrow, just to be safe. I'm sure we're okay for tonight. Let's clean up and get dressed; I wouldn't mind popping in a few minutes early on J.B. and Betty."

Susie slipped out of Andy's back rub and tickled him on the chin. "Another one of 'Sleuth Sussman's Crime-stopping Tips?' Maybe we'll catch them just as they're putting the blood-soaked knives into the dishwasher."

"Get thee to a shower."

"At once, my liege." Susie swiped a last potato chip and headed for the bathroom.

There couldn't have been much doubt about the Cranstons' alibi for the last ten days. For nearly an hour J.B. flooded Andy and Susie with pictures of their grandchild's birthday party—the poor kid must be seeing flash cubes in his dreams. Sussman supposed the photos could have been dated, even though J.B. had torn them fresh out of a package, claiming he'd just that minute returned from the Fotomat. He tried to construct the scenario for an elaborate hoax involving rented kids and bogus birthday parties; it made him feel slightly ridiculous as J.B. goo-gooed over the pictures. Cranston seemed so thoroughly smitten by grandchild fever that Andy, having carefully observed the behavior of Susie's parents as his sister-in-law approached babydom, was convinced that he couldn't be faking.

"Well now," J.B. drawled, placing the stack of pictures at the base of his Remington rodeo sculpture behind the coffee table, "all this baby talk must be givin' you two young'uns some ideas. How long you been tied up?"

"Oh, about six months," Andy said.

"Hell, you're jus' about ready to have a little one yourself, then." He patted Susie in the tummy. "Unless you got one cookin' already. I used to be able to tell them things right off, but my instincts've gotten rusty."

"Sorry, nothing in the oven," Susie said primly. She pulled her beige turtleneck sweater tightly over her blue jeans and walked over to the bar. She helped herself to a Heineken; she had a feeling it was going to be a long night.

"We're a two-career family," Andy explained. "Susie's my agent; I can't afford to have her out of work."

"Aw, that's what they all say. My little girl, she told me jus' last year, 'Daddy, I worked hard and went to college, I got me a well-paying job and a wonderful husband—' Hell, I told her, that's why I sent you to college in the first place." J.B. swallowed a handful of cashews. "For the husband, that is."

Susie gave J.B. a dirty look but Cranston, comfortably ensconced in his couch, master of his domain, waved her off. "Now listen, honey, I bet you're one terrific agent. You ever want a job sellin' real estate, you come straight to me. But listen to ol' J.B. You get yerself a little one inside, mark my words—" He grabbed Andy by the arm. "This' boy'll find a way to make ends meet. He won't have no trouble at all."

"J.B.!" shouted Betty from the kitchen. "Get that big foot outta your mouth and help me set the table."

"My foot's right on the floor where it belongs—"

"MOVE!" Betty instructed, and J.B. moved. "My goodness," she added, as he grabbed a stack of paper napkins, "you think you'd been dragged kickin' and screamin' into the 1990s." Betty stepped out of the kitchen, where she'd been frying some breaded veal chops. She was wearing an apron over her jeans and checkered blouse. "Honestly, Susie, he's not that way at all at work. His top salesperson's a woman. If she took a maternity leave he'd probably have a conniption fit."

"We're perfectly supportive of all our employees," J.B. muttered. He set the napkins underneath the forks, then went back to the kitchen counter and started to put the food on the table. "If Joanne wants to have a baby and miss six months of commissions, that's perfectly fine with me—"

"Be careful with the beans, J.B., they're hot."

J.B. set a string bean and onion casserole on the table, while Betty checked the veal chops. They appeared done to her satisfaction. She took them out, put them on a platter, and announced that dinner was officially served.

"Absolutely delicious," Andy said, after he had sampled the veal and the beans and the potato pancakes and some homemade blueberry muffins. "Murray warned us you were a world-class cook, Betty. He wasn't kidding."

"Oh, yes." Betty's voice dropped visibly at the mention of Murray. "We surely enjoyed his visit, Andy. It's just that he left us kind of suddenly."

"We were wondering about that. We got the package, of course. I'm sure Murray appreciated you sending it along."

"Mmph," J.B. said, chomping down a mouthful of veal. "What the hell's with that friend of yours, anyway?" Betty stared hard at J.B., who finished chewing his food, then took his wife's hand. "Excuse me, dear. Andrew, we were most enthralled with your chum. We're just a tad curious why he blew out of town in the middle of the night, didn't even leave a down payment on a condo."

"I thought he talked to you about the package—"

"Hell no! I'd left a message for him the day before; there was no one home. The next morning I woke up, there's a box by the door. There's a note—says if he's not back by tomorrow we should go ahead and mail it to you. What was in that thing anyway?"

"Oh, nothing important. Just some personal papers. I don't know what the big deal was." Andy helped himself to another veal chop and some more potato pancakes. "You didn't see him or hear him leave?"

"I heard an alarm go off," Betty said. "Or maybe it was just that darn clacking from his typewriter. Those personal papers must have been his life story, the way he was going at it." She walked over to the refrigerator, grabbed the water pitcher, and refilled everyone's glasses. "I'm sure I heard the shower go on, though—once I'm up, I don't fall back to sleep again. There was some shuffling around, then I heard the door slam and the car leave."

"Did you hear more than one person?"

"I don't think so." Betty sounded embarrassed. "I wasn't listening for that type of thing."

"That's not what I meant," Andy said gently. "Were you aware of anyone entering the condo before the alarm went off, or even afterwards?"

"No. I just thought, well that crazy cousin of Barb's is sure up early. Then I heard him come up the stairs and drop something by our door."

"You didn't tell me that," J.B. groused.

"Well, it took me a few minutes to collect myself. I put on a robe and got out of bed; I heard the car outside. By the time I opened the door he was gone." Betty nibbled delicately on her salad. "You don't think anything's wrong, do you? Maybe I should call Barbara—they were cousins."

"No, don't bother," Andy said. "Hell, when Murray finds out I'm here for the ski race, he'll probably show up at my doorstep, looking for a free pass."

"Heh, heh, heh," chortled J.B. "That dang ski race, I bet we moved five units this month just on account of that." He wiped his hands on his paper napkin. "Your pal snuck out of town before he'd bought himself some property, Andy—we can't let that happen to you."

"I'll have to check it out with the expert skier, here," Sussman said, glancing at his wife.

"Hell of an investment, specially if you're buildin' a family." J.B. patted Susie on the knee. "Gives you a beautiful place the whole gang can enjoy—the kids don't have to run off to Fort Lauderdale or Palm Springs. Course you got a little catchin' up to do."

Susie glared at Andy; she was starting to turn red. "Well, it's something to consider," Sussman said. "Course, if we had kids, they'd probably take over the place anyway, send us off to Scottsdale for the winter."

"Nah, nah. Family that plays together, stays together. Speakin' of which . . ." J.B. turned to his wife. "Betty, did Murray ever catch up with that little cousin of his?"

"I don't believe he mentioned it if he did."

"Jus' curious. The morning before we left for Seattle, I stopped by the Village Deli. I was beginnin' to wonder myself and there I was, walkin' by where she worked. I asked a gal up front if anyone had seen her."

Sussman dipped a piece of potato pancake in his applesauce and took a bite. He tried not to seem too interested in the little cousin; he concentrated on the food and waited for J.B. to finish his story.

"Murray had a cousin named Dani," Betty explained, breaking the lull. "She had a crush on one of the ski instructors and came up here to stay with him. Dani's father was furious; he'd cut her off completely."

"Ol' Sam can sure get hisself an attitude," J.B. said with a horselaugh.

"So much for family harmony."

"Not typical," J.B. insisted. "You take a look at all the beautiful young families enjoying residence on this mountain. Stop by my office in the morning—"

"J.B.," Betty said, giving him a playful slap on the head. "We don't try and close our guests."

"Oh, all right." J.B. poured himself some more beer. "Anyway, like I was saying, I stopped over at the Deli. I asked one of the gals at the counter about Dani; she tells me she never heard of her. But as I'm about to leave, she says wait, there's another gal jes' walked in, talkin' to the manager. This one used to work there a coupla months ago, she oughta know Dani. So I wait till she's finished and I catch her jes' as she's walkin out."

"Do you remember her name?" Sussman asked.

"Hell, I don't know that I even asked. Cute little thing, though. I asked her if she remembered Dani Kaplan."

"Did she?"

"Well, at first she got defensive, said she'd never heard of her. But hell, I been forty years in real estate; if I can't tell when someone's lyin' outright, I oughta turn in my license. I grabbed her and said, 'Listen, honey, that gal's a friend of mine, an' you ain't tellin' me the truth. If she's in trouble, I want to know.' " J.B. cradled his beer mug and took another gulp.

"Well?" said Betty. "What did she say? Why didn't you tell me this, J.B.?"

"There wasn't nothin' to tell. The gal says she and Dani was friends, but Dani left town and she hasn't seen her in weeks. I says are you sure? I still had her by the wrist. She gives me a sweet smile, says yeah, she's sure. I gave her my card; she promised to let me know if she heard anything." J.B. picked his napkin off the floor. "Then a fella waves at her from across the street—she says that's her friend and she's got to go. She shook loose and ran off. Gal was a little stronger than I thought."

"Do you know who she met?" asked Sussman. He wondered if Cranston was suspicious at his sudden interest in Dani, but J.B. didn't seem to mind.

"Nah. She went into the mink store, I didn't get a good look. I had work to do—if Barbie Kaplan's that worried about her daughter, she should have just called us in the first place." J.B. brought his fork to his mouth, saw that he had cleaned it off completely, and dropped it back on his plate. "Well now, all this intrigue sure gives me an appetite. Honey, since we ain't gonna sell any condos tonight, how about a little dessert?''

Outside the Cranstons' condo, at the cul-de-sac at the end of the street, Andy and Susie looked around the rented Camry before they unlocked the doors. It was snowing lightly; both the street and the car were dusted. If anyone had been nosing around, they would have left prints. Susie slid into the passenger seat. She struggled to keep her eyes open until they got home, she had matched J. B. Cranston beer for baby album.

"So," Andy said, buckling her seatbelt, "it seems Beth from the deli's still at large. Or was, a week ago."

"You're assuming it was Beth?"

"She'd just quit working there. She was Dani's friend. We know she was hiding something." Andy watched as his wife yawned in complete skepticism. "If you believe Murray's account of things."

"If you believe Murray's account of things, Beth probably kidnapped him and took him to Paris, to keep him from Sara and Mrs. Kaplan."

"Well, at least give him some credit for narrative accuracy." Sussman put the car into gear and pulled away. "The apartment was just like he'd written; all that Western art, the Remingtons. And J.B. and Betty were drawn perfectly."

"Au contraire, Pierre." Susie flipped the visor down and looked in the mirror. It wasn't a pretty sight, in her opinion. Her cheeks sagged, her eyes were baggy. She tried a smile, but it only emphasized her weariness. It occurred to her that since she'd been married, she hadn't worried much about makeup at the end of an evening. She thought about a little rouge, but just didn't have the energy. She pushed her bangs over her eyes and put the visor back up.

"All right, Susan. What picky item did I miss, probably pertinent to the case."

"It's not picky. According to Murray, J.B. was Mr. Mountain Macho. Cussed around with his parochial values, completely supported by the little woman."

"I didn't detect any cracks in the marriage."

"C'mon, Andy! He's all bluster. He gets out of line, Betty cracks the whip."

"Suse, he's not exactly henpecked."

"That's not the point."

"What is the point?"

Susie took a deep breath. "The point is, Andy, it's the type of thing Murray would leave out. In Murray's world the men are totally confident, completely in control. The women are non-voting subsidiaries."

"Maybe he just figured J.B. would be a more entertaining character without help from Betty—"

"Of course, that's exactly what Murray WOULD think." Susie yawned again and tilted her seat back. "That's why he's such a swine."

Andy glanced quickly at Susie, then shifted his eyes to the road. The new snow had made the going slippery; he wasn't sure how the Toyota would handle. "I don't suppose, darling, that it would be politic to suggest that your attitude toward J.B. might have been colored by his interest in our future as progenitors of the Sussman line."

"Oh, please!" Susie sat up long enough to elbow Andy in the ribs, then sank back into the seat.

"Watch it, you'll put us in a ditch." Sussman slowed down as he reached the turnoff to their condo. "Seriously, though. I'm not blind. I sat through three days of your parents in Chicago, trying their best to be subtle."

"My parents were very subtle. Besides, they've got Carol to worry about. Wait'll they get stuck baby-sitting a few times—"

"They won't care. They'll love it."

"We'll be safely in New York."

"There is no such thing. And wait till we visit my parents in Florida."

"What difference does it make what our parents think?" Susie's eyes were wide open now. "Are we supposed to have a baby to please our parents?"

"Of course not."

"Well then. The subject is closed."

"Um . . ." They were at the condo now, it was a single unit chalet at the end of a line of similar chalets that stretched an entire block. "What about to please ourselves?"

"Aw, Andy." Susie snuggled next to him. "We've been through that a hundred times. It's hard enough at work; after six months they're just beginning to accept me. If I get pregnant now, there'll be nothing left of my career."

"That isn't true. You're still my agent. I won't fire you."

"Andy, I didn't put in three years of law school and two summers clerking and three years doing grunt work just so I could become a cottage industry at age thirty-two."

"You don't have to become a cottage industry. It's not exactly a permanent problem, you'd only be off a couple of months."

"You expect me to just pop out a baby and go back to work? Who'd take care of the child?"

"We could get a nanny—"

"A NANNY?"

"Look, I'm just saying it's a possibility. Lots of women have babies and go back—"

"Andy, just because I don't want to have a child right now doesn't mean I'm completely devoid of motherly instincts!"

"I've never had any doubts about your motherly instincts—"

"Can't I just get my feet on the ground in New York and feel that my career's going in the right direction?"

"Sure. It's only that you can be a lawyer the rest of your life—"

"I know," Susie said. "I know how much time's on the clock." She sunk back in the seat. "Look, can we just save this discussion for a more appropriate moment."

"I was hoping an appropriate moment was about to arrive."

Susie kissed Andy, then reached over and opened his door. "Sussman, it's a good thing I'm still in love with you."

"I'd be in trouble otherwise?"

Susie pushed him out into a snow bank, then slid over and followed him out the driver's door. "You'll never know." She helped him off the ground and the two of them staggered toward the front door. "Oh, and Andy?"

"Yes, my darling?"

"There was one other teensy discrepancy I picked up from our conversation with the Cranstons."

"Can it wait till morning?" Sussman unlocked the door and escorted Susie inside.

"I doubt it. I'll be hung over and won't remember anything."

Sussman picked up Susie and carried her into the bedroom. He set her down gently on the bed and started humming Brahms' "Lullaby."

"Well? You want to hear this clue or not?"

"Is it important?" He lifted Susie's legs and pulled the bed-spread out from under her.

"Maybe." Susie sat up and unzipped her parka. She tossed it on a chair, then took off her boots and stretched out on the bed. "Betty said that on Murray's last morning, when he dropped off the package, she heard the car start outside and then he was gone."

"So?" Sussman took his jacket off, tossed it in a corner, and started to undress.

"Murray didn't have a car, Andy. He'd returned the Land Cruiser and walked back to the village that afternoon. And according to the note, he was supposed to meet whoever sent it on the slopes. He wouldn't have needed a car."

"Hmm." Sussman sat down on the bed and snuggled against Susie. "Intriguing." He pulled off his shirt. "Should we write that down?"

"One of us will remember it."

"It'd better be you." He started to help Susie off with her turtleneck. "Hey, Suse?"

"What?"

Andy kissed her on the lips. "I'm feeling really appropriate."

"I'm feeling really drunk."

"Aw . . ." Andy turned off the light. "How about appropriately drunk?"

"Uh, maybe. Rub my back."

Sussman did as he was told.

"A little lower."

"Sobering up?"

"Just enough."

Sussman pulled Susie close to him. He rolled the blankets over their head.

Outside, the snow was falling harder. A few cars glided down the street; they were silent on the snow. A station wagon stopped for a moment beside the condo, it was obscured by the blizzard. It pulled up beside the Camry, stopped, then drove away.

No tracks were left.

By morning, the street would be clean and white.

21

Andy Sussman woke up to an eerie silence. It had snowed two feet overnight; an ever-so-slight dapple of snowflakes continued to fall from a slate-gray sky. He groggily rolled toward his alarm clock. It was 7:45. He hadn't intended to sleep this late, but the room was dark and he was woozy from the night before. Beside him, Susie was still in dreamland.

He opened the shade a few inches. Everything was a dull white, as far as he could see. The few cars that were parked on the street were barely visible underneath mounds of snow. There was no traffic, except for an occasional skier gliding by and a few curious gawkers like himself surveying the effects of the storm.

Sussman pulled on a pair of sweatpants and his Sorrel boots. He walked through the living room and slid open the porch door, which had a view of the slopes. He slogged outside, kicking a pile of snow away from the door. The mountain looked deserted. Only the bottom lifts were running, and the chairs were empty. All of Sunburst was starting late this morning; the first skiers had an hour's wait ahead of them.

Andy kicked off the Sorrels, headed for the kitchen and put some water in a teapot. Everything was so still and quiet, it was like Christmas morning. He had left the porch door open a crack; he breathed in the crisp mountain air. He picked up the phone and dialed the ski school. The most tangible benefit of the blizzard was that he could call off the ill-advised ski session with Casey Wright, a commitment he'd regretted the instant he'd made it.

"Why don't we make it this afternoon?" Casey suggested,

interrupting Sussman as he tried to beg off. "The back bowls'll be open by noon. Baby, until you've skied the bowls with fresh powder, you haven't skied!"

"Sorry, no can do," Sussman said. "I've got interviews with skiers lined up, I've gotta get 'em taped before the practice runs start. I'll be tied up until three o'clock—I don't think it's enough time."

"Make it two, we'll call it a half-day."

The teapot started to whistle. Sussman hurried over to turn it off before it woke Susie up. "Look, Case, I'll think about it, okay? I've got breakfast cooking, I'll talk to you later." Sussman hung up the phone; the instant he did so it rang again.

"Got your boots on, Andy?" It was Kevin Cumberland.

"They're in the general vicinity."

"I've got great news! We're gonna ski the back of the west ridge today."

Sussman reached into the cupboard for a teabag and pondered Cumberland's announcement. "The west ridge is wilderness, Kevin."

"Yeah, for three more months. Listen to this, Andy—I rented a helicopter for the afternoon!"

"Kevin, you're nutso. I can barely ski down a regular mountain."

"No sweat, I'll be with you all the way."

"Forget it, Kev, I've got interviews this afternoon—"

"The racers are all stuck in Denver, the storm shut down Stapleton. Our session with Casey's off. We've got nothing else to do!"

Sussman opened up a packet of Earl Grey, set it in a cup, then poured hot water over it.

"Sussman, you there?"

"Yes, Kevin, I'm here. Which is possibly the best place for me. Have you thought about avalanches?"

"No problem. We'll start from the top—there's nothing above us. We'll cut straight across, I've got the route all figured out. We'll end up at Sunburst, we can ski right back to the village."

"Kevin, you are a crazed human being."

"A professional crazed human being. And as a special bonus, I put in a call to my buddy at the police department. It's quiet as a monastery in there right now. Get ready, I'll pick you up in

fifteen minutes. We'll chat with Craig, then we'll catch the
whirlybird at ten-fifteen. What do you say?''

Sussman dunked his tea bag in the hot water. ''I dunno. Let's
talk to your guy first, then we'll see—''

''Great! Be there in a snap.''

Andy hung up the phone and sipped on his tea. There was, he
thought, a curious phenomenon emerging in his life. He was
thirty-five, slightly past his peak in terms of recklessness. Yet there
seemed to be forces that were pushing him toward risk and adventure at a time when by all rights he should be settling into a
sedentary family life. He thought about Susie and the baby issue.
He knew it was not fair to blame these wacko schemes on a lack
of dependents—a little backbone on his part and the letters N O
would go a long way toward resolving matters. Still, he couldn't
help but feel that were he a father, people would attribute to him
a greater sense of responsibility, deserved or not. They would not
blithely suggest that he go off stalking giant anacondas on the
Grand Inini River or go helicopter skiing in the Rocky Mountains. It was, he admitted, a strange rationale for having a child,
but it seemed apropos at the moment.

Nonetheless, Sussman donned his ski outfit: long undies, jeans,
a turtleneck, and a sweater. He figured he would at least go as
far as the talk with Cumberland's pal. When he'd gotten his information, he could always beg off. He left a note for Susie that
he'd be tied up most of the day. He didn't explain where he was
going; he'd call her when he got finished with the cops. Then he
slung his skis over his shoulder and went outside to wait for Kevin.

A thought occurred to Andy while Kevin Cumberland skidded
off in his Porsche toward the police station. What if he could
convince Merle Summers to substitute this afternoon's ski tour
for the French Guiana trip? It was a natural for ''Adventure!''
A last trek down a wilderness terrain, soon to be overrun by
greedy developers. Who said that every segment had to be filmed
in some God-forsaken jungle in an underdeveloped country full
of armed insurgents? He wouldn't have any trouble convincing
Kevin to bring a cameraman along. It would be great publicity
for him, not to mention the salary he'd earn for being the guest
Adventurer.

Besides, if this murder case proved to have any merit the show could be topical—it could be a ratings smash. The possibility that he might turn Murray Glick's wild-goose chase to his own advantage struck Sussman as poetic justice. Of course, if it hadn't been for Murray, Sussman would not have had to worry about French Guiana to begin with—or wilderness skiing. Still, he was determined to make the best of the situation. He would enjoy telling Murray about it whenever Murray finally showed up. If he showed up. Sussman wondered what the Sunburst police could tell him about that.

Andy followed Cumberland into the police station; there was only a skeleton staff on duty. A receptionist manned the telephones, giving mostly weather information to tourists. A desk sergeant sat behind her, sipping coffee and reading the sports section of *USA Today*. Cumberland gave him their names and walked straight back. "Craig!" he yelled as he approached the back of the room.

A tall, stocky man with a red mustache looked up. He was sitting at his desk, tying a dry fly. The fly was clamped in a small portable vise, illuminated by a bright lamp with a magnifying glass built into it. The fly was not quite finished; there were some loose feathers at the tip.

"Glad to see our tax dollars at work," Cumberland said.

"Hey, I've been here all night. Some skiers got stranded on the road in, I had to stay on dispatch till two-thirty. By that time, there was no sense leaving." The officer turned around from his fly clasp and saw Sussman. "Hi, I'm Craig Gustafson."

"Andy Sussman." Sussman extended his right hand. As they shook, the name kicked in; it was the same cop Murray had talked to the night before he disappeared. Andy alternated his glance between Cumberland and Gustafson. Perhaps he should think twice before getting on a helicopter with these guys. "Looks like a work of art," Andy said, taking a closer look at the vise. "Yellow stone fly?"

"Good call. Kev, you didn't tell me your boy was an angler."

"The dude is a veritable Renaissance man of sport. You should have seen him on the downhill run yesterday."

Sussman grinned sheepishly. It had been nine years since he had last held a fly rod in his hand. He'd been sports anchor at an independent station in Reno. He'd woken up at four in the morning to cover opening day in the Eastern Sierra, he'd learned more about fly-fishing than he'd ever hoped; in particular, he had learned the perils of cheap waders in forty-degree water. "This for sale?" he asked, leaning over the fly.

"Nah. Used to moonlight a little, but I couldn't fill the orders. I've got a few extra, though; you can have this one when I'm done."

"Hey, pack a fishing rod along this afternoon," said Kevin. "I heard there's some cutthroats up there; it's probably near spawning time."

Sussman rolled his eyes.

"God, I wish I could go with you," Gustafson said, turning the light out. He loosened the vise and slid it to the back of his desk.

"Take the afternoon off," Kevin said.

"Can't. Gotta stay on duty for snow emergencies. Wait another hour, people'll get tired of sitting around. The accidents start to roll in around noon, plus the snow starts to melt, then freezes in the afternoon and pulls down power lines. Spring storms are a bitch."

"It's your choice. Last chance to ski a virgin forest. This time next year it'll be condo city."

"Don't tempt me. Now what was it you wanted?" Gustafson turned toward Andy. "Some avalanche death a couple of months ago, that's what Kevin said over the phone. It wouldn't be that ranger accident, would it?"

"That's it exactly. The Allanson kid." Sussman sat quietly for a moment, waiting for Gustafson to speak, but the cop didn't offer anything. "See, we're doing a little background report on the annexation of the west ridge. Evidently, this ranger was opposed to it. He got in a shouting match with some congressman about an Impact Statement that was allegedly censored. The accident happened a few days later."

Gustafson pulled a manila folder from his desk drawer; he had taken it from the file before Sussman and Cumberland arrived. "I looked through it again—didn't see anything to suggest it was more than an accident." He flipped it to Andy. "And that environmental angle doesn't do much for me. Plenty of people were opposed to the lease. They had a rally over by the gondola last month, I saw a lot of Smokey hats in the crowd. Nobody got themselves killed, though."

Sussman leafed through the file. "Was an autopsy done?"

"Standard examination." Gustafson took the file back and found the report. "Death due to asphyxiation."

"Were there any other marks or wounds on the body? To indicate he may have been assaulted in any way?"

"He was alone in the wilderness. I don't know what could have got to him, except a bear or a deer."

Sussman did not want to insult the policeman's intelligence, but he had been trying for several days to construct a scenario in which Allanson's death had been planned and carried out. Someone would have abducted him, there would have had to have been some marks on his body. But the coroner's report indicated nothing, and it was too late to gather further evidence.

"Now here's something you might be interested in," Gustafson said. He lifted a thermos from the back of his desk and poured himself a cup of coffee. "About two weeks ago, we had a tip. Very similar to the Allanson case. New snowfall, same conditions. Someone reported that a skier had skied off the boundaries near the west ridge, got caught in a snowslide."

Sussman looked straight at Gustafson. "Another body?"

"Turns out there wasn't. We called in the ski patrol, wasted half a day. Nerves were getting strained by the time we got home."

"Who called in the tip? Did they actually see the skier?"

Gustafson sipped on his coffee. "Claimed they had. Left a name, but we were never able to track him down."

"Had there actually been an avalanche?"

"There'd been a slide, but like I said, no body." Gustafson pulled the file toward him and skimmed through it. "Found some marks on the snow, though. Someone had definitely been there before us."

"Ski tracks?" asked Cumberland.

"Yeah. Cross-country tracks, too. But they were faint. It was windy, there was snow blowing around. It was hard to tell when they'd been made."

"Was anybody reported missing?" Sussman asked.

"Nope. Never had a single inquiry."

"Did you get any more tips?"

"The guy called back once, that was it."

"You're sure it was a guy?"

"Both calls were from guys. But we don't know if it was the same person. The calls weren't taped, different people answered them. Anyway, he asked if we'd found this skier, and we just said no. He hung up and never called back."

"Do you have a date on that call?" Sussman asked.

"I could check. It was logged in." Gustafson got up and walked over to another desk.

Sussman drummed his fingers on the desk top. It would have been easier to just ask Gustafson if he remembered talking to Murray; he'd surely know if the lost-skier incident was before or after his visit. But Sussman had a feeling that the less official connection he had with Murray Glick, the better off he'd be. There was another way of finding out. He still had the envelope the manuscript had come in; the whole thing was back at the condo. He was sure it had a postmark on it.

"Here we go," Gustafson said, returning from his desk with another file. "March 9, the first call. March 11, the second call. Any particular reason for asking?"

"Oh, we just wanted to check a few dates with the networks, regarding the filing of leases on the land and the provisioned Impact Statements and the transfer of certain Forest Service personnel and a few other things—"

"Boys," Cumberland said, bailing Sussman out, "we got a helicopter date in half an hour. Andrew, does that about sum up your inquiry?"

"Absolutely." Sussman gathered the Allanson file into a neat mound and returned it to Gustafson. "Hey, Craig, mind if I make a few quick phone calls. I gotta clear this ski trek with my wife and my boss."

"No problem," said Gustafson. "Dial nine for an outside line. Go to the next cubicle—you can have a little privacy."

Sussman ducked over to the desk in back of Gustafson; he called Susie first. She sounded remarkably spunky; she had just gotten out of the shower. As he described Cumberland's plan, it occurred to him that he should have asked her along in the first place; she was undoubtably the better skier and would probably enjoy it more.

"That's all right, I wouldn't want to impose on your boys' day off," Susie said, without any hint of irritation.

"I'm sure you could come along." Sussman poked his head

out of the cubicle and waved at Cumberland. "Hey Kev, we got room for Susie?"

"The more the merrier."

But Susie declined; she had some business of her own to look after. "I already called the ski school, Andy. I arranged for a private lesson with Sara."

"Really? Good work there, Miss Marple."

"My last detective chore for the trip. Besides, it's the best way to see the mountain. And I want to get a few stories straight."

"I'll bet."

"Have fun with Kevin," she said. "The rest of the trip you're mine."

"You got it, babe." Sussman hung up the phone. He walked back to Cumberland and filled him in on his "Adventure!" proposition. Kevin seemed amenable, especially when he found out he'd get paid. Andy picked up Gustafson's phone and tried his luck with Merle Summers in New York.

"Colorado!" said Merle, incredulously. "U.S.A? Andy, what am I supposed to tell my advertisers?"

"Tell them this is a world-class story, Merle. It's the last wilderness trip ever on a pristine mountain. How would you like to have taken the last raft down Glen Canyon? The last backpack through Hetch Hetchy?"

"But it's a ski resort, Andy."

"Not yet it ain't. Besides, think how much you'll save on transportation and medical expenses."

Merle was silent for a moment; Sussman could sense the gears starting to mesh in his mind. "Let me see . . . Andy, are there any grizzlies up there?"

"Grizzlies?" Sussman looked at Kevin.

"Not unless one wandered down from Yellowstone," Cumberland said. "Perfectly safe, believe me—"

"There's been some unofficial migratory reports," Sussman told Merle. "Huge footprints. Plus some timber wolves and a rare strain of trout—"

"No teeth," Merle muttered.

"TEETH?"

"On the trout. What about the natives, Andy? Any crazed locals holed up there? Maybe a polygamist?"

"Merle, you're a sick man."

"I'm just trying to find a way to make this work for you. We have viewer expectations to consider. Now what about the avalanche angle? You think there's a chance you might actually run into one?"

"Yes, Merle, there's an excellent chance. There've already been several avalanche deaths this winter. I'm sure it would make for great footage. Would you like us to take some dynamite along and actually set one off for you?"

"Do it off-camera," said Merle. "And don't get us stuck for the rescue; I understand the Forest Service charges a fortune."

Sussman sighed. "Does this mean we're on?"

"On a conditional basis. See if you can rustle up a cameraman. Let me talk to Cumberland—we'll work out a preliminary agreement. If the footage works out, great. If not . . ." There was a pause at the other end of the line.

"I understand." Sussman handed the phone over to Cumberland and walked over to another desk. He had thirty minutes till the helicopter ride. He figured if they could delay things another half-hour, he could probably pull this off. He picked up another phone and called his production office. It was almost too easy. He was able to scare up a cameraman plus the ski-cam. The cameraman was thrilled; he'd be ready in forty-five minutes.

Sussman walked back to Gustafson's desk. The cop was at the front of the room, talking to the desk sergeant. Cumberland was still on the phone with Merle, finalizing a quick oral contract for his participation.

Sussman pulled the trout fly toward him. At this exact moment, opening morning in the High Sierra didn't seem like such a terrible thought, leaky waders and all. It sure beat hopping out of a helicopter and onto a steep mountain full of freshly fallen snow.

On the other hand, Sussman thought, as he watched a few flakes of snow blow outside the window, Kevin's helicopter was a decided improvement on the jungles of French Guiana.

"Ready to roll?" said Kevin, hanging up the phone.

"No, but let's do it, anyway."

Sussman zipped his parka and pulled on his hat. His skis were sharpened. His insurance was paid up. He didn't know where his passport was, and he didn't want to find out. It was time to assault the mountain.

22

Susie Sussman stood at the ski school meeting place, in front of a wooden sign with the number 7 painted on it. She supposed that to be accurate she should have waited at number 8 or 9, but a little modesty wouldn't kill her. She looked at her watch; it was a few minutes before one o'clock. She was right on time for her half-day private lesson.

"Susie Sussman?"

Susie turned around and saw a ski instructor standing behind her, dressed in bright yellow ski pants and the regulation Sunburst parka. The girl's short red hair sprouted a few inches below her yellow-tasseled knit ski cap. She was pretty and perky, as advertised. "Sara?"

"That's me." Sara patted Susie in the behind with her ski pole. "C'mon, let's hit that powder before it gets skied off. We'll talk on the lift. Follow me!"

Susie snapped her bindings on and glided after Sara; the instructor took quick, powerful strides and was already several yards ahead of her. They met up at the base of the number three chair; it was part of a two-lift sequence that would take them up to Dragon's Head. From there, Susie hoped, they could run several of the expert slopes, then cut across to lift seven and over to the back bowls.

The line at three was packed, but Sara skied right to the front, where the ski classes alternated in. She motioned Susie over and a few moments later they were on the chairlift. Susie figured that the time saved from liftlines was reason enough for the lesson. Moreover, the eighty bucks was going to come straight out of

Murray Glick's pocket, if she had anything to say about it—if Glick was going to lie back and let the suspense mount, he could damn well treat her to a week of skiing.

"We're real excited to have you guys up here," Sara said, as the chairlift creaked upwards. "I saw the tape of your husband running the downhill, I was impressed. I skied it the other day— the top portion's a bear. Then someone told me you were the expert skier."

"I'm way out of practice, Sara. That's why I signed up." Susie had made no attempt to disguise her marriage. Andy was familiar to the ski school people by now, and Kevin Cumberland had been carousing with many of them at night—he was probably the source for her reputed skiing prowess. "I'm just hoping Andy can get through the week without breaking a leg. Maybe we'll make it an annual event."

"You should get him on the European Tour. France, Switzerland, Italy. Just gorgeous—you'll get treated like royalty. With the dollar so low, it's the only way to go."

"God, I'd love it. But Andy could never get away the whole winter—he's got basketball games every week."

"Ugh. A bunch of smelly gyms, you're stuck inside all the time." Sara shook some snow off her cap. "Maybe he should get a new agent."

"He better not," Susie laughed. "I'm his agent."

"Oh, God, I'm sorry!" Sara pulled the safety bar over their heads. "You'll probably want to push me off after that."

"I get much worse from my own law office, believe me."

When the lift reached the end of its run they hopped off and glided to the right, toward a sign with a blue square on it that indicated an intermediate slope. "We'll take Dragon's Head, just so I can check you out," Sara said. "Then we'll head over to seven and get to the bowls. Show me some turns, ski the bumps on the bottom. No need to get fancy."

Susie did a couple of quick stretching exercises, then edged up to the top of the run and pushed off. She carved a few turns into the hill, she felt completely at ease. The skis beneath her seemed as natural as jogging shoes. She picked her line and headed straight for the moguls; they were barely visible underneath all the new snow. She bobbed in and out of them, losing her balance just once when she leaned into the hill, but recovering without any visible slip. When she got to the end, Sara was just a few feet behind her, whooping and hollering.

"All RIGHT! We are in for a GREAT afternoon, girl!"

Susie kicked some snow off her boots. "How'd the turns look?"

"Wonderful. Poling could be a smidgen better on the steep part."

"I'm always weak with my poles—"

"Hey, gives us something to work on. Otherwise I'd feel useless."

They skied down to the number seven chairlift. The line was slightly shorter than at the bottom lifts, but it was taking more time; the lift had stopped entirely a few moments ago. The lift operator, a tall guy with a scraggly blond beard, was shouting into the phone and chewing on a Slim Jim. After a few more seconds of animated conversation, he walked into the shelter at the base of the lift, pushed a button, and the lift resumed running.

"Everything cleared up?" asked Sara, as she alternated into the line with Susie.

"Fella forgot to jump off at the top," said the operator, squinting through yellow tinted sunglasses. "You ladies headed for the back bowls?"

"Absolutely."

"Soo-perb! I skied Sundowner this morning. Hey, you see Casey Wright, tell him not to forget me. I'm gettin' stir-crazy down here." An empty chair came by and the man positioned it while Susie and Sara got on.

"Will do, uh . . ." Sara looked back at the nametag on the man's scruffy army surplus jacket.

"Chris Banner!" the man shouted. "I been waitin' three weeks!"

"I'm so terrible with names," Sara said, as the chair whisked them up the hill and out of earshot. "It's embarrassing."

"Happens to everyone. What's he waiting for?"

"Ski school. A lot of the people running lifts are waiting for jobs to open up."

"There's hardly any time left for this year, is there?"

"They always hire a few extra right before the Easter rush. And once he gets on staff, he'll be in good shape for next winter. He might as well hang on another month." The lift stopped for a moment. The wind whistled through it, blowing some snow off a pine tree and sprinkling it in their faces. The lift cable creaked, the chair swung back and forth. Susie hung on to the safety bar, but Sara didn't seem flustered. "So how come you requested me?" she asked. "I don't remember having any of the CBS people in my classes."

"Oh, we had a friend from Chicago—that's where we're from. He gave you a special recommendation."

"No kidding. Who was it?"

Susie hesitated; she was reticent to draw distinct lines between Murray and herself and Andy, but curiosity had gotten the better of her. "Uh, he's a friend of Andy's, actually. His name's Murray Glick—"

"Oh, the detective!" The chairlift started moving as if on cue. "I was wondering what happened to that guy. He stood me up."

"Murray? I didn't think he'd missed a date in his life."

"Well, it wasn't exactly a standup. He was in my group and we went out for dinner and, uh . . . well, we were definitely going to have dinner again and go skiing, and then he just never called."

"Now that's unusual—for Murray, anyway." Susie winked, but Sara didn't seem to catch on. "He does have this reputation as a Casanova back home."

"Well I didn't figure him for Dudley Dooright. I was just surprised he left like that—I never saw him anywhere on the mountain again. He didn't stop by the office; he wasn't hanging around the village anywhere."

"You checked after him?"

"Sure. I mean, we had a nice time. When I didn't hear from him I thought maybe I'd been a little, uh . . . brusque. I called the number at his condo, but all I got was someone's answering machine. I even called his office in Chicago."

"You must have been quite fond of him," Susie said, trying to avoid a tone of outright incredulity. She'd assumed all of Murray's amorous adventures were total fiction; this was the first sliver of doubt.

"Well, he was kind of fun. Hey, he's *YOUR* friend." Sara gave Susie a friendly tap in the boot with her pole. "Anyway, his secretary had no idea where he was—he'd told me he was on a case; you'd think she'd know. If you run into him, I'd like to give him a call."

"I'll see what I can do." Susie forced a smile. "He calls Andy all the time—"

"Maybe I'll find out about his Christmas cruise. The new resort's going to be such a circus, I might just bag it and spend Christmas floating to St. Thomas with the world-famous detective . . ." Sara reached over to Susie, who had turned away and was leaning precipitously toward the side of the chair. "Uh, Susan? You all right, girl?"

"Excuse me." Susie sat up straight. "Must have been the croissant I had for lunch."

"Natch."

"Little stomach bug." Susie smiled weakly, but she knew she was coming off as patronizing. She sounded like her mother, who would become sickeningly polite whenever Susie brought home a boy who fell something short of Prince Charming.

"Listen," Sara said, as they approached the dropoff point, "I'm a little confused here. First you tell me Murray's this close friend of yours—you go to the trouble of requesting me for a private strictly on his recommendation. But the idea that I actually like him seems to have put you in total shock."

"No, no. I mean, not total shock. It's just . . ." Susie lined her skis parallel to the hill and prepared to hop off. "It's just, sometimes when you really KNOW a person, you never figure—" The chair passed the dropoff point; Susie jumped off and skied about thirty yards from the lift. Sara caught up with her in three quick glides and leaned over her shoulder.

"So he's not your ideal dreamboat, is that it?"

Susie sank down into a pile of powder. "See, I've seen the guy in action. And I admit he has his good qualities. But, uh . . ."

"Semi-dreamboat?"

Susie silently wiped the snow off her face.

"A raging, conceited, chauvinistic swine?"

"Bull's-eye." Susie struggled to get to her feet. She planted her ski poles in the powder and managed to gather enough momentum to get out of the snow. "I suppose you'd have to spend a little time with him—"

"I thought I had." Sara turned toward the ridge. "C'mon, let's get moving before you get petrified." She led Susie toward the main run, then headed for an open meadow. "Plant the left pole." She skied beside her and demonstrated the proper technique. "Don't sit back in the powder. Worse thing you can do, especially in the bowls."

"Gotcha."

Sara rapped Susie in the behind with her poles. Her teaching technique had turned crisp and professional, almost aloof. "Keep the weight over the skis. Follow me." She glided ahead of Susie and led her through a thin patch of Douglas firs; the shortcut left them about fifty yards from the lift to Sundowner. Sara took a few quick glides and left Susie well behind her.

"Wait up!" shouted Susie, trying to figure out how to patch up this relationship before Sara guided her off a cliff. She shoved off as powerfully as she could, but she didn't catch Sara until she reached the chairlift. There was practically no line; Sara had already alternated in. Susie caught up just in time to be whisked up the hill again.

For a few minutes they rode in silence, watching the snow-covered trees go by. The air was getting colder, the sky was clouding up again. It looked like more flurries were on the way. "Sara," said Susie, placing an arm on her shoulder, "listen: I didn't mean to be so hard on Murray. He does have some endearing qualities. I'm not normally so critical—"

"That's none of my business—"

"Listen, I can tell you he's a first-rate detective. He's solved two cases for my husband. He's loyal to his friends. Believe me, he's perfectly capable of being charming and witty—"

"Gosh," said Sara, slapping herself on the knee. "Wouldn't you know it? I'm perfectly capable of enjoying the company of charming and witty guys."

Susie shrugged; she took her stocking cap off and shook the snow from it. She stared straight below her, at the skiers criss-crossing the slopes.

"All right, all right," Sara said. "Look, Sue, I'm no Brownie. I knew Murray wasn't up for the *Cosmo* centerfold. And he never got to see the inside of my apartment, if that helps my standing any—"

"That's none of MY business," Susie said, although she believed it. She was convinced that if Murray had gotten past first base with Sara, it would have been duly reported in the manuscript.

"But you've got to admit, he can be a lot of laughs."

"Uh . . ." Susie strained for a believable lie. "Sure. Mirth aplenty."

The lift was approaching the top; it went over a ridge and started descending for the last few yards of the ride. "Maybe you'd have to spend some time around here to appreciate him," Sara said. "People can be so one-dimensional—all they want to talk about is skiing. Snow conditions, jobs, racing reports—especially with the Cup here this week. Our whole lives are sealed into this little mountaintop in the clouds. Tips up!"

They jumped off the lift and skied to the right. They found themselves on the rim of Sundowner bowl, one of the three back bowls of Sunburst mountain. It looked like a large amphitheater carved into the hillside, but instead of benches the bowl was filled with moguls. Even with the foot and a half of new snow, you could see the tips of them protruding like icebergs.

"Ready?" said Sara.

"Um . . ." Susie scanned the bowl, looking for trails or some type of visible fall line. She saw skiers shooting in and out of the moguls at random. The going was treacherous—every few seconds a curse floated up from below.

"Follow me!"

Sara took off and Susie struggled to keep up. The bowl was steep, the fresh powder camouflaged the deep ridges between the bumps; it was like walking blind on a street full of open manholes. Susie skied cautiously; she tumbled several times. But after a few turns she began to feel the coordination return to her body, as if someone had pushed a button causing her strength and motor reflexes to revive all at once. She forgot about falling and took a direct line down the bowl, darting in and out of the moguls, dodging a few other skiers who had come unglued, swishing and swerving while Sara whooped her encouragement.

The next hour was spent skiing every square foot of Sundowner. The subject of Murray never came up, although as Susie rode the lift for her fourth run, she was still trying to rationalize the attraction. Sara was in a leisure-time profession. She was surrounded by smooth-talking ski-types. Just maybe, Susie thought, a detective from Chicago who leads cruises in his spare time would be enough of a curiosity to hang onto for a while. Murray was perfectly capable of leaving a wonderful first impression. They'd only had one date. As for Murray's account of it, well the whole sequence involving Mrs. Kaplan at the condo had to be a fake. Susie wanted to ask Sara about it, but it seemed impossible without telling her that Murray had included her in his souped-up memoirs. Maybe she SHOULD know that, Susie thought, but somehow she didn't want to send Sara's feelings crashing down too hard.

By the time they'd finished their fourth run, it was getting close to three o'clock. The bowls closed at three-thirty, the rest of the lifts shut down at four. Susie was totally exhilarated; even if they went home tomorrow the trip would have been worth it. And there were still two bowls left for the rest of the week.

"Ready to call it a day?" asked Sara. "Sundowner's only got a couple of runs left." They were standing at the top of the bowl, looking in the opposite direction. By skiing off a trail to the right, they would end up at lift seven, which would channel them back onto the main slopes.

"I think I might take one more run. It's not like I get out here every day."

"I have to get back. I've got some paperwork, plus scheduling to work out. I've got tomorrow morning open, not that you need another lesson—unless you want to do a semi with your husband."

"I'll have to check Andy's schedule. It sure was fun, though. If we get some more snow it might be worth doing again."

"Give me a call. Oh, and if you see Murray . . ." Sara smiled and put her hands on Susie's shoulder. "I assume you do come in contact with him now and then, despite everything."

"Oh, yes. In fact, I have this suspicion we'll run into him soon."

"Out here?" Sara's face lit up. "I thought he was finished with that case of his, that's why he left." She reached inside her parka and pulled out a card and a pen. She scribbled a phone number on the back. "Here, that's my home number. Tell him I didn't appreciate him disappearing on me."

"Will do." The two women hugged for an instant, then Sara backed off and waved goodbye. She took a couple of strong, gliding strokes and disappeared over the ridge. Susie watched her for a moment, then descended into the bowl. Her legs still felt springy, she calculated that if she worked quickly she could squeeze two runs in before the lift closed. She went flying around the moguls, darting downwards nearly on a straight line. It was her fastest run by far.

When she got to the bottom, she saw the lift line was more crowded than before. Most of the skiers knew that the day was ending, and Susie now doubted she could get in her extra run. She skied to the end of the line, hesitant to look for a chairlift partner. She figured if she yelled "single!" as was the custom, she'd immediately get hit on by some well-tanned ski Adonis who couldn't see the ring underneath her mitten. It was not the way she wanted to end her day. She had decided to simply wait her turn and ride up alone when she felt a tap on her shoulder.

"Excuse me, miss, are you single?"

Susie turned around and saw a young skier in an ice-blue parka; a girl, she figured, in her late teens, although it was hard to tell. The kid was a few inches shorter than her and wore a blue knit balaclava pulled over her face. A few strands of red hair showed through the eyes.

"Sure," said Susie. There didn't seem to be any polite way to refuse her. She seemed shy enough, and Susie guessed she could put up with her for ten minutes on the lift.

"Thanks." The girl skied beside her and didn't say another word as they edged their way up the line. They got on the chair and Susie pulled the safety bar over their heads. The youngster looked at her and smiled, then looked away.

"Nice day," Susie said, but got no response. "Aren't you a little hot in that thing?"

"A little." The girl tugged at the wool mask to get some more room around her mouth.

The lift continued upwards. The girl looked at Susie again. She cleared her throat, she seemed to be working up to something. "Would you like to ski back down the mountain with me?" she said hesitantly. Little puffs of breath came through the mouth-holes of the balaclava; it reminded Susie of the Camel sign in Manhattan.

"I don't think so. I'm going to try and ski the bowl again. Thanks anyway."

"I'm excellent company."

"No, really." Susie leaned away; she wondered if she'd mis-calculated. It must be a boy, some teenage kid, probably trying to impress his friends on a bet. "I'm married, actually. Sorry."

"Life is so unfair. Would this help change your mind?" The kid reached into his pocket. He pulled out a pistol with a silencer on it. He pointed it straight at Susie's heart.

Susie gulped. She looked down at the bowl below her; she squirmed in her seat. "Are you kidding?" she said. "It's broad daylight—"

"Quiet." The high-pitched voice was firm. "I can kill you right here—leave you on the lift and ski off. You're only worth slightly more to us alive than you are dead."

Susie didn't answer. She could only guess how much this person knew about her. She decided not to mention Andy's name; it could only put him in jeopardy. "Look, junior, I made copies of everything. They're with lawyers and editors. Why don't you put that away, go home and watch MTV?"

The kid grinned wretchedly behind the mask and pushed the gun closer to Susie; she felt it right between her breasts.

"Who are you?"

There was no answer.

"Do you have any idea who you're messing with—"

"Do exactly as I say." The kid jammed the pistol even closer. "When the ride's over, ski off to your right. Ski beside me, like we're old friends."

"Where are we going?"

"You'll see."

Susie looked up; the ride was over. She raised her tips and got ready to hop off. She thought of making a run for it. The kid had slipped the gun inside his parka, but she could see the outline of his hand tight against it.

"Head straight down Cherry Picker. When the trail splits, turn left. No tricks."

Susie did as she was told. She skied gracefully, her turns were quick and clean. She hoped that if she took a steep line the kid might stumble and give her a chance to escape, but he skied perfectly. Or maybe it was a she. Susie looked at the mask, trying to piece together features. Had Sara set her up? Carvall? She thought about Dakota-person. Or Casey, whom she hadn't met. The kid certainly skied well enough to be a ski instructor or ski patroller. Maybe he was older than she'd guessed.

"See the path to your left?"

"Where?"

"By that patch of firs."

Susie looked to a small clearing. She could see a narrow, snowy trail leading off the main slope.

"Go."

Susie tried to guess her location. She was near the western boundary of the ski area, probably not far from where Rick Allanson had disappeared. If she was going to make a break for it, she would have to do it before she got on that trail.

But there was no chance. Her assailant had the gun trained directly on her. The slopes around them were empty. Most of the skiers had headed back down to the village. There wasn't a ski patroller in sight.

"GO!"

Susie took a deep breath. She skied down the slope and veered left, onto the trail. As they skied deeper among the fir trees, it narrowed to a pair of tracks and sunk into the freshly fallen powder. Susie slogged straight ahead. It was like cross-country skiing, with a slight downhill pitch. The light was waning.

Up ahead, maybe fifty yards, an adult figure waited on cross-country skis. The person had a definitely masculine look, although the head was covered by a woolen mask. Susie stopped, bending down to tighten a buckle on her boot.

"Move it," said the kid. "Now!"

Susie squinted ahead into the shadows. In the background, she heard a long, mournful drone. It sounded like an outboard motor. It was coming from in back of them. It was getting louder.

"C'mon!" shouted the adult from down the trail. The voice was definitely male. The rest of the message was drowned out by the approaching motor.

"Geddown!" shouted the kid, his voice rising an octave. He shoved Susie hard sideways. She fell into the snow, face-first. She choked and twisted, but the kid held her down; she thought she was going to suffocate. She felt the binding on her right ski release. She heard the droning get closer, until it was almost on top of her.

It was a snowmobile.

The kid let go of her and stared straight ahead, while Susie struggled to get up. Across the way, the other man had ducked out of sight.

The snowmobile stopped a few feet from Susie. The man on

it was tall, he wore a helmet, and had a rugged blond beard. He leaned toward them and shouted over the roar of the engine. "Hey, yo! You all right down there?"

The kid kept his right hand inside his parka, hiding the revolver. "We're fine."

"Hey, atta boy! Listen, you see a pack of snow machines, maybe fifteen minutes ago?"

"Nope. You're on ski area property, you better beat it—"

"No we ain't. This here's a National Forest. We got permits—"

Susie pulled herself out of the snow. She knew there were no snowmobile permits in the area; she'd read the warning signs at the ranger station. She looked at the snowmobiler. He wore yellow shades underneath his helmet. He looked a little like the lift operator she'd seen earlier with Sara.

"Listen," squeaked the kid, his voice starting to waver, "I haven't seen your friends. Now get out of here, before I call a ranger."

The snowmobiler revved his engine. "Fine, buddy. Up yours, too." He put the machine in forward and roared away. Then, just as the kid turned back toward Susie, he made a quick U-turn. He pointed the snowmobile directly at them and gunned it full throttle.

"Hey!" The kid reached for his gun and fired wildly, then leaped backwards in the snow. Down the trail, the other man got up and started skiing toward the scene, his gun drawn.

"Yo, babe!" the snowmobiler roared over to Susie and came to a dead stop. "Jump on!"

Susie pushed herself upright. Her right ski had released and sunk into the snow. Her left one was still on. She hopped toward the snowmobile. A few feet away, her assailant struggled to regain his equilibrium.

"C'mon, sweetheart, move it!"

Behind them, the other man was gliding closer. He stopped and fired a shot; it splintered off a tree behind them. The snowmobiler pulled out a gun of his own and fired back. He missed, but the man was forced to take cover behind a fir tree. "Get rid of the ski!" he shouted to Susie, as she leaped onto the snowmobile.

Susie kicked off her left ski and straddled the snow machine.

The driver revved it once, then roared off through the woods. "Hold on!" he shouted, swerving back and forth. Susie heard the report of gunshots, there were two of them. She heard a ping as a bullet snapped into a tree behind them. She didn't have time to be terrified. She held onto the driver's waist as he guided the snowmobile deeper into the woods and up the slope.

They drove on for what seemed like hours, but it was only a few minutes. The kidnappers were on skis—they had no way of getting back up the mountain. The snowmobile flew across a ridge; they were now a good half-mile from the Sunburst boundary. It pulled to a stop in a glen, deep in the woods. The late afternoon light filtered through the fir trees—a few warm rays reached Susie's chilled face. The driver turned the motor off. "Sorry about the rough ride, babe. You okay?"

"I think so," Susie mumbled. She stepped off the snowmobile and stared at the man's jacket. It was definitely the lift operator she had seen before; he wore the Sunburst identification badge that said "Chris Banner." Wrong, Susie realized; a churning in her stomach told her what her eyes had missed.

"Glad to hear it. Incidentally, that's one gorgeous-lookin' outfit, Susela. Cover of *Ski* magazine for sure. Maybe *Vogue*. Glad someone has taste in the family."

Susie stood rigid in the snow. "You shameless, sleazoid parasite. You've been here the whole time."

The man took off his helmet. "Now, now. To everything there is a reason—"

"I swear to God, I'm going to see that you're hung off the back of one of your cruise ships and keel-hauled through the Panama Canal."

"I'll take that to mean you're glad I could make it." The man took off his sunglasses, then flashed the most demented grin that Susie Sussman was ever happy to see.

It was Murray Glick.

23

"Try and contain your excitement," Murray said, as Susie clenched her fist and turned various shades of red. "I know it's been a harrowing afternoon."

"Murray!" Susie kicked the back of the snowmobile and stumbled into the snow. "For God's sake, where have you been?"

Murray cupped his right hand to his ear. "Did I hear 'thank you, Murray? I'll always be indebted to you, Murray'?"

"You damn near got me killed, Murray!"

"Aw, Susela." Murray got off the snowmobile and helped Susie back to her feet. "It's a good thing I followed you up to Sundowner. You should be more careful who you ride with."

"Get your slimy hands off me." Susie slogged away from the snowmobile in a fury and sat down on a fallen tree trunk dusted with snow. "How'd you know I was in trouble?"

"You were followed up the lift by two masked banditos. One of them had a familiar grunt."

"Which one?"

"The tall one."

"Where'd you recognize him from?"

"A similar encounter." Murray pulled a Slim Jim from the pocket of his snowmobile jacket. "Care for a bite?"

"Yech. Who is he?"

"That I do not know."

"Come on, Glick."

"I don't, really."

"Were you following me, too?"

"I knew you'd signed up with Sara. I figured you'd head for the bowls."

"Did she tell you that?"

"Sara? Haven't spoken to her in weeks."

"So how'd you find out—"

"It's my business to find things out."

Susie slumped back on her tree trunk. Her parka was already soaked through with snow. Her ankles were sore—her custom-made ski boots were decidedly uncomfortable when there were no skis attached to them. "Murray, could you please take me back to the condo? I'm an absolute wreck."

"Sweetheart, take my word for it, even in a moldy tree trunk, dressed in waterlogged goose down and polyester, you are a total knockout."

"Murray, I AM totally knocked out. Please?"

"No can do, Susela. We can't be seen together. Fill me in on your progress, then I'll call you a taxi."

"Fill YOU in?" Susie kicked some snow at Murray. "I'll fill you in: Your friends are chasing you halfway across the country. Your business is going bankrupt. Your poor secretary can't pay the bills."

"I appreciate Peggy's problems, which were regrettably unavoidable. She can look forward to a wonderful bonus." Murray unzipped his snowmobile suit and pulled out a mini-carton of Minute Maid grape juice. He stuck in the straw and took a long slurp. "Care for a sip?"

"No! Damn it, Glick, start talking. Someone tried to kill me—"

Murray sat next to Susie on the log and handed her the juice. "Drink up. And don't forget I almost got killed, too, if that makes you feel any better."

"It doesn't." Susie took a sip from the grape juice. "Who tried to kill you?"

"Los banditos."

"Who are they?"

"I told you, I don't know. The circumstances of our first meeting weren't conducive to formal introductions."

"Murray . . ." Susie looked him squarely in the eye. "I can't believe this. Andy was actually worried about you."

"Just Andy?"

"Andy's my husband. If he's worried, then I'm worried."

"Glad to know the marriage is still strong."

"It can withstand even you." Susie edged down the log.

"Murray, I read your miserable excuse for a memoir. Not that I wanted to read any more, but could you please explain what happened after page 112?"

Murray took the grape juice back and finished it in one swallow, then scrunched up the carton and stuck it in his pocket. The sky was turning dark, there were a few flurries in the air. A stiff wind was coming out of the west. "You want the whole spine-tingling story?"

"Just the salient points. And it better include a damn good reason for dragging us out here."

"Very well, Mrs. Sussman." Murray cleared his throat. "Wednesday morning, 5 A.M. Dawn broke cold and ominous. Maybe it was just the chill in the air, maybe it was the fresh blanket of virgin snow, but I had a feeling that someone wanted this day to be my last. I hoped it wasn't the Man Upstairs."

"Save it, Glick—"

"I read the letter over to myself: Come to the gondola, 6 A.M. Alone. I slipped on my thermals and ski suit. I thought about my Colt .38, locked in my desk back home. But it was too late for wishes—this case would be solved mano a mano. I zipped up my parka. I slung my skis over my shoulder and walked off toward Sunburst Village—"

"You LIE!" Susie said, thumping Murray in the ribs. "You were met at the condo by someone in a car. Betty Cranston told me—she was wide awake."

Murray broke into a grin. "Susan Sussman, you are one foxy sleuth. You've exceeded my greatest expectations."

"Murray, *PLEASE* tell the truth."

Murray reached into his jacket and pulled out a Mars bar. "Snack?"

Susie started to push the candy away, but her stomach was growling. She snatched it from Murray, broke it in two, and gave him back the smaller half. "Now talk, buster."

"Yes, ma'am. Fact is, Brian Ellsworth met me at the condo. He's the ranger—"

"I know who he is."

"He had one of those beeper devices they use when they're skiing off into the woods. We'd customized it the night before; we could fit it in a place where nobody would look. Right in the, uh—"

"Spare me."

"Fine. I was wired up. Brian stayed in the parking lot, I followed instructions. I got to the gondola at six. It was closed. I was waiting at the base, munching on a sweet roll. Fella came up from behind, stuck something cold and round in my back. Told me we're going for a ride. I listened. He marched me off to the parking lot, into a Dakota pickup. Blindfolded me, drove us up to a trailhead."

"And led you off into the forest?"

"They've got their technique down. About a mile in they stood me up against a fir tree, shot some knock-out drops in my arm and left me for dead. An hour later, the cannons went off at Sunburst."

"What cannons?"

"The Forest Service fires two seventy-five-millimeter war-surplus artillery guns into strategic spots on the hill after a storm. Sets off controlled avalanches, makes things safe for the clientele the rest of the day. Listen for 'em tomorrow morning, bright and early."

Susie took a deep breath. She tried to fight off the image of lying deep under a pile of snow, hearing the cannons go off, suffocating slowly to death. It was going to be hard avoiding nightmares for a while.

"See, whoever pulled this off had it figured. They knew Sunburst's target areas after the blizzard and they knew when the cannons are fired. They sedated me, left me just on the National Forest side of the border. Then, while the cannons were booming, they skied uphill and set a ground charge that would bury me. The next day the ski patrol gets an anonymous tip."

"Rick Allanson was killed the day after a snowfall," Susie whispered.

"So were you and I. Almost."

Susie looked up; the snow was starting to fall in larger flakes, it was clinging to the trees. "But this time Ellsworth was tracking you?"

"He knew right where they were heading; it was almost exactly where Allanson had disappeared. He got up there by snowmobile, pronto—"

"But he didn't see the kidnappers?"

"He was busy digging me out. They'd set their slide and gone,

I was lucky he got to me as soon as he did. You can see I'm still a little frostbitten.''

Susie took a closer look at Murray's face. He'd bleached his hair and beard, but she could see the skin was rough and blotched in places.

"Not to worry, darling—a few weeks in Mazatlán ought to speed up the recovery.''

"Who's worrying?'' Susie said, but her voice faltered. It was the first time she'd actually seen Murray injured in the course of an investigation. "Murray, you could have told us—''

"No I couldn't. It was important that they thought I was snuffed. The death of Rick Allanson, the lease of the west ridge, the disappearance of Dani Kaplan—they're all tied together, Suse. And I'm the only one who suspected it.''

Susie got up from the log; the snow had seeped through her pants. "Murray, you could have told Andy. An anonymous phone call, a letter, something. No one would have known—''

"I sent you the manuscript,'' Murray said innocently.

"Oh, please! You're lucky I don't sue you for the extreme abdominal pains it caused me—''

"Now, now, let's try to have some literary objectivity.'' Murray zipped his parka back up; the weather was deteriorating. "I will admit that I thought you'd be more likely to come if I instilled a certain sense of urgency.''

"The possibility didn't escape us.''

Murray shook his scraggly beard and chortled like an emaciated Santa Claus. "Well gosh, Suse, Andy needed a change of pace; he spends way too much time indoors. I saw his tape, he looked pale. I hope he spends a few more days on the mountain.''

"Murray,'' Susie shivered, "will you PLEASE take me home before we both freeze to death.''

"We won't freeze. I'm wearing extra thermals, I'll be happy to peel you off a pair. I took all the precautions.''

"So I heard.'' Susie scooped up a snowball and fired it at Murray. "That's from Terry Tollison. Who doesn't know you've been spending the last month romancing a cutie-pie ski instructor.''

"Terry understands that my work sometimes puts me in awkward situations. For which I'm getting paid good money by a very sweet lady.'' Murray wiped the snow from his jacket.

"Murray, you are such a trip." Susie walked back to the snow-mobile and sat down on the seat. "I talked to her, too, by the way."

"Barbra?"

"Bar-ba-ra."

Murray grinned. He pulled out his Slim Jim and gnawed a piece off the tip. "Susan, I can't tell you how impressed I am. Truth is, I've been looking to open up an office here in Sunburst. You'd be a natural. You could ski all morning, Andy could fly out for the weekends."

"Glick, is the word 'shame' in your vocabulary?"

'This is a tough business, sweetheart. I do my job, I don't ask questions. I take risks. If an occasional client finds that attractive or sensuous, I can't exactly help that, can I?"

"Murray, are you listening to me? I talked to Barbara Kaplan—who, as you well know, is not exactly Glencoe's answer to Joan Collins."

Murray walked back to the snowmobile. "Maybe you caught her on a bad day."

"I asked her, Murray. She did NOT fly out to Sunburst for a secret rendezvous."

"Well for cripes sakes, Suse. You didn't expect her to admit it, did you? To a perfect stranger?"

"Glick!" Susie reached for the key to the snowmobile. "Take me home."

"Not yet."

"I'm cold!"

Murray put his arms around her, warming her with his snow-suit.

"I'm going to scream."

"You'll wake the bears out of hibernation."

"Then I'll faint."

"Just hang tough for a few more minutes, Susela."

"Take . . . me . . . back!"

"I can't. I'm still dead. And you wouldn't be inviting Chris Banner back to your place, would you?"

Susie freed herself from Murray's bear hug and shoved him against the seat.

"Okay, okay—just get me up to date on your dauntless investigations, then we'll get you home."

Susie sat back on the snowmobile. She finished her half-a-candy bar. She shook the snow out of her mittens, then told Murray about her interviews with Barbara Kaplan and the Cranstons. She tried to summarize Andy's talk with Casey Wright, but she was tired and sore and couldn't recall much. Finally, she described her discussion with Jack Carvall. It was then that Murray's eyes lit up, especially when he heard about the Dakota screeching out of the parking lot.

"You didn't see the driver at all?"

"Sorry."

"What about Carvall's plans? Did he say where he was being reassigned after the office closes down?"

"I told you, no. He seemed evasive about it."

"Could you find out?"

Susie shook her head. "Sorry, pal. You're alive, I'm off the case."

"I'm not alive, Suse. Not as far as a killer's concerned—"

"Carvall might BE the killer. He might have been the other kidnapper. I'm not going to waltz back into his office—"

"Talk to the ranger girl; she sounded sympathetic. Call her, meet her in the village. You don't even have to set foot in the ranger station—"

"Murray! Does the fact that my life is being threatened bother you in the least?"

"Would I be here if it didn't?" Murray took Susie's hand. "I am your protector, Susan Sussman, wife of my best friend." He helped her back on the snowmobile. "And don't forget Dani Kaplan. If I'm right, her life's at stake, too." He climbed onto the snow machine and sat in front of Susie, taking her hand. "Suse, I'd advise staying off the slopes for a day or two. Hang around the village, keep Andy company. And tell him to keep a sharp eye on our friend Mr. Wright. He's going to be your insurance policy for the next few days.

"CASEY?"

"Absolutely. To whatever extent Casey's involved in all this, his motive is to become a big shot at Sunburst. The World Cup ski race is the most important thing ever to happen here. He can't let any harm come to you or Andy."

"Even if his own hide's at stake?"

"Not until the race is over. He'll find a way to stall you at least that long."

"And what happens after that?"

"There won't be any after that." Murray started the snow-mobile. "Trust me." He put the machine in gear and glided out of the glen. They plowed through the woods, toward the ski slope, which was still hidden by the thick forest. When they reached the edge, he brought the engine to an idle.

"Murray," said Susie, as she caught a glimpse of an empty ski run through a clearing fifty yards in front of her, "this is not home. Take me to the condo; no one's going to know who we are. It's dark, it's nearly a blizzard."

"Sorry, Suse. Someone might be watching. Andy could be standing outside waiting—he'd give me away. I'll take you down to the bottom of three. You can walk back from there."

Susie started to protest, but Murray revved up the motor and made his way down the slope. He stuck to the edge of the ski area, winding down the mountain until he got to the bottom of lift three. It was the westernmost of the bottom lifts; there was a well-worn trail leading back to the village, a half-mile away.

"Murray, I am NOT going to walk all the way back there in my ski boots—"

"I'd give you my cowboy boots, but they're too big. You'll be fine in those; just loosen the buckles a little."

"Forget it. Start the motor."

"Sorry, babe." Murray lifted Susie off the snowmobile and set her upright on the trail. "Just keep those legs pumping, you'll be home before you know it."

"Thanks a bunch," Susie muttered. "What about my skis? They're out in the middle of the woods."

"I promise you a brand new pair. Pick out whatever your heart desires—I'll reimburse you as soon as the case is over."

"You're damned right you will." Susie took a few tenta-tive steps down the trail. "Murray, is it safe to walk back by myself?"

"I'll keep an eye on you."

"How are we supposed to get in contact with you from now on?"

Murray winked.

"Should we ask for Chris Banner?"

"Chris is retiring. I'll be in touch." Murray revved the snow-mobile.

"What about J. B. Cranston? And that girl he talked to? And Sara? And the cop Andy was with—"

"Relax, Susela. Enjoy your walk. Say hello to Andy."

"Murray," shouted Susie, as he started to pull away. "Some day, if there's a God in heaven, if there's any justice—"

"Sweetheart, my whole profession is predicated on the existence of justice. Au revoir!"

Susie stood still for a moment, watching as the snowmobile disappeared into the snow and the darkness. She started to walk, feeling the boots pinch against her toes and ankles; it wasn't comfortable, but she'd make it. She looked over her shoulder, into the swirls of snow. She could tell from the drone of the snowmobile that Murray hadn't strayed far.

Susie swore under her breath as she clomped along the path. The thought of a Jacuzzi and a warm cup of cocoa inspired her every step. Her anger began to drain away. A half-mile wasn't so far, especially compared to where she had been a few minutes ago.

It occurred to Susie that she actually felt some solace in the fact that Murray Glick was looking out for her. It was odd, but as much as she despised him, she felt confident that she'd be perfectly safe as long as he was around.

Susie didn't quite know how to account for that.

But she had a suspicion that if things had come down to trusting Murray Glick, her life was in need of some serious adjustments.

24

Andy Sussman gently peeled off his blue jeans, then his long johns, then his wool socks and underwear. He extended a toe into the bathtub; the water stung, but the pain was hard to pinpoint. His entire body was covered with welts and bruises. His right knee felt like two pieces of a jigsaw puzzle that had been forced together but didn't quite fit. His back was an electronic switchboard gone awry, sending pain signals indiscriminately through his arms and legs. He lowered himself into the tub carefully, a pore at a time. He found a complimentary vial of bubble bath and poured a few drops of it under the running water. He let the bubbles foam up around his battered bod; they stung even more, but the aroma relaxed him. He turned the water off and reversed his position, resting his feet on the faucet and his head against the end of the tub.

He closed his eyes and breathed in and out slowly, evenly, opening his fists, relaxing his muscles. He felt the pain begin to dissipate. He heard the door to the condo open. He wanted to yell hello, but he couldn't quite stir his vocal cords to action. He conjured up the idea that Susie had returned from shopping, that she had a bag full of pasta and her special tomato and mushroom sauce, with a tossed salad and garlic bread somewhere in the picture. He could actually smell the aroma when he was interrupted by a sharp twinge of pain originating from his right toe. "Ouch!" he cried, opening one eyelid.

"I'm getting in," Susie said, without so much as a hello. "Move it or lose it."

"Hey! Take off your damn ski boots!"

Susie looked down at her feet. "Details," she mumbled. She unloosened the buckles and removed the boots, tossing them weakly toward the hallway. She stripped away two layers of socks; the toes were red with blood. "Andy," she said, making a feeble attempt to remove her sweater, "could you possibly help me off with this?"

"Susan, look at me," Sussman groaned, looping his right leg over the tub wall. The leg was a gruesome sight; it was bruised and scratched, there was an ugly welt over the shinbone.

"Please?" Susie said, speaking through the back of the light blue ski sweater that she had managed to pull over her shoulders.

"You would not believe what I've been through," Andy said. He leaned over the edge of the tub and tugged at Susie's sweater. With great effort he pulled it over her head and lobbed it onto a towel rack. "Kevin Cumberland is a totally berserk human being. They lowered us from the helicopter by rope ladder, right onto the edge of a precipice. We skied straight downhill, through snow up to our necks, with these freaking tree stumps sticking out all over the place. The mini-cam got caught on a pine branch and damn near strangled me."

"Help me off with these pants," said Susie. She zipped the bib of her designer overalls open and pushed the suspenders sideways. The pants were soaked through; the zipper stuck in a few places but she somehow forced it down. Andy pulled on the legs and she slid out of them. She was standing now against the towel rack in her bra and long johns.

"Then we fell into a damn stream," Andy continued. "Can you believe it? 'Just build up some speed and shoot over the moguls,' Kevin says. Some mogul! It was a half-exposed boulder, we fucking landed right in the middle of a creek! The water's thirty-five degrees, we're soaked to the bone. Fortunately Kevin's got an extra change of wool undies in his backpack—we've got to strip down in the middle of a snowstorm at 9,000 feet."

"I have two pieces of news for you," Susie said, removing her underwear and lowering herself into the tub. It was a luxury size unit, according to the condo brochure, which meant that it could accommodate two people if they lay on top of one another. Susie slid next to Andy, leaving both of them canted toward the sides.

"Listen to me, Suse. After we change clothes, the storm kicks up worse; we can barely see in front of us. And the snow gets into the main camera unit's cables, so that's totally useless. Then Jerry the cameraman sprains his wrist so we've got to help him carry everything the rest of the day. In the meantime, our only footage is six hours of mini-cam; you'll get seasick just watching it—and the last twenty minutes of that is a couple of rednecks trying to chase us off the mountain—"

"Someone tried to kill me," Susie said, taking a handful of soap bubbles and lathering them over her hair and face. "That's my first bit of news."

"Someone what?" Andy grabbed Susie by the shoulders. He pushed her sideways a few inches so he could look directly at her.

"Kill me. I was abducted after my lesson with Sara. They were going to drug me and leave me in a snowdrift."

Andy shook some soap out of his eyes. "Who?"

"I don't know. They didn't leave a card."

"Jeez, Suse." Sussman's voice dropped to a whisper. "Why didn't you say something?"

Susie gave Andy a look that would have vaporized a weaker man.

"Well how'd you get out of it?"

"That brings us to news flash number two. A certain detective who'd been reported MIA turns out to be still among the quick."

"Aha." Sussman pushed himself backwards in the tub so that Susie still lay on top of him, her head resting gently on his chest. "Well, that's certainly good news. How is he?"

"Andy!" Susie aimed an elbow directly south.

Andy squirmed sideways, barely saving future generations of Sussmans. He kissed Susie on the nape of the neck and began to massage her shoulder. "There, there. Doesn't that feel better?"

"Doesn't even begin to compensate."

"Give me time, babe."

"You should live long enough."

Andy kissed Susie again; he held her closer. He considered an advance toward lovemaking, but he guessed there was a reasonable chance that one of them would drown in the attempt. He bathed her instead, lathering the bubble bath all over her body, tenderly cleansing the blood that had caked around her feet. When he had finished, he retreated to his position at the back of the tub and coaxed some details out of her. His mind didn't absorb everything. His legs still ached and his back was getting sore from lying underneath her. He was most interested in Murray's rescue. He repeatedly asked Susie where Glick had gone—surely he must have dropped some kind of hint. It was only when she emphasized her total ignorance to his whereabouts by jamming a bar of soap into his navel that his mind snapped back to Susie's account of the abduction. "Suse, describe the guys that kidnapped you."

Susie breathed in deeply; she sunk a few inches into the tub. "The kid was maybe five-six. Late teens, maybe college. I thought it was a guy, now I'm not sure. He wore a ski mask and a blue parka. Not anyone we'd met, unless it was Dakota-person. The other guy was taller and older—I didn't get a close look."

"Honey, listen. I think those were the same two that tried to run us off on the way down."

"What are you talking about?"

"I told you. On the way out, these two guys came by, one on cross-country skis, one on downhill. They were a mess, looked like they'd rolled down the hill headfirst. The smaller one had a torn suit, sopping-wet parka. And a ski mask—we could see him pull it over his head just as we skied up to him."

"Did they pull a gun on you?"

"No. They seemed panicky, though. Younger one started chewing us out about skiing in a National Forest, until Kevin told 'em we were with CBS and if they didn't get the hell out of there and leave us alone he was going to call the sheriff and have 'em both arrested for trespassing."

"What'd they say to that?"

"The kid was shook-up. Rattled off a few obscenities, but the older guy calmed him down. He jabbed him with a ski pole and whispered something. They backed away and took off downhill. I just figured they were a couple of locals. Damn, if I'd have known—"

"Andy—" Susie sat up in the bathtub, accidentally squashing Sussman's kneecap.

"Ow! What?"

"Didn't you say you got it all on the mini-cam?"

"Oh, yeah." He rubbed some bubbles onto his knee. "Yeah, Jerry'd taken it from me in exchange for the big unit after he hurt his hand. He was standing behind us, taping the whole thing. It probably won't look like much; it was snowing and getting dark."

"I have great confidence in the miracles of modern technology. Why don't you call him up and make sure he keeps the footage?"

"Will do, babe." Andy leaned toward the faucet and ran some more hot water into the tub. "I'll get hold of him first thing in the morning."

"Dearest," Susie said, "do the words 'attempted murder' instill any kind of a sense of urgency in you?"

Andy looked at Susie, who was now standing up in the bathtub. If the words "attempted murder" had not instilled a sense of urgency in him, the plastic scrubber that she was aiming at his noggin certainly did. "Susan, I will call Jerry right away." Andy pulled himself out of the bathtub with considerably more alacrity than he had thought he possessed only a few seconds ago. He draped a towel around himself, limped over to the telephone, and called up the production headquarters. Fortunately there was an engineer on duty who had the hotel phone number of Jerry the cameraman. Sussman called him up. Jerry had just returned from the hospital, where he'd gotten his wrist taped. He had the minicam tape with him and would be happy to give it to Sussman, if Sussman wanted to walk over to his hotel and get it. Otherwise, he'd bring it over to the studio in the morning.

Andy looked out the window. There was a full-scale blizzard blowing now, the wind was piling the snow up in drifts outside the window. He told Jerry he'd pick the tape up in the morning, then limped back into the bathroom, where Susie was nearly invisible underneath a sea of bubbles. "Sweetheart, Jerry has the tape. There's a small glacier forming outside our front door. Do you mind if I pick it up in the morning?"

A blob of bubbles nodded in what Sussman interpreted as affirmation.

"I'll look at it first thing. We'll blow up whatever parts we can, see if we can get a better look at those guys. I can take the tape over to the police department and show it to Gustafson."

Susie stuck her head out of the foam. "You trust him?"

"He's a friend of Kevin's."

"Did he know I was skiing with Sara in the bowls?"

"How would he? Unless—" Sussman thought back to his interview that morning. Gustafson had told him to take another phone for privacy, than walked over to another desk. "There's a possibility he could have listened in. If I had to make a guess on pure instinct, I'd say he's okay."

Susie rinsed some suds out of her eyes. "Andy, maybe we should wait."

"I thought you were in such a big hurry."

"I mean, to give the tape to the cops. Seeing as you're not one hundred percent sure. I'd rather we held onto it a day or so and showed it to, uh . . ." Susie started to cough.

"Showed it to who?"

"I think by that time a certain detective might possibly get hold of us."

Sussman finished drying himself off. He walked into the bedroom and slipped on a pair of sweatpants. He turned the heat up a few notches; he was beginning to feel toasty and comfortable despite his aches and pains. He found a set of matching sweats in Susie's dresser and brought them into the bathroom. "Is it my imagination, or do I detect some well-disguised confidence in the master sleuth?"

"At least we know he's not trying to kill us," Susie said. "Intentionally, that is."

Sussman took Susie's ski sweater from the towel rack and folded it neatly. "Can I assume, then, that we're going to make an attempt to follow through on his assignments?"

"I just want to get this over with, at minimal risk to ourselves." Susie opened the plug and the water started to drain out of the bathtub. "I'll call Carol Bevins. I'll try and get her to have lunch at the village. If you want to keep tabs on Casey Wright, that's up to you." She stood up and turned on the shower for a few seconds to rinse off the soap bubbles. When she stepped out of the tub, Andy wrapped a towel around her and held her close against him.

"Darling, listen: there's no sense taking any risks at all. Pack up, I can have you back to New York on the next plane—"

Susie shook her head. "I thought about it, Andy. If someone really is intent on killing me, they could follow me back to New York. I'm probably safest right here. With you."

"You're sure?"

"I'm sure." Susie hugged Andy tight. "They won't try it again. Murray's right—no one with a business stake in Sunburst is going to let anything happen to us during the World Cup."

"Right," said Sussman. "Not this week, anyway." He gave Susie a kiss, the two of them walked hand in hand out of the bathroom. "And by the time the race is over, the whole case will be closed. We have the word of the master sleuth."

"Of course," Susie said.

"Nothing to worry about."

"Absolutely."

"Nothing."

"Nada."

Andy and Susie looked at each other for a moment, traded uneasy smiles, and headed for the kitchen. "In the meantime," Sussman said, as he scrounged around for some dinner, "how would you feel about a quick trip to Switzerland?"

25

Murray Glick flopped over in bed, his toes sticking out over the edge of the blankets. It was 7 A.M. Streams of sunlight spilled over the mountains and filtered through the thin white drapes and battered shades of his efficiency apartment. He groped at the Sears coffeemaker that rested on top of his battered old Olivetti. He opened one eye and saw that the red light wasn't on yet. He'd programmed it for seven-fifteen. He was owed fifteen minutes more sleep. Sometime in the not-too-distant future, hopefully on some deserted Caribbean isle, a soft breeze tickling his toes and a beautiful girl by his side, he was going to make up for it. But not today.

He sat up in bed and surveyed his spare accommodations. He'd inherited a few pieces of furniture from the former tenants who hadn't paid the rent: a small dinette set, a couple of lamps. He'd splurged on the mattress, a full-sized Sealy Posturepedic. When you're six-foot two, pushing thirty-five, and dependent on a functioning spinal cord, you don't fool around with rollaway cots.

There was no phone in the room. Murray was not expecting any calls. A radiator at the far corner did a pretty fair imitation of a woodpecker every night; it actually provided some heat, usually in sporadic bursts that would turn the place into a tropical rain forest. Murray supposed that it was good to suffer these kinds of indignities from time to time. It kept him sharp and in touch with the grittiness of his profession. Mainly, though, it served to remind him what he had worked so hard over the last five years to avoid. As the red light flickered on the coffeemaker, Murray resolved that he had had about enough of this. It was Thursday. The World Cup race was Sunday. It was time for him to come back to life.

But where? And for whom? It was a question to be considered carefully. He needed the maximum effect. It was not every day, after all, that a Jew got resurrected.

Murray poured himself some coffee and tore the cellophane wrapper off a sweet roll that he'd bought at a 7-Eleven the night before. There were several people with whom he needed to have heart-to-heart discussions, but the approach had to be subtle. He had to be careful not to flush out the actual murderer/kidnappers before he'd assembled his case. He needed to work the outer levels of the conspiracy, sending ripples toward the core, until Someone (or more than one) burst into public view.

Murray pulled out a pen and jotted down names, candidates for a visit from the Ghost of Detectives Past. Casey was out. So was Carvall. Both of them were too central, although the Forest Service supervisor lingered in his mind. Carvall would have known exactly when and where the avalanche cannons were fired, and he'd been vocally supportive of the west ridge expansion. Still, it was a long leap from there to a murder. More importantly, what if Carvall did have Dani Kaplan in his custody? Murray was being paid to find the girl; he was afraid his sudden reappearance might cause Carvall to panic. He reluctantly drew a line through his name and moved on to Craig Gustafson. He wondered if the cop had been holding back information all along, or if he was just too stubborn to admit he'd fucked up. Murray pondered the question. He wasn't crazy about waking up the local police. Pursuing a closed murder case after he'd faked his own demise would only get him in more hot water.

Then, of course, there was Beth. Murray was certain she knew where Dani was. But where was Beth? He'd dropped by the Village Deli a week ago in his Chris Banner disguise and asked around; he'd been greeted by an ignorance so total that he was immediately suspicious. He guessed Beth still had friends there. He guessed someone was keeping her informed. But what did she need to know? Who was she keeping track of? And how would he find her? Short of staking out the deli in the faint hope that she'd drop by again, Murray was stumped.

At the bottom of his scratch pad, he wrote down two names.

The first was Sara Felder. From a professional standpoint, he couldn't overlook the possibility that she'd been involved in setting Susie up. Yet, deep down, Murray considered that unlikely; he knew it was just an excuse to see her again. Not that that was any great crime. The girl was crazy about him, after all. He could have her over for dinner. Pick up a pizza, some sleek candles, a bottle of Chablis. His powers of analysis and deduction might be inspired by an evening of romance. Murray smiled wistfully; he tapped the arm of his shabby wooden chair and looked around his rat trap of an apartment. He drew a line through Sara's name. Romance would have to wait.

He looked at the second name and circled it. He decided that a morning appointment would be most convenient. He showered, shaved, then rummaged through his closet until he found the proper attire. He took a last gulp of coffee, headed for the door, then stopped. He walked back to the bed and pulled a Colt .38 Detective Special from underneath the pillow. He'd paid cash for it a week ago at a sporting goods store a few miles out of town. He'd had to fill out a form and provide identification. It was a risk, but it had already paid off once. He had a feeling it wouldn't be the last time.

Murray kicked some freshly fallen snow off the sidewalk. The chic ski village was several miles away; surrounding him was a collection of apartment buildings and convenience stores, a life-support system for the not-so-glamorous Sunburst personnel: retail clerks, maids, lift operators. He'd been residing on this block for three weeks now. Immediately after his escape he'd stayed with Brian Ellsworth, in a cabin near the ranger station, but Ellsworth's transfer had come through faster than expected. Murray had found the efficiency advertised on a bulletin board at a church and rented it under the name of Chris Banner. He'd managed to slip in and out without attracting much attention. Hopefully, he would be back in more upscale digs before long.

Murray walked down the block, dressed in dark green pants and a matching long-sleeved shirt; a little oval in the right breast read "Chuck." On the back of the shirt, in script, were the words "Rocky Mountain Mineral Water." Murray had filched the uniform from a laundry truck outside the water company's loading dock several weeks ago, in anticipation of just this situation. The only thing he needed now was an actual Rocky Mountain Mineral Water truck. Murray hiked about a half-mile; the neighborhood grew more affluent, he found a water truck making its morning deliveries. The driver had parked it at the corner and was walking toward an apartment with two five-gallon plastic containers slung over his shoulders. When he had disappeared inside the apartment building, Murray slipped inside the truck. He found the key in the ignition. He marvelled at how nice it was to be in a community where people didn't lock up their cars like vaults every time they ventured a few feet away. He could live in a place like this. He waved to a school bus full of kids across the street, he shouted hello to a woman walking her dog. He turned the key. He started the truck and drove off toward Sunburst Village.

Murray steered carefully up the snowy, sloping roads, stopping finally at a curb in front of a two-story condominium at the end of a cul-de-sac. He felt a twinge of nostalgia. He still had the key to Barbara's unit; there was a strong temptation to let himself in, fix himself an omelet, and take a steaming hot shower. Instead, he looked in the mirror, adjusted his sunglasses, and tugged at his blondish beard. He pulled the cap over his forehead. He wasn't terribly worried about the disguise; it was only meant to get him up the stairs and into the Cranstons' condo. Still, he liked to be efficient. He slung a water bottle over his shoulder and headed up the stairs. He knocked on the door.

"Who's there?" shouted Betty Cranston.

"Rocky Mountain Mineral Water," Murray answered, dropping his voice a few notches.

"Coming." Betty opened the door; she was dressed in dark blue slacks and a beige cable-knit sweater. "I thought our delivery day was Friday."

"The schedule got staggered because of the ski race, ma'am. We've got expanded service for all the skiers and media. We'll be back on the regular schedule next week." Murray walked through the hallway toward the kitchen. He had meant to carry on this charade for just a few seconds, then give Betty a big hug and corral her husband for a short seminar on Colorado real estate. But he altered his plans when he got to the kitchen. There was a visitor there, talking to J. B. Cranston.

"I don't give a flying fuck about the goddam race!" shouted

a middle-aged man, wearing cowboy boots that didn't quite match
his gray business suit. He wore a heavy overcoat despite the cozy
temperature inside the condo. "I'll rip the balls off that little son
of a bitch."

"Sam, Sam, get ahold of yourself," said J.B., his voice sliding
into a smooth, southwestern drawl. "Hell, he ain't so little either.
Have some orange juice—Betty squeezed it fresh."

"No thanks, dammit. Let's go—"

"Gotta have some vitamin C if you're gonna go pickin' fights
with youngsters. Specially ones with arms like cement mixers."

Murray walked across the kitchen, the water bottle hiding his
profile. He was happy to see that the bubbler was nearly empty;
it would give him an excuse to change the bottle, instead of just
dropping the new one off and leaving.

"You're a day early," J.B. said, flashing a patrician glare. He
loosened the collar on a silver dress shirt. A fleece-lined parka was
sitting on the dining room chair. Murray guessed J.B. had been
about ready to head for work when Sam Kaplan had barged in.

"Schedule's changed for a few days," Murray mumbled,
glancing at Kaplan as he walked over to the bubbler. He recognized him from the pictures in the condo downstairs. They had
been taken years ago, but Sam was still slim and muscular. Murray guessed he played a lot of handball or racquetball. The tan
suggested a Florida golf game. The receding hairline and drawn
forehead suggested about fifty years of age and a missing daughter.

"What the hell are we waiting for?" Sam said. "If he's involved with that race we oughta head over and settle our business
before the press gets there—"

"Speaking of land values," interrupted J.B., casting a casual
glance Murray's way, "you should see what's happening on the
other side of the ridge."

"I know EXACTLY what's happening on the other side—"

"Hot damn, pardner, with interest rates being what they are,
we could work a closed-end deal on a series of lots near the proposed lifts—"

Sam started to shout a protest, then looked over at Murray.
He sat down at a bar stool next to the counter and took a sip of
orange juice. "Sure, sure," he said. "Mortgage rates look like
they're headed up again, J.B. I'd buy in now."

Murray lifted the empty bottle off the bubbler. He pulled the plastic red tab off the fresh one and slung it upside down onto the stand without losing a drop of water. He knew that Sam had caught J.B.'s hint and changed the subject. He straightened the bottle, waved goodbye, and headed for the door. He figured if he made a quick effort to dispose of the truck, he could jog back and catch Sam before he made his next move.

Back outside the condo, the street was quiet. Most people had been smart enough to get their cars in their garages before last night's snowfall. The cul-de-sac was a circle of white, except for the Rocky Mountain water truck. As Murray drove it out of the lane and up the street, he saw a light blue Ford station wagon pull to a stop at the bottom of the circle. Murray drove a half-mile, then parked the truck and jogged toward the Cranstons' condo. He made it back in about ten minutes. The blue Ford was parked two driveways down.

Murray didn't approach the Cranston/Kaplan unit directly. He walked up the front walk of a unit several doors down, out of the Ford's sightline. He edged around the side, then cut through two backyards until he was directly behind the Kaplans' garage. Crouching in the snow behind a fir tree, he peered at the Ford. It was a new Taurus. There was only one person inside, he couldn't tell if it was a man or a woman. He tried to get a read on the rear license plate. It was covered with snow; he could make out a 2 and a B and that was it. He did notice that the license was framed by a bright-red plate holder, probably attached by the dealer. He couldn't make out the lettering, but he noticed a decal of a grizzly bear on the side of the plate frame.

Upstairs, Murray heard the Cranstons' front door slam. He heard voices. They were were approaching the garage. He heard Sam bark out at Cranston, "I have every right to walk in there and ask a few questions."

"Sam, you're out of control."

"I am NOT out of control!"

"Listen to me, Sam. I know Casey. He doesn't respond to threats. He'll have you hauled right out of there—"

"You're way off, J.B. The last thing he wants is trouble. We'll sit down like professionals. I'll be very dignified. I'll make a fatherly request and then he'll tell me where my daughter is. And then I'll kick the living shit out of the little pecker!" There was a pause, then Murray heard the car door slam and the engine start. The car roared out of the garage and onto the street.

Murray, still squatting in the snow, watched Sam Kaplan drive off. A few seconds later he saw the Taurus wagon pull out from behind a snowbank and drive after him. Back at the garage, J. B. Cranston shook his head, muttered something unintelligible, and walked back up to his unit.

When Cranston was safely inside, Murray stole around the back of the garage and let himself into the Kaplans' condo through the patio door. He walked quickly toward the guest bedroom. He'd stuck an extra pair of jeans and a sweater in the back of one of the dressers. He took off the mineral water uniform and stowed it deep in the drawer, then changed into his new clothes. He combed his hair. He thought about shaving off the beard, but there wasn't time.

He walked into the kitchen, picked up the phone, and tapped out a number. Sam Kaplan, it appeared, had finally decided to take Dani's situation into his own hands. Murray wondered how much Barbara had told him—he wondered if she even knew Sam was out here. He waited for his call to be answered. He waited five rings, then hung up. He was convinced that Sam's idea to confront Casey Wright was ill-advised, especially with someone tailing him. Setting off fireworks with Casey might cause someone to panic. He picked up the phone and dialed again, this time trying his friend's office number.

"CBS World Cup, production department," answered a secretary.

"Andy Sussman, please." There were a few moments of silence, then Sussman picked up the phone. "Hello, old chum," Murray said, and then, without waiting for an answer, "Don't say a word. I'm still officially in rigor mortis."

"There's at least one vote for you to stay that way."

"Listen up, Andrew. I need a small favor."

"Not a chance."

"I knew I could count on you. I want you to call Casey Wright. Tell him you need to meet him immediately."

"Forget it."

"Tell him you need some type of production shot. Just get him away from his office. Get him up on the slopes somewhere."

There was a momentary pause. "Why?"

"I can't tell you. I'll explain later—"

"Explain NOW, dammit. Where are you? What the hell's going on—"

"Just do it." Murray hung up the phone. He could tell that Sussman was irredeemably pissed off at him. Still, he knew Andy would come through; it was one of the advantages of such an enduring friendship. He would make it up to him somehow. In the meantime, there was another matter to clear up. Murray searched the kitchen for the telephone book, found the yellow pages and opened it to "Automobile Dealers, New." He searched the large display ads until he found what he was looking for. "Clyde Collins Ford, Number One in the Rockies." It was a full-page ad, lined by gold and red piping. In the middle of it, a grizzly bear roared beside a new Ford Probe.

Murray copied the address down. He locked the patio door. He exited from the front entrance and walked toward the village. From there he would catch a shuttle bus that would get him within a few blocks of his apartment; then he would pay a visit to Clyde Collins Ford.

It had been a long time since he'd been to a Ford dealership, Murray thought, walking briskly over the snow-covered path. He'd been driving foreign cars for years back in Chicago, despite the snow and the salt and the deteriorating highways. But what the hell, his Maserati was getting on in years. He'd been hearing great things about the new generation of Fords.

True, Murray did not consider himself a Ford Motor Company kind of guy. But he had the feeling that today they might have just the car for him.

26

Susie Sussman stood outside Clem's Claim, anxiously looking down the street, waiting for Carol Bevins to arrive. She had held deep reservations about fulfilling Murray's instructions, her assurances to Andy notwithstanding. In the end, she'd decided that a few minutes over lunch was not too great an inconvenience, especially if it helped push this whole business to a conclusion. What's more, she was beginning to feel a spark of anger, and not just at Glick. Two people had tried to kill her; she suspected they weren't finished. She was damn well going to do her part to see that they were apprehended, even if Murray would doubtlessly reap all the benefits.

So she'd called Carol at eight-thirty that morning, hoping to reach her before Jack Carvall arrived. She'd succeeded, but only by a few seconds. Bevins had hinted that she had some information, then suddenly clammed up. She'd suggested that they have an early lunch and had agreed to meet here at eleven o'clock. It was now eleven-fifteen. Susie paced in front of the restaurant, breathing a high altitude sigh of relief when she saw the familiar brown uniform and Smokey hat jogging toward her from down the block.

"I parked back by the gondola," Carol explained. Her cheeks were red, her breath spilled out in abbreviated puffs. She carried with her a cheap leather portfolio. "I thought I'd lose myself in the crowd better." She looked over her shoulder, then across the street. "In case someone was following me."

Susie had not anticipated that anyone would tail an interim forest ranger, but she scanned the street anyway. "Did you see anyone?"

"No," Carol admitted sheepishly. "Maybe I'm getting paranoid; I'm not used to this spy stuff. Let's go outside."

Susie and Carol walked through the swinging saloon doors of Clem's Claim. Behind them, on the street, a blue Taurus station wagon pulled up. It stopped, then rolled forward and parked across the way, in front of a fashion boutique. No one got out.

Inside Clem's, the two women sat down at a wooden table at the back of the room. The place was dark and musty, the lighting was dim. A glimmer of brightness shone through the snow-blocked windows. A waitress came by and they both ordered chef's salads. When she'd left, Carol pushed the battered portfolio across the table. "I guess you should take a look at this."

Susie silently zipped it open. She pulled out a photocopied document and held it up to her eyes, trying to catch a few stray sunbeams. It was an official letter from the Forest Service. It acknowledged the resignation of Jack Carvall, effective the end of the month. "So Jack's bailing out," Susie said, handing the letter back to Carol. "What's he going to do?"

Carol shrugged. "I don't think he's required to explain his career plans to the Department of Agriculture."

"Did he say anything to you?"

"Not a word. He's still supposedly waiting for reassignment. This came in the mail after he left yesterday. I could read it through the envelope. I steamed it open and photocopied it."

"Good work." Susie took a sip of coffee. "So. A Forest Service administrator suddenly resigns, just as his office is being closed to make room for a ski development."

"I thought it was kind of curious." Carol took her Smokey hat off and set it down on the table, nervously rubbing the edges of it with her right hand. "On the other hand, maybe he just didn't want to be transferred. They could have sent him anywhere. This is such a gorgeous place, I'm wishing I could stay myself. Maybe he just found something else to do."

"An unexpected opportunity in the private sector? Gee, I wonder who might have opened their hearts to him."

The waitress came by with their salads, but Bevins didn't have much of an appetite. She nibbled on some lettuce and drank her coffee. She glanced at her watch. "Susan, I really can't stay too long. There's no one at the station except Jack—"

"I'm sure he can handle the public for a few minutes." Susie looked at the letter again. "I have this feeling he can put up with just about anything for a few more weeks."

Carol picked nervously on an olive and stared straight at Susie. "I'm not sure I want to know why. Look, Susan, I just wanted to help you with your article. I'm kind of caught here. I do have a job, and I'm up for promotion, and Jack IS my boss—"

"Just give me a few more minutes. I know Carvall had an interest in the new ski area. He was involved in the Environmental Impact Statements—"

"I overheard your interview. Jack did approve of the sale. But I don't see how that would have any connection to his leaving, unless he, uh . . . unless—"

"Unless he had some financial incentive in seeing that those Impact Statements reflected the Sunburst position."

Bevins pushed her chair backwards. "Listen, I really do have to get back. Even if you're right about all this, Jack still initials my job ratings. Do a great story, I'll look for it in *Sierra.*"

"There's just one other question, then I'll let you go." Susie took Carol by the hand and pulled her back to the table. "When I interviewed Jack the other day, there was someone else in his office. They left a few minutes before me, through the back door. I think they drove off in a Dodge Dakota pickup, with a big dent on the driver's side. Do you have any idea who that was?"

"Sure. It was his girlfriend. Lizzie something—"

"What'd she look like?"

"Oh, a little smaller than you. Red hair, shoulder length. Kinda young, I bet she wasn't out of college. Jack's thirty-two."

"What kind of relationship was it?"

"What do you mean?"

"Were they serious? Did they live together? Did he have other girls?"

"I'm not sure—I haven't been here that long. The first few weeks she used to come by all the time, then I didn't see her for a while. I thought they'd broken up. Then she came back the day you were there and they started arguing. I haven't seen her since."

"Do you remember what they were fighting about?"

"I never heard much. I don't pry. Listen, I really do have to go."

"So do I." Susie signaled the waitress. After paying the check, she led Carol outside the swinging doors, into the bright sunlight. "Carol, thanks, you've been a big help." She scribbled her phone number onto the lunch receipt. "Here. If you find out anything else, give me a call. I'm with my husband; we'll be here through Sunday."

Carol folded the receipt and put it in her purse. "Staying for the big race?"

"Oh, I'll probably skip it and head for the back bowls. The slopes should be empty—it'll be a perfect time to ski."

"Makes sense to me." Carol started down the street. "Take care, Susan. Thanks for lunch."

"Bye-bye."

Carol Bevins started to walk away, then stopped dead in her tracks. 'Sue!'' She walked back toward Susie.

"What's the matter?"

"It's her." Carol pointed to a store across the way.

"Who?"

"Lizzie what's her face. Light brown sweater, red hair, walking by herself."

Susie stared straight ahead. The village was crowded; there were dozens of skiers wandering around in their parkas and stretch pants. She saw a red-haired girl approaching, about half a block down. The girl lingered in front of a ski store, looking at the fashions in the window. She walked slowly from store to store. She stopped in front of the fur shop and stayed there several seconds; Susie could sense that she was imagining herself in a luxurious stole. Finally, she left the window and walked toward the curb. She opened the driver's door of a new, powder-blue Ford wagon and started the motor.

"Looks like she's got new wheels," Susie said.

"Figures. Jack probably bought it for her. She must've got tired of the pickup."

"Come on, let's take a ride." Susie grabbed Carol by the arm and pulled her down the street.

"Hey! I gotta get back to work."

"Carvall can hold the fort—"

"He'll be furious—"

"Come ON!" Susie pushed Carol toward her rented Camry. "Hurry, before we lose sight of her."

Bevins got in the passenger side and Susie started the car.

Traffic was slow. Skiers crisscrossed the street, delivery trucks servicing the restaurants were clogging the intersections. They caught sight of the Taurus wagon just as it made a right turn.

"We're in luck," Susie said, "I thought I'd lost her." She crept up to the intersection and turned right. She saw the blue wagon up ahead. Keeping a few cars between them, she followed it for several blocks. When they got to the edge of the village, she saw it turn onto Antelope Avenue, a major thoroughfare, and speed off. Susie picked her way through traffic, ran a yellow light, and got onto Antelope. Again she thought she'd lost the Ford, but she caught sight of it about a hundred yards up the road, slowing down and heading west.

"What's out that way?" Susie asked. She tried to keep a few cars between her and the Taurus, but the traffic was thinning.

"Just a few small towns. Douglas. Sheep's Creek. Mostly ranchers, a few worn-out mines." Up ahead, the wagon signaled a turn. "Susan, where are we going? Why are we doing this?"

"It has to do with the death of that forest ranger a couple of months ago."

"You think she's a MURDERER?" Carol grabbed Susie by the arm. "Don't you think we should call the police?"

Susie shook Carol's arm away and followed the Ford as it turned off the highway, onto a country road. She stopped and looked in both directions; she saw the wagon heading north and followed it. She wondered for an instant if she was taking a foolish chance. She could always turn around and report what she'd learned to Murray; he couldn't expect her to carry this out any further. But her adrenaline was pumping, she didn't want to turn back. All she needed was Lizzie's destination—just an address, then she'd be finished. Glick could follow things up and that would be that. "I'm not quite sure the police can be told yet," she said. "There'a another person at risk here—a young girl is missing."

Carol turned to Susie with a look that registered somewhere between terror and disbelief.

"Don't worry. We'll just see where they're staying, then we'll go home." Susie kept her eyes on the road. About a half-mile ahead, she saw the Ford turn off onto a smaller road. She slowed down as she approached the junction, then followed the Ford's path for a few hundred yards. The road curved into the woods; it was difficult to see through the snow-covered firs. It forked into two smaller lanes. The Taurus was out of sight.

"Let's go back," Carol said. "Let's call the police."

"We'll give it one shot. Acey-deucy, right or left. If we've lost her, I'll turn around and go back." Susie looked again to both sides, then turned left. She drove the Camry slowly—it skidded through the snow. The road curved through the trees, it didn't seem to lead anywhere. Susie was about to turn around, but decided to give it a few more yards. She brought the Toyota around a ninety-degree bend. A large clump of snow dropped off a pine tree, onto her windshield. She stopped and turned on the wipers. When the snow had been cleared away, Susie and Carol found themselves staring through their windshield at a woman, standing in the middle of the road.

The woman had pulled an ice-blue parka over her sweater. Her car was parked off to the side. She was holding a twelve-gauge shotgun and pointing it directly at the windshield of the Toyota. "Get out and get your hands up," she shouted. "Or I'll blow you both straight to hell."

27

The Sunburst commercial district was several miles from the ski village, just a few minutes from the interstate. Murray cruised down Haley Avenue, past a hardware store and a supermarket. He was driving a '79 Pontiac Bonneville that he'd bought for five hundred dollars, another accessory to his bargain-basement life. The Bonneville's engine was knocking, the lifter valves were just about shot. A few drops of melted snow leaked through the window on the driver's side. This anonymity business was beginning to grate on him; he was glad he only had to keep it up for a few more days. He was hoping the car would last him through the weekend.

About a half-mile past the K Mart, Murray saw the big blue rotating sign for Collins Ford, flashing the time and temperature. It was twelve-thirty. He had wasted nearly an hour back at his apartment, searching through his belongings for a misplaced ID, a plastic Commerce Department badge that had wedged into a side pocket of his hanging suitcase. He hadn't needed it in years, but it was about to come in handy.

He parked his car about a block from the dealership and walked onto the lot. He casually inspected a new Probe, examining the sticker, looking through the windows at the interior until he caught a salesman's attention.

"Howdy!" said a middle-aged man, his pudge belly crammed into a pair of overly tight designer jeans and a fleece-lined parka. "How ya doin'? Can I sell you a Ford today?"

"No," Murray said honestly, "I'm afraid not."

The man let out a horselaugh and slapped Murray on the back. "Well then, maybe I can give one away!"

"For that I'd be willing to listen." Murray saw a new Taurus wagon a few yards down and wandered over to it.

"Friend, the deal I'm gonna give you, I might as well be givin' it away—"

"I'm touched," Murray said. "True charity is a such a rare virtue."

"Har, har." The salesman pounded Murray on the back again. "A comedian, I like that."

Murray took a closer look at the Taurus. It was exactly the model he'd seen a few hours ago, except this one was white. "Sell a lot of these?"

"Yes indeed, it's a very popular model. In fact, it's the only one left."

"Do you have one in powder blue?"

"I'm sorry sir, we don't have a powder blue one on the lot. We could order it, have it here in a week. In the meantime—"

"But you sell a lot of the powder blues?"

"Yes sir, we sell all we can get. What did you say your name was, friend?"

"Murray."

"Howdy, Murray, my name's Max." Max shook Murray's hand heartily. "We've had a factory backlog, Murray; it'll take us a few weeks to get your color in. In the meantime, why don't we take this honey for a test drive."

"Actually, Max, I've already driven the car—"

"Well that's great! Done all the research, I bet. Read the Consumer Reports. Hell, they done my whole job for me. Murray, let's not waste time—let's talk turkey!"

"Fine, Max, fine. Only I did have one question—"

"Fire away, Murray!"

"Well, I'm from Chicago, see. But I'm moving to Sunburst—"

"That's GREAT! You'll love it here—"

"And I was wondering, Max, with the insurance changes and everything, how long does it take to get license plates on a new car up here?"

The salesman gave Murray a puzzled look. "Oh, I don't know. Six weeks, maybe. Don't quote me on that. You get temporary registration, of course—"

Murray did some quick arithmetic in his head. The blue Taurus wagon already had plates; it would have been bought back in January, maybe December.

"Murray, you know what? I think we've got a medium-blue wagon right on the lot! You can't hardly tell the difference between that and the powder blue."

"I don't think so, Max."

"Just take a look—"

"Max," Murray said, draping a long arm around the salesman, "we need to talk."

"Sure, Murray! C'mon in my office. The medium blue's right in the showroom."

"Powder blue, Max. Not medium blue."

"Powder blue, absolutely."

Murray followed Max into his office, a tiny cubicle inside the main showroom.

"Now, Murray, let's talk dollars." Max grabbed some folders from the shelves behind his desk.

"Let's not." Murray opened his wallet and flashed Max the Commerce Department badge. It was old and frayed; he had borrowed it from a retiring federal agent six years ago when he was handling industrial espionage for a private firm back in Chicago, well before his Northbrook Court days. He presumed, correctly, that Max would not give it a close examination.

"Well, well." Max's face turned a deep red. He pulled the door closed. He showed Murray to a chair opposite a desk. "Have a seat, Murray. You know, despite this case of mistaken identity, I have this feeling we can still be friends."

"That would please me greatly, Max."

"You want some coffee? We got some fresh brewed."

"No, thank you. Now Max, listen carefully. We're doing some investigating on the selling practices of certain salesmen on certain models of cars during the past several months."

Max leaned forward in his chair. He fumbled for a cigarette.

"Certain models of cars, Max, that were difficult to obtain. That a customer might be willing to pay extra for. Like a new, powder-blue Taurus station wagon."

"Murray, you can be assured, I've done nothing, uh . . ." Max puffed on his cigarette. "Nothing irregular."

"I'm sure you haven't, Max. Now, just to be friendly, how about getting me the records of all the powder-blue Taurus wagons you've sold in the period between November 1 and January 30. And please, Max, be discreet."

"Right away, sir." Max trundled out the door, into the main

office. He came back five minutes later with a stack of computer-generated invoices. "Here we go, Murray. I want to emphasize, we do things strictly by regulations. I've been working here nine months; I have great admiration for Mr. Collins."

"Fine, Max. I'm sure you're doing an outstanding job." Murray thumbed through the invoices. The salesman had brought records for all the Taurus wagons, but Murray quickly found the color code and pulled out invoices for the powder blues. There were thirteen of them. Murray inspected each one until he found what he wanted. On January 28, Collins Ford had sold a powder-blue Ford Taurus station wagon to Jack Carvall.

"Anything I can help you with?" Max offered. "Code's a little tricky."

"No, thank you," Murray said, waving him off. He had a yearning for a cigar, but resisted the temptation. He didn't think it fit in with the image of a Commerce Department inspector. He read through Jack Carvall's invoice. Although Carvall had signed it, the car had not been sold to him personally. It had been sold to a business, "Sunburst Concessions," of which Carvall had identified himself as president. It was located on Lodestone Avenue, which was part of the ski village. Murray didn't know from the address number exactly where it was; he wasn't even aware of the street names. "Max," he said, handing over the invoice, "could you photocopy this for me?"

"Yes sir!" Max grabbed the invoice. "Sure you don't want some coffee?" Murray shook his head and Max hustled back outside, returning a few moments later with the copy. "Anything else I can do for you, friend?"

"That's it, Max."

"Nothing wrong, is there? I can get more information—"

"I don't believe it's anything serious, Max. Thanks for cooperating."

"Glad to help! Sure I can't interest you in that wagon? I bet you really did like it. Am I right?"

Murray got up to leave. "Sorry, Max, all part of the job. Good-bye, now—"

"How about the new T-bird? Take a test ride, Murray, you'll fall in love!"

"Max, if I test ride the T-bird, there's an excellent chance you'll never see it again."

"I'll take that chance! Hell, Murray, you're a civil servant—"

"So long, Max." Murray walked out of the dealership, casting a fleeting glance at a convertible Thunderbird in the showroom. He thought about his creaking Bonneville. He wondered how difficult it might have been to "test-drive" the T-bird for a few days. Max would probably be too scared to report it missing until after the weekend, by which time Murray would have returned it with a full tank of gas.

Safely down the street, Murray pulled a long cigar out of his pocket, clipped the end off, and lit it. He took a deep draw and let a smoke ring rise into the air. It was a good thing he was such an honest guy, he mused to himself. He got into his old beater, revved the engine, and plugged along toward his efficiency apartment. He guessed he would never get a medal. He'd never get a street named after him. But he knew that if guys like him ever let their standards fall, the world would be in one hell of a mess.

28

Andy Sussman stood by the kitchen counter in his condo, tapping his right index finger next to the telephone. It was three o'clock. He had not heard from Susie since before lunch. He had given her specific instructions to call after her meeting with Carol Bevins, but he hadn't heard a thing from her all day.

Outside, the late afternoon sun was beginning to edge behind Sunburst peak, a few snow flurries were starting to fall. Sussman was clearly worried, and aggravated as well. He had followed Murray's instructions earlier in the day and called Casey Wright. Casey, convinced that CBS had finally seen the wisdom in his idea for a guided tour, had led Andy and two cameramen on an interminable two-hour loop of the slopes, complete with a trip to the back bowls, which Sussman negotiated with extreme difficulty. His body, already bruised from Kevin Cumberland's insane ski tour the day before, now resembled a black-and-blue bas relief of the moon.

Sussman had returned from the tour to find no messages awaiting him, except for a note from his producer that interviews with the Swiss ski team would be lined up for tomorrow morning at ten. He had phoned Clem's Claim—he'd given them a description of Susie. They were relatively certain she'd been there, although it was the girl in the Smokey hat that the waitress remembered. According to her, the women had paid the tab and walked out, nothing unusual. He had called the ranger station and asked for Bevins. She wasn't there. She'd gone out for lunch and hadn't come back. Sussman had turned tense and jittery; he'd sat by his office phone for an hour, then returned to the condo to see if Susie had left a note.

She hadn't.

Andy had passed another hour viewing and re-viewing the mini-cam videotape that Jerry the cameraman had given him that morning. As expected, the tape was shaky. Visibility had been low to begin with; it was snowing and getting dark when they'd crossed paths with the two skiers. The VCR at his condo didn't allow him to blow up frames, although he did freeze the tape at a few spots and crawl in front of his TV screen, trying to identify Susie's assailants. He was more successful figuring out who they weren't than who they were. Both of them wore ski masks. The taller man didn't have the muscular torso of Casey Wright, or the hefty girth of J. B. Cranston. The smaller one didn't resemble anyone he knew, although he was beginning to think that it was a girl; he recalled the red hair, longish for a boy, that he'd seen before she pulled the ski mask on. He tried to make out her figure underneath the parka.

He thought about the two women connected with the case. He doubted whether Sara could have been involved; Susie surely would have recognized her, after skiing with her all afternoon. He had pulled Murray's manuscript from the bottom of his suitcase and read over his description of Beth. The light brown hair didn't match, although that could easily be disguised. Sussman began to consider the possibility that both of the skiers were hired killers.

He pondered his next move. He was reluctant to call the police. Part of him was fearful of what he might find out: a car crash, an avalanche. Another part of him just didn't want to involve Sergeant Gustafson, whom he still suspected might somehow be involved.

And then there was Murray. Sussman wanted to believe that his friend was on top of everything, serving as his wife's Unseen Protector, as promised. Perhaps they were together right now, uncovering some vital information—snarling at each other, no doubt, yet safe and sound and ready to wrap up the case.

But what if they weren't? Murray certainly hadn't given any indication of seeing Susie when he'd called that morning. How would he even know she'd made the appointment with Carol Bevins? Andy stared at the phone, waiting for it to ring, hoping that when it did he would hear his wife or, failing that, his buddy.

It didn't ring.

It was time to do something. How could he get in touch with Glick? By this time, Murray must have made himself known to someone. Sussman called his production headquarters; there were no messages. On a hunch, he picked up the phone and tapped out the Cranstons' number. Betty answered it. Before Sussman could get a word in edgewise she'd told him how wonderful it was to hear from him again and invited them back for dinner and asked if he'd heard from his mysterious friend Murray. Andy told her he wasn't sure about dinner, he'd have to ask Susie, but as it happened he did have some news about his pal. "There was a message from him when I got in today," Andy explained, "but I haven't been able to track him down, and as it turns out, I've had an emergency come up—"

"Is everything all right, Andy? Is there anything we can do—"

"I think I can manage. But I would like to get a hold of Murray, so if you or J.B. happen to see him, could you please have him call me at my condo?" He gave her the number. "As soon as you see him."

"Well of course, I'll do it right away. Say, does this have anything to do with Sam?"

"Sam?"

"Sam Kaplan. The father of the little girl Murray was looking for. He flew into town last night, steaming mad. He was ready to go after Casey Wright with a hatchet, but I guess he never found him."

"Is that right?" Andy suddenly realized why he had spent two perfectly awful hours with Casey. "Where's Sam now?"

"Gosh, I don't know. He went over to J.B.'s office after he missed Casey. I think J.B.'s trying to calm him down a little."

Sussman paused briefly, wondering if he should call J.B. at work. He thought better of it. He speculated as to when exactly Sam Kaplan had gotten into town. Perhaps he'd arrived earlier than Betty thought—in time to squeeze in some late afternoon skiing. He thanked Betty for the information. He promised to have Susie call her about dinner as soon as she got in, then said goodbye.

Andy had another thought. He dialed the ski school and asked for Sara Felder. According to the office, she was out on a group lesson. She'd be back at four. He left a message: "If you see

MG, call immediately. Susie S.'' He left their number. The secretary said she'd leave it in Sara's message box.

Sussman walked over to the refrigerator and found himself a beer. He twisted the top off with his palm. He took a swig, he paced back and forth in the kitchen. He walked over to the phone, but he didn't know who or where to call. He thought again about the police, but he wasn't ready for them just yet.

Andy took his hand off the telephone. He figured he'd better leave the line open. He walked over to the couch and let himself sink into the center seat. He sipped on his beer. He sat back and waited.

Murray Glick walked along the streets of Sunburst Village, peering into the windows of the restaurants, ski shops, and boutiques. He was late. The damn Bonneville had choked and sputtered all the way back from the car dealership, finally chugging to a halt a block from his apartment. He had managed to push it over to a curb and left it there, then taken a bus into the village.

Strolling casually, Murray took careful note of the street signs. Sunburst Way. Snowflake Lane. He found Lodestone Avenue; it ran straight into the gondola station. Finding street numbers presented more of a problem. The merchants didn't seem to believe in addresses; putting numbers above the doorways was evidently too pedestrian for such a chichi resort. The one shop that did have an address was Dr. Feingold, the cosmetic surgeon; it was 534 Lodestone. Sunburst Concessions, according to the Ford invoice, was 562 Lodestone. Murray looked up and down the street. There was no Sunburst Concessions in either direction; he'd assumed all along that it was a corporate name. He walked up the street and found himself staring into the window of the Village Deli.

The place was nearly empty; it was late afternoon, the demand for sandwiches had dropped. A few people stood by the counter, ordering hot chocolate or coffee or a bottle of New York Seltzer. Murray walked over to the counter and tried to sneak a look at the cash register, thinking there might be a business name and address printed somewhere.

"Can I help you?" said a husky young kid from behind the counter. He had sun-bleached hair and a bronze complexion. He looked around eighteen, which meant that he must be about twenty-one. Murray hadn't seen him before. Most of the sandwich slingers were girls, although Glick supposed that it was not a bad idea to have a few guys working at night.

"I hope so. I'm applying for a job at Sunburst Concessions. Ordering and purchasing. My aunt knows Mr. Carvall, I'm supposed to look him up."

"Who?"

"Jack Carvall. He's the owner."

"I don't know any Carvall," the kid said, wiping some crumbs off the counter. "Mr. Grabow's the manager; he's probably the guy you want to talk to, but he's gone for the day. Can you come back tomorrow morning at eight?"

"Sure," Murray said. "Grabow, huh? This IS Sunburst Concessions?"

"That's what it says on my paycheck. Must be some kind of official name. As far as we're concerned it's just the deli."

"Right," said Murray. "Thanks a bunch, pal." Bingo, he thought, as he walked out of the shop. Jack Carvall had a business going on the side. Not exactly a threat to Baron Hilton, but Murray had a suspicion that Sunburst Concessions had had some rather large cash influxes lately. He jogged down the street and around the corner, past Clem's Claim. It was crowded with tourists and après-skiers. He stopped; he saw a familiar face. It was Sara, hoisting a glass with a bunch of skiers. Murray guessed it was her lesson group for the week, they had probably come straight off the slopes. He figured that Sara got treated to a lot of post-lesson drinks over the course of a season. He couldn't blame her. Or her clients.

Murray thought about joining her. He owed her some sort of an explanation for his disappearance; he wanted to see her before he left. He wouldn't even have to identify himself. He could write a note, drop it by her table. Dinner for two tonight at Lorenzo's, for old time's sake. He was sure she'd make it.

But something held him back. He was nearing the end of this caper—it was no time to get soft. He'd put up with fleabag apartments, crumbling Pontiacs, raggedy clothes in the attempt to maintain his cover. And now, finally, he had the missing piece of the puzzle. There was no sense taking a risk.

Murray took a last, longing look at Sara, then headed back down the hill. He didn't look back.

29

Susie Sussman sat on the floor of a drafty den, shivering slightly, watching a rerun of "Laverne and Shirley" on a snowy color television. She didn't know exactly where she was, only that it was within a mile or so of where she and Carol Bevins had been apprehended. The house was old and run down. The floors were creaky, the walls looked like they could use a fresh coat of paint. She was sitting on a frayed, rumpled beanbag, a few feet in front of a wobbly coffee table. Carol was next to her, leaning on a sofa cushion. Both of them had their hands tied behind their backs and their legs bound at the ankles.

"Beth's going to the store," announced a young woman, poking her head inside the door to the kitchen. "What do you want for dinner?"

"Lobster Newburg would be nice. Maybe some rice pilaf. Croissants, half a cantaloupe, and some orange sherbet. And some white wine. Maybe a Riesling."

"I don't think Swanson's makes all that, but I can ask."

"Please do," said Susie.

"I'll have the turkey Tetrazzini," said Carol Bevins, who seemed more familiar with Swanson's specialties.

"That we can manage." The girl smiled. She was slim, with light blond hair that was turning brown at the roots. She looked all of about twenty years old. She went by the name of Leah, but Susie Sussman had recognized her immediately from the pictures in her mother's house. "Would you like the turkey, too, Miss Ettenger?"

"Surprise me." Susie leaned back on her beanbag. "How

about putting some news on, Leah? I actually saw this show when it was an original.''

The girl shrugged. She changed the channel to the local news, then walked back into the kitchen. Susie could hear her talking with Beth, relaying the dinner orders.

Susie squirmed on her beanbag, trying to find a comfortable position. The ropes were beginning to dig into her wrists. She wondered if she should let Dani Kaplan know that she knew her real identity. Susie certainly wasn't going to blurt it out while Beth was around, but perhaps when she was gone there would be a diplomatic way to broach the subject.

Carol Bevins, meanwhile, was as grim as could be; her dinner request was about the only sentence she had spoken since her abduction. ''Well, I'm sunk,'' she muttered, as she heard the front door slam and Beth drive off.

''Carol, you're going to be fine.''

''Sure. If that crazed bimbo doesn't shoot us, she'll get Jack to give me a reprimand. I'll probably get drummed right out of the Forest Service or sent to some miserable outpost in the Okefenokee.''

''Carol,'' Susie said softly, ''Jack Carvall is a criminal. He may have killed a man. He's going to be caught, and you're going to be fine.''

''Who's going to catch him? *Sierra* magazine?''

Susie took a deep breath and glanced back toward the kitchen. Dani Kaplan was standing by the refrigerator, sipping a soft drink, looking at them through a crack in the door. ''Carol, has Beth always had red hair like that?''

''You mean Lizzie?'' There was a trace of sarcasm. ''As far as I know.''

''How far is that?''

''Just the month I've been working here.''

Susie adjusted her back to the beanbag. She tried to recall Murray's description of the girl who had worked at the deli. Short brown hair, very protective of Dani. Suspicious of Dani's father. This had to be the same person. How she had become connected to Jack Carvall, Susie had no idea. But she wished Murray had gotten the description right—if she'd been able to equate Beth with Lizzie a few hours earlier, she might have saved herself an ambush. ''Oh, Leah,'' Susie shouted toward the kitchen.

Dani poked her head through the doorway. "What? You want a Coke or something?"

"How about if you come in and talk with us for a few minutes. Watch the news. It's better than sitting there, staring at the fridge."

Dani didn't seem too excited about the prospect, but she sloped out of the kitchen and sat down on the floor, a good five feet from Susie and Carol. On the television, the weatherman was predicting another foot of snow before the World Cup race on Sunday.

"Leah," said Susie, "do we look like dangerous people to you?"

Dani sipped on her soda and stared through the television.

"For goodness sakes, Leah—Carol's a forest ranger."

"I used to know someone over at the Forest Service," Dani said coolly, sneaking a glance at Bevins. "I don't remember seeing you there."

"I've only been there a month," Carol said. "Look, I wasn't going to a costume party."

"She came in to replace another ranger," said Susie. "A man named Rick Allanson. He died in an avalanche. Did you know him?"

"I might have." Dani turned quickly away, her face reddening.

"His death was a terrible accident. At least that's what we were told."

"I'm sure whoever told you that knew what they were talking about," Dani whispered.

"Brian Ellsworth told us. He was a very close friend of Rick's. Did you know Brian, too?"

Dani shook her head. "I think maybe I heard his name."

Susie pushed herself off the beanbag and edged toward the girl. "You know, Leah, when something bad happens to someone we care about, it's natural that we might want to crawl into a hole and hide for a while. It's hard to face those kind of things."

Dani continued gazing at the television. The sportscaster was on, talking about the snow conditions for Sunday's race. A tape was shown of several of the skiers arriving at Sunburst in a limousine. Susie noticed a CBS camera in the background. "I'm not hiding from anything. I like it out here just fine. Sunburst's way too glitzy for me."

"Leah, I think it's natural that there might be some feeling of blame. I can understand that you might want to hurt whoever was responsible for what happened."

"I don't know what you're talking about." A tear started to stream down Dani's face. "Why would I want to hurt anyone?"

"I don't know. But I can't help but notice that Carol and I are tied up by our arms and legs, after being hauled away at gunpoint. Some people might consider that bordering on hurtful."

Dani stared at Susie and Carol, but she didn't make any move toward unloosening their ropes. "Beth said you followed her back from town. She said you were dangerous."

"You seem to put an awful lot of trust in Beth."

"Beth's my friend. Sometimes I think she's my only friend."

"I'd think a bright, pretty girl like you would have plenty of friends." Susie saw another tear welling from Dani's eyes. For a moment, she felt like a counselor at summer camp again. She wanted to put her arm around Dani and take her for a walk through the woods, explaining that her problems weren't nearly as traumatic as they seemed. Of course, the problems at camp had been a lot easier. Boyfriends. Parents that didn't understand. Sneaking a cigarette, or maybe even a joint. "Leah," Susie asked, "how did you and Beth get to be such good friends?"

Dani turned around and faced the television.

"Was she a friend of Rick's, too?"

"She hardly knew Rick."

"That's a little surprising, for someone that spent so much time at the ranger station. I'd have thought they would have known each other quite well."

"What are you talking about? Beth and I worked at the deli." Dani got up and headed for the kitchen. "What would she know about the Forest Service? Look, I don't know who you are, but you'd better get your story straight."

"It's becoming straighter all the time." Susie raised her voice as Dani disappeared behind the door. "And I do know who YOU are . . . Dani."

No one said a word. Dani turned slowly back to the doorway, her fists clenched. "I should have figured that out by now," she said, almost to herself. "Beth was right about you."

"Beth's going to get you in deep trouble—"

"She saved my life!"

"She's using you."

"You're a liar—" Dani slammed the door closed.

"Dani," Susie shouted, "you'd better think hard about what you're doing. Kidnapping is a serious offense."

"So is murder!"

"You bet it is!"

Outside, a car pulled into the gravel driveway. Susie heard the car door open, then slam shut. Beth hadn't been gone long; there must have been a convenience store nearby. "Dani, we're here to help you," Susie shouted, but she got no response. She heard Dani walk toward the front door. "You're going to have to believe us—"

The front door creaked open. Susie heard muffled voices from the foyer. She wondered if she had told Dani too much. She wondered if she had gotten through to her at all. She heard the two voices move toward the kitchen. There was some rustling around as the oven was opened and some glasses were taken from the cupboard. The telephone rang.

"Hello?" The voice was Beth's. For perhaps two minutes she didn't say a word. When she did, she spoke in a muffled tone; Susie couldn't pick up anything intelligible. Finally, after another extended silence, Beth slammed a drawer closed. She said loudly and with great irritation, "You DON'T need to. Just stay away!" She slammed the phone down.

"Who was that?" Dani asked.

"Never mind," Beth snapped.

Susie perked her ears, trying to catch more of the conversation, but all she could hear was the clatter of dishes and the banging of cupboard doors. She wondered who had been on the phone. She guessed it was Jack Carvall; she expected to be seeing him soon. She wondered if anyone else would be paying them a visit.

Susie shifted her hands behind her back, trying to loosen the ropes. They were still uncomfortably tight, she could feel the abrasions on her wrists. She adjusted her back against the bean-bag. She glanced at Carol Bevins, who had closed her eyes and was either asleep or too depressed to talk. She watched the news show credits rolling across the television screen. She leaned back and waited for her TV dinner.

30

Murray Glick sat at the rickety kitchen table in his efficiency apartment, penciling notes onto the back of a Burger King napkin. He had circled three sets of initials, signifying Jack Carvall, Beth, and Casey Wright. A series of arrows connected the circles; most prominently, a double-sided arrow connected Carvall and Beth. Murray shook his head; he never would have guessed it. Carvall must be pushing thirty-five, the girl was barely out of college. Not that he hadn't been attracted to her himself; he might have made a serious move, had he not fallen so hard for Sara. But that was excusable, he was just a red-blooded American male on a road assignment, subject to all the attendant spiritual temptations. Carvall, by contrast, had romanced an impressionable young girl into a blind loyalty that included kidnapping and murder.

Or had he? Perhaps it was Beth who saw a handsome, well-educated Forest Service administrator and decided that he could be a man of unlimited potential—if, like Lady Macbeth, she could convince him to seize the moment. A bribe here, a murder there. It was an intriguing concept—an inspiration, thought Murray, to get back to his manuscript, which he was convinced was of higher literary merit than Susie Sussman gave it credit for and would be a great addition to his detective enterprises. He could envision a cross-country book tour: appearances on all the talk shows, signings at the big chain bookstores, drawings for free Caribbean cruises.

One the other hand, Murray mused, as he stared at his doodlings, the intrigue might all be in his imagination. Perhaps neither Beth nor Carvall had been cajoled into this. Perhaps they were simply two people made for each other.

There were still others to consider, of course, most prominently Casey Wright. Murray had meant to call Andy for a report on their ski tour—not so much because he expected any new information, but to apologize for ruining his friend's morning and to check on Susie's progress. Murray still suspected Casey had a hand in this—if he ever managed to trace a cash-flow trail, he expected to find Wright at one end. But he might not find Dani Kaplan, and that was what he was being paid to do.

Murray figured that the path to Dani began at the door of Jack Carvall. He'd called the Forest Service earlier; Carvall was in, but busy with a line of visitors. He guessed that it was Beth who had driven the Taurus that morning; she'd probably switched from the Dakota after the foiled attempt on Susie's life. In all probability, she'd returned by now to wherever she was hiding Dani.

Murray didn't think that merely following Carvall would lead him to Beth. He doubted that they were living together, or had been since Dani Kaplan had disappeared. He wondered if Dani even knew Carvall—perhaps she'd heard his name while working at the deli, but he guessed she knew nothing of their relationship. He assumed that contact between the two of them had been carefully regulated, and would be until they finished whatever business remained. He needed to flush them out. He had a feeling that the man most likely to help him do it was residing at a luxurious condo at the end of a cud-de-sac outside Sunburst Village.

The Kaplans' unit was several miles away, but Murray didn't bother trying to get the Bonneville started. He figured that the best he could do was have it declared a National Monument— maybe he could get some kind of a tax break. Besides, he'd decided it was time to get his image back on the uptick. He'd shaved his beard and put on a clean pair of jeans. He gave his leather boots a quick shine. He splashed on some aftershave, grabbed his ski parka, and headed for the bus stop.

Murray had a scheme which he intended to set in motion the next morning. Jogging the half-mile from the village to the condo, he considered the best way to elicit Sam Kaplan's cooperation. He stopped a few yards in front of the unit to catch his breath, then walked to the front door and knocked hard. There was no response. He heard voices inside. He knocked harder, but still no one answered. Reluctantly, Murray pulled the key out of his pocket, unlocked the door, and slipped into the hallway.

"I don't WANT to call the police," Kaplan was saying to J. B. Cranston. "What are the police gonna do?"

"They'll find her, and they'll do it without getting you arrested for murder."

"I'm not going to KILL him, for Chrissakes. Besides, I don't need all that publicity."

"What publicity? It's a small town, it wouldn't even make the Denver papers—"

"There's a goddamn ski race on national television this weekend! There's reporters all over the place. You get the cops hauling in one of their officials, next thing it's bouncing off the satellite, my daughter's gonna be dragged in front of the whole country—"

"My, my," said Murray Glick as he walked into the living room, "it's nice to know that Dani's interests are finally being considered." He stopped and stood in front of the couch, a few feet from J. B. Cranston and Sam Kaplan.

"Well, hell's bells!" J.B. said, looking startled for only a moment. "Look who blew into town! Damn, Murray, I figured you'd be back for the big race. Grab yerself a tall cold one, I bet you and Sam have a lot to talk about."

"Who the hell is HE?" gruffed Kaplan.

"He's your cousin, ain't he? Or aren't you talking to that part of the family, either?"

"Cousin my ass—"

"Mr. Kaplan," Murray said, keeping his distance, "my name is Murray Glick. I'm a private investigator. I was hired by your wife to find Dani."

J.B.'s smile dropped about a foot and a half. Sam stood rigid, his hands on his belt, shaking his head in disgust. "Will you look at that?" he said. "Barbie really splurged this time, didn't she? A real live shamus."

"I think you'll find that your wife gets a satisfactory return on her investments."

"Yeah, I'll bet." Kaplan walked over to Murray, eyeing him like a racehorse at auction. Glick's face was sweaty, his ski sweater wet from the jog over. Kaplan brushed a few loose pine needles from his back. "This must be a real treat for you—a few weeks at a place like this. Next week it'll be back to warehouse thieves and barroom floozies."

"I'm terribly homesick, Sam. I'm dying to get back to my gutter in Chicago. That's why we're going to solve this thing in the next twenty-four hours."

"We?" Kaplan flashed J.B. a look of total cynicism, but Cranston only stood there, still as a stone. "Sure," Sam said, "I'll play along. Where's my daughter, shamus?"

"She's with a friend. At least she thinks she is. Sam, does Barbara know you're out here?"

"That's none of your business."

"My business is exactly what it is."

"Listen, I'm Dani's father—"

"Something you've only recently discovered, from what I understand—"

Sam Kaplan took a step toward Murray, his right hand balled into a fist, but before he could aim it anywhere J.B. leaped in front of him and shoved him onto the couch. "Relax, will ya, Sam! You're gonna give yourself a heart attack—"

"I'm fit as a marine!"

"And dumb as a donkey."

"Don't waste yourself on a lowly shamus," Murray said, dusting off his collar. "You're up against murderers and kidnappers."

"Murderers? She ran off with a damn ski instructor—"

"Listen up," Murray said matter-of-factly. "I know who Dani's with. I think I know how to find her. But I'll need your help."

"Just point me at the sonuvabitch."

"Not now," Murray said. "Not yet—"

"When?"

"Tomorrow morning. We'll have Casey distracted with the practice runs; we can take care of the guy we really want, one-on-one."

"And just who is that?"

The front door swung open and Betty Cranston hurried in, dressed in jeans and a sweatshirt. An apron clung loosely to her belt—she hadn't bothered to put on a jacket for the dash downstairs. "Murray, my goodness, I thought that was you!"

"Hi there, Betty," Murray said sheepishly, as Betty gave him a hug and kissed him on the cheek.

"Hold on, honey," J.B. said, pulling his wife away. "Seems our friend Murray ain't no cousin of Sam and Barb's after all. He's a private detective; Barbie hired him to look for Dani."

Betty backed away slightly; she didn't seem as shocked as J.B. had been, but she looked at Murray disapprovingly, like a teacher whose star pupil had been caught copying his essay from *Reader's Digest*.

"Folks, I am sorry," Murray said. "I was on assignment. There's some dangerous people involved here, I'm sure you'll understand once we get to the bottom of this." He looked at J.B., waiting for some acknowledgment, but Cranston didn't appear to be in an understanding mood. "I do appreciate the help you've given me. Not to mention the fried chicken."

"You could've up and told us the truth," J.B. said, still holding Betty's hand. "We loved the little girl; we would have helped you anyway."

"I was hired to do a job. I had to take precautions. I'd only known you a few days."

"You think WE were involved?" Betty said, blushing.

"Personally, no. But I'm a professional. There's a life at stake."

"Than why the hell are we standing here?" growled Sam. "Let's move it—"

"Just give me a chance—"

"I've got a roast in the oven," Betty said, tugging on her apron. "I only came down to tell Murray that his friend Andy called. He says it's an emergency and you'd better call him right away—"

"When was that?"

"Oh, it was this afternoon, about three-thirty."

"Excuse me, folks." Murray headed for the main bedroom.

"Hey!" shouted Sam. "That's my—"

"I need a little privacy. J.B., make sure he doesn't run off." Murray slammed the bedroom door shut behind him. He grabbed the phone from the night table and dialed Andy's condo. The phone barely rang once.

"Hello?"

"It's Murray. Speak."

"It's about time. Where the hell are you?"

"The Kaplans' condo. What's going on?"

"They've got Susie."

"Who?"

"How should I know? She went out for lunch with Carol Bevins and neither of them came back."

"She didn't call?"

"Nope. I checked the restaurant. They saw the two of them walk out—that's the last I heard. Murray, what the hell's going on? I thought you were supposed to be looking after her."

"Not to worry, Hoops—"

"Do you know where she is?"

"I'll find her."

"You lost her."

"Andy, gimme a few minutes, I'll call you right back."

"Murray—"

"Back in five, Hoops." Murray hung up the phone. He cursed himself for losing track of Susie—not that it was entirely his fault. He'd been on the move all day. She'd just walked a few blocks for lunch; how could she have been abducted in broad daylight? He looked in his wallet for a phone number. After all the weeks on this case, all the careful planning, had he finally slipped up professionally? Or had he just run out of luck? He checked his watch; it was a few minutes before six. He hadn't intended to act tonight. Now he would have to force the issue. He dialed the ranger station, hoping the absence of Carol Bevins had kept her boss at the office later than usual.

"Carvall speaking," answered a voice on the seventh ring.

"Harvey Weinberg, here, Chicago *Tribune*. We're doing a sidebar article for the main race coverage—"

"Listen, pal, we're closed. I'm leaving in a few minutes—"

"Don't hang up! See, Mr. Carvall, we're taking a cross-country tour down the west ridge tomorrow—kind of a last trek before it gets bulldozed for that new ski area. I'm sorry, it was kind of a last minute assignment, but we wanted to get a few maps and things and maybe a short interview—"

Murray heard a long sigh from Carvall's end of the line.

"I promise we won't take much of your time."

"Can you make it here in half an hour?"

"I think so. Where exactly are you?" Murray listened patiently to directions he didn't need, then promised he'd be there within thirty minutes. He thanked Carvall profusely, then hung up and called Sussman again. "Andy, can you get over here in five minutes?"

"No. Susie had the car."

"I'll pick you up, then. Gimme directions."

Sussman gave them. "Murray, where're we going?"

"Beats me. Ranger station first."

"Do you know where Susie is?"

"Five minutes, Hoops. Be ready."

"Murray, I'm worried as hell—"

"Piece of cake, pal." Murray hung up the phone and walked back into the living room. He found Sam and J.B. pacing by the kitchen. Kaplan was holding a highball glass; there was an open bottle of Jim Beam on the counter.

"Are you gonna get your butt in gear or what?" Sam said. The drink didn't seem to have mellowed him out much.

"As it happens, yes. Get your coat—we're going for a ride."

Kaplan grabbed his overcoat, a heavy, black, fur-lined job, made for Chicago winters. A scarf and a pair of gloves bulged from the pockets.

"Where to?" asked Cranston.

"You're off to dinner with Betty."

"Hell no, Murray! We got kidnappers, here—"

"You'd just be in the way. Stay by the phone. If we're in trouble, I'll try and call. I won't say anything. I'll ring once and hang up, then ring again and leave the line open. That way you can trace us if there's any problems. Understand?"

J.B. nodded, but he looked unconvinced.

"Got your keys, Sam?"

"You mean my wife didn't rent you a brand new Caddy—"

Murray saw a set of car keys lying on a small table near the door and scooped them up.

"Hey! Gimme those, I'll drive—"

"Shut up and follow instructions." Murray walked over to Kaplan. He faced him chest-to-chest. He stared him down with a violence that left no doubt as to who was in charge. "Sam, I will drive. Now move it."

Sam pulled his gloves on and walked to the door.

"So long," Murray said to J.B. "And thanks, pal."

"Happy hunting," muttered J. B. Cranston. He patted Kaplan on the back. "Do what you're told, Sam." He walked outside and up the stairs to his own unit. "Good luck!"

"We'll take it," Murray said. He flipped the keys in the air and caught them in his left hand. He grabbed Kaplan's coat sleeve and led him to the garage. "C'mon, Sam. Let's go get your daughter."

31

Andy Sussman and Murray Glick sat in the front seat of Sam Kaplan's Buick Regal, waiting in the nearly empty parking lot outside the ranger station. It was seven o'clock. The sky was clear; for the first time since he had been at Sunburst, Andy could see stars from one mountain peak to the other. But the wonders of a crisp alpine night held little attraction for him; the heavens seemed cold and empty without Susie by his side. "What's keeping him in there?" he said, tugging at Murray's elbow.

Murray took a long drag from his cigar; a puff of smoke floated out the open sun roof. He aimed his binoculars toward the office window; it was partially blocked by a curtain, he could barely make out the silhouettes of two people in the room. "Unfortunately, we're forced to rely on the extemporaneous acting ability of Sam Kaplan. Not the way I'd have written the script, but we'll make do."

Andy nodded and slumped against the door. Kaplan's job had been simple enough. He was supposed to stomp into Carvall's office in a rage, tell him that he knew Dani had been kidnapped, and that Carvall and his girlfriend had her. He'd say nothing about the murder of Rick Allanson—that would be for Carvall to admit at the proper time. Sam would threaten to call in the state police if he didn't take him to his daughter immediately. "What if Carvall puts up a fight?" Sussman asked. "Maybe he's got a gun in there. He's already killed a guy, if you've got it figured right."

"Relax, Andrew." Murray peered through his binoculars again. "They're both still upright. Even if Carvall has a gun, he won't plug him right in his office. He's gotta come out. There's only two doors and they both open into the parking lot.''

"How can I relax—"

"Susie's fine, take my word for it. Carvall's the trigger man, not Beth.''

"I already took your word that you'd look after her—"

"Andy, all I asked her to do was talk to the ranger girl. I don't know what she did or where she went. She should have come straight home.''

"Dammit, Murray, this isn't HER fault.'' Sussman turned away from Glick. Outside, he could see the ski slopes in the distance. The glimmer of lights from the cars and stores and condos lit up the background. He reached back for the binoculars and stared at the office window.

"Andy, listen to me.'' Murray cuffed his friend gently on the shoulder. "We'll find her. Two hours, you and Susie'll be back in the condo drinking hot toddies. Tomorrow morning you'll be out on the slopes, skiing the back bowls. Maybe we'll take a group lesson with Sara.''

"Forget it. I'm burning my skis.''

"Nah, Hoops, the fresh air does you good. That bronze mug'll look terrific on television. Wait'll the race Sunday—the broadcast'll be a smash, you'll be expanding your audience. You could get an Olympic spot in '92—"

"I don't know how to thank you, Murray.''

"Hey, it's nothing. Wait'll the book comes out, you'll both be heroes.''

"The book?'' Andy put the binoculars down and stared at Glick in utter incredulity. "The BOOK?''

"I'm calling it 'The Big Freeze.' I'll finish up the last hundred pages when I get home. I've been taking notes—I just have to figure out the ending.''

"Murray, you cannot be serious.''

"Of course I'm serious. It'll go great with the cruises and the retail business. Maybe even get optioned for a movie. It's got everything—murder, beautiful girls, a glitzy ski resort. I've already contacted several publishers.''

"Murray! I don't suppose you've given the slightest bit of thought to the rest of us—"

"Of course I have. I've always got your best interests at heart, Andy—you know that.''

Sussman looked back at the ranger station, but nothing was stirring. "Murray, I do NOT want any of this going public. In the first place, it's an invasion of privacy. In the second place, I'll get skewered by CBS for getting myself assigned out here, as if I don't regret it enough already. They'll probably stick me back on Celebrity Network Superteams—I'll never see the inside of a sports arena again."

Murray took a deep draw from his cigar and let go several staccato bursts. "Andrew, don't worry so much about your image. Have some faith in the redeeming power of literature."

"That's how I ended up in this mess."

"Now, now—" Murray lurched forward and took the binoculars back. "Hang on, they're coming out."

The front door to the ranger station opened and Jack Carvall stepped outside. He was not wearing a parka, just a maroon turtleneck sweater and bluejeans. Behind him came Sam Kaplan, his bulky overcoat open to the waist. Carvall had his hands in the air.

"What the hell?" muttered Sussman. He watched as Carvall edged gingerly across the parking lot. When they got within fifty feet, he saw the gun in Kaplan's hands.

"Damn amateurs," growled Murray, slamming the binoculars onto the car seat. "Can't follow the simplest instructions. Come on." He got out of the car and walked toward Carvall and Kaplan, with Sussman following a few feet behind. The four of them met about twenty feet from the Buick. "Well, hello Jack," said Murray, waving at Carvall. "I don't think we've ever been formally introduced. The name's Murray Glick."

"Yeah, yeah," muttered Carvall. "I was afraid you'd turn up again. Would you please tell this crazy sonuvabitch to put his damn gun away?"

"Sam, you crazy sonuvabitch, put your damn gun away."

"Shove it up your ass," said Kaplan.

Murray shrugged. "What can I say? He doesn't listen."

"Kaplan," Carvall said, craning his neck around as Sam shoved the pistol deeper into his back, "your daughter's fine, believe me. You want to keep her that way, you do what I tell you—"

"Shut up and get in the car."

Carvall glanced at Murray.

"I'd listen to the man, Jack."

Carvall scowled; he walked slowly toward the Buick. Glick and Sussman followed a few steps behind.

"Not you guys," said Kaplan. "This is just between us."

"The hell it is," said Andy. "They've got my wife—"

"I'll make sure she gets a cab back." Kaplan shoved Carvall into the driver's seat.

"Goddammit, Kaplan, that's enough!" Sussman made a move toward Sam, but Murray grabbed him and pushed him backwards several feet while Kaplan got into the Buick's passenger seat. "Murray, what're you doing?"

"The man's got a firearm, Andrew, in case you didn't notice."

"He can't shoot all of us—"

"He can shoot one of us, and I'd prefer it not be you or me." The engine started in the Buick. "Don't move, Andy." Murray jogged over to Kaplan's side of the car, just as it was about to drive off.

"Outta the way!" Kaplan shouted through the open window.

"Just wanted to wish you fellas a nice ride." Murray walked over to the rear bumper of the car and gave it a friendly tap. "Give us a call when you get there, Sam. Just to let us know you made it safely."

"Beat it. And send Barbara a refund."

"I don't think she'll ask for one," Murray said with a smirk.

"Fuck off." Sam Kaplan kept his gun trained on Carvall. "Let's go, Smokey."

Carvall backed the car up. He eased it past Murray, then put it in forward and roared away as Glick stood waving goodbye.

"For God's sake," Sussman said, catching up to Glick as he wandered off to the other end of the parking lot. "Are you just gonna let 'em drive off?"

Murray puffed on his cigar.

"The guy tried to KILL you, Murray."

"Andrew, one thing I've learned after six years in this business is that my adversaries tend to want to dispose of me one way or another. I try not to take it personally." Murray took a last look as the Buick disappeared down the street. "C'mon, we got work to do."

"Where?"

"Here." Glick led Andy to the only other vehicle in the lot, a black Dodge pickup truck. "Looks like a Dakota to me." Murray examined the driver's side. He ran his finger along the door. "Some recent body work, yes? A new coat of paint?" He grabbed the door handle. It was unlocked. He reached inside and pushed the hood release.

"Great, Mur. By the time you get it hot wired they'll be five miles away."

"Within range. Get in the driver's seat. When I tell you, pump the accelerator."

Andy Sussman did as he was told. He looked through the windshield as Murray worked feverishly with the distributor cap, shuffling the wires like a blackjack dealer. Less than thirty seconds went by before Murray yelled, "Hit it!" Sussman tapped the gas pedal and the Dakota roared. Murray slammed the hood down and jumped into the passenger seat. "Ándale, muchacho!"

"Where to?"

"Take the main road out to 13; it's the only route heading out of town."

"Then what?"

Murray reached into the inside pocket of his parka. He pulled out a small radio receiver, about the size of a walkie-talkie; a pair of earphones were attached. "Pick up a little speed, we should catch up. This baby's good within a ten-mile range."

"What is it?"

"A signal receiver. Same device I used with Ellsworth. I slapped the bug under Sam's back fender—we can trace 'em if you just gain a little over the next few miles."

Sussman pulled out of the parking lot and sped down the street, barely pausing at the stop signs as he got to the outskirts of town. He reached the entrance to State Highway 13. He pulled into the left-hand lane and floored it.

It was seven-twenty on a Thursday night. The skies were clear, there was hardly any traffic. Andy hoped there weren't any cops in the neighborhood. He watched the speedometer jerk up from 50 to 60 to 70. He flew down the highway, his foot clamped on the accelerator, his eyes on the road.

32

Murray Glick was hunched over in the passenger seat, the headphones clamped over his ears. He and Andy were heading west; they had slowed down to about fifty miles per hour. There wasn't much traffic on the road, mostly trucks en route to one of the other ski areas, or cutting over to I-70. A few of them honked as they passed the black Dakota but Andy Sussman, clutching the steering wheel, paid little attention. "Picking up anything, Mur?"

"We're getting warmer. They've stopped; the beeps are getting louder all the time."

Sussman slowed as they passed a county road. "Here?"

"I don't think so. It's still getting stronger, keep going."

Sussman hit the gas pedal and pushed up to 80. The road was straight and flat. He didn't see any lights, except an occasional car coming the other way. The next intersection was miles ahead.

Susie Sussman was finishing a Swanson's chicken potpie when she heard a car pull into the driveway. Beth had disappeared into the kitchen, leaving Dani to stand sentry in the den, armed only with a container of yogurt. "Expecting company?" Susie asked.

Dani shrugged; she looked back toward the kitchen. A moment later Beth hurried out, wielding a Smith & Wesson pistol. "All right, meal's over." She pointed the pistol straight at Susie and said to Dani, "Tie 'em up."

"Okay," Dani peeped. She hadn't said a word to Susie or Carol since Beth had returned from the store, except for a mumbled "Here . . ." when she handed them their dinners. Now she took the plates back and put them on the coffee table. She picked the ropes off the floor and retied Susie's hands behind her back.

The doorbell rang.

"Stay here," Beth said. "If they make a move, shout." She walked back through the kitchen, still holding the pistol.

"You might want to loosen these a little," Susie said, when Beth was out of earshot. "You may need us soon."

Dani ignored her and finished tying Carol's hands.

"I don't know who she's expecting—"

"That's none of your business."

"How could anybody possibly know where I am?"

"Just shut UP," Dani said.

"You know, Dani, I'm trying my best to like you. We are risking our lives for you—at least try and be pleasant."

"Don't make me laugh." Dani spoke with conviction and Susie wondered if she was ever going to get through to her, or if it mattered.

About a mile and a half after they had passed an intersection marked "County Trunk W," Murray told Sussman to slow down. "I'm losing it," he said. "Back up."

Sussman did a U-turn and headed back toward W. He stopped at the intersection. The road went north and south. He tried south.

"Nope," said Murray, after about a hundred yards, holding the headphones tight against his ear. "Try the other way."

Sussman turned around and crossed the highway again. "Any stronger?"

"A little . . . Nope, weaker now."

The road curved in a semi-circle, bending around a small hill and almost returning, then it came to another crossroads. Sussman stopped. "Where to now?"

Murray got out of the Dakota and looked around; he figured he could spend the next two hours exploring the sideroads. He took a couple of steps in each direction. The road was thick with aspens and a few firs. He walked back to the truck and pulled himself up to the top of the cab to get a better vantage point. There was a gentle ridge in front of them. He thought he saw the twinkling of lights on the rise, about a mile in the distance. He climbed back down and got into the truck.

"Any sign?"

"Keep going north. Stay on the main road another mile."

Sussman put the Dodge back into forward. The road was

bumpy—the Dakota needed a new pair of shocks. "Hear anything?"

"Back in business," said Murray. "We'll be there soon."

Susie had settled into her beanbag; she was watching a game
show when the commotion began. She heard the front door slam
and then open again. She heard Beth screaming some obscenities
that were drowned out by the sound of furniture being knocked
over. Dani, who was still standing guard, edged over to the
kitchen door to eavesdrop. There was more scuffling. Susie listened earnestly for Andy's voice or Murray's, but the first voice
she recognized was that of Jack Carvall.

"Just put the gun down and let him see the girl—"

"What girl?" Beth said, "there's no one here but me."

"Bullshit!" shouted another voice. "I know she's in there."
There was more shoving, then a shout, then a gunshot—Susie
could hear the bullet ricochet into the kitchen. She rolled off the
beanbag and lay flat behind it. There was silence for about fifteen
seconds, then she heard the sound of someone kicking a table
aside.

Dani hurried back to Susie, her hands and arms were trembling. "Get me out of here," she said, her voice breaking.
"Please. They'll kill me."

"Who will?"

"My father's in there with Jack Carvall. He's with the Forest
Service. He's the one who murdered Rick."

Susie tried to work her hands free from the ropes. She could
feel them start to give. "How do you know?"

"I saw it. He took Rick away—"

"Untie us. Fast."

Dani fumbled with the ropes on Susie's hands. When she'd
gotten her untied, the two of them worked on Carol's hands and
legs.

"Dani!" shouted Sam Kaplan from the kitchen.

"Oh shit," Dani said. "Hurry, we can make it out through
the window."

"Dani," said Susie, "you don't need to run from your father—"

"Hold it!" Sam Kaplan barged through the kitchen door,
brandishing his pistol. "Dani! Stay where you are." Sam turned
back toward the kitchen. "Get in here, both of you."

Carvall and Beth staggered into the den. Beth was bleeding from the lip and holding her right hand. Carvall had a welt on his left cheekbone, but he wasn't showing any signs of pain. He glanced quickly around the room. He saw Susie and Carol—he glared wickedly at them.

"Dani, get behind me," Sam said, waving the pistol at her.

"No! Shoot me, go ahead!"

"Dani—"

"Do it now!" Dani sobbed. "You might as well."

"Dani, these people are murderers—"

"You're the murderer!" Dani backed toward Susie. "You had Rick killed, just so you could make a few crummy dollars on another real estate deal."

"Dani, that's a damn lie—"

"Oh come on, Sam," said Jack Carvall. "She knows all about it. Might as well tell her the truth."

"You shut the hell up—"

"You MONSTER!" cried Dani. "I don't know you! Why don't you just go away and leave me alone forever!"

Sam looked at his daughter, while pointing the pistol straight at Carvall. "Dani, honey, listen to me. I didn't kill anyone. I have no idea what you're talking about."

"Oh, please," said Beth. "You were in on the development plans for the west ridge right from the start. You gave Casey the money to bribe Carvall."

Sam Kaplan was turning crimson—the gun was starting to shake in his hand. "I had no dealings with that damn ski resort. I sure as hell never talked to that pansy-assed ski instructor—"

"That's just what you wanted everyone to think," Beth said. "Even your daughter. But the truth was, you were the point man for Kozlo Realty. The only thing keeping you from millions of dollars gained at the public's expense was an Environmental Impact Statement. And Rick Allanson was writing that statement, and it was going to blow your whole corrupt project right off the mountain."

"Dani," said Sam, "that is a total lie. Look at me. You may not always agree with me. You may not like everything I do, or the way I do it, but have I ever lied to you?"

Dani stared at her father. "I don't know," she said, crying softly. "I can't believe anything anymore." She turned to Susie. "What do you know about this?"

"I'm getting educated every minute," Susie said, not eager to make her own speculations public, especially while she was facing the business end of Sam's revolver.

"Ignore her," said Carvall. "She's just a reporter—she knows what I told her. Listen to me, Dani, this is for your own good. Those Impact Statements had to be changed. For the good of everybody, not just a few tree huggers. Jobs depended on it. Real jobs for an area that has no economy besides the ski industry."

"I'll try and hold back my tears," sneered Beth. "You got a big fat bribe for trashing Rick's statement. Casey got a promotion. Kaplan got rich."

"And Rick Allanson got murdered." Dani stood up straight and faced her father. "And you told them to do it—"

"I don't even know who the hell Rick Allanson is."

"Sam, you're a damn good actor, you know that?" said Carvall.

Sam stuck the gun in Carvall's ribs. "Maybe I'll pretend to pull the trigger."

"Think you can do it yourself?" said Beth. "It's a lot easier to just give the orders, isn't it? Like with Rick Allanson. He threatened to blow the whistle on you, so you sent the word down from Chicago."

"That's a bunch of bull—"

"Only there was one mistake," Beth said. "Rick wasn't alone when he got assaulted in his own apartment." She turned to Dani. "Was he?"

Dani had slumped against the far wall, underneath the window. Her face was a deep red from crying. Susie edged closer to her. "So you saw it all?"

Dani snuffled back some tears. "They didn't know I was over there. We'd been friends a couple of weeks. He was so intense about what was happening at Sunburst, I just wanted to get to know him better. And Casey was so arrogant. Then Rick told me about the bribes—"

"What bribes?" snapped Sam.

"Hah!" scoffed Beth. She was still holding her injured arm; a small trickle of blood dripped from her mouth. "You know what bribes—you paid them."

Dani looked at Beth, then spoke to her father. "Rick stayed late at work one day. It was after seven, it was dark. Casey came into Carvall's office through the back door. They went out to the woods, behind the station. Rick followed them. He saw Casey give him an envelope. He overheard them. Casey said the money came from Sunburst Corp; there'd be more when the Impact Statements were straightened out. Carvall said he'd take care of it." Dani's voice faltered. "After Rick told me that, I didn't want to be anywhere near Casey. I packed up. I didn't tell him where I was going. I went over to Rick's and slept on the couch. I was just going to stay a few days and then find another apartment. I was there two nights and then . . ." Dani sniffled again. "It was about four in the morning . . . I was asleep in the living room and I kind of heard the door open . . . I barely had my eyes open . . . I saw this guy go into Rick's bedroom. A minute later he was pushing him out the door. I could see who it was, but I was so scared . . ." She started sobbing and buried her head in her arms.

"Sweetheart," Sam said, "believe me, I had nothing to do with any of that."

"C'mon, Kaplan," laughed Carvall, "why the big secret? You've got the gun. Plug us all. Bury us under the floorboards."

Sam turned toward Carvall. "Nobody'd miss you, scumbag, believe me—"

"Come on, pull the trigger—"

"Daddy, DON'T! Don't kill anybody else!" Dani stood up and started to walk toward her father.

"I haven't killed anyone. Now sit down—"

"Give me that!" Dani lunged toward her father.

"Dani!"

But Sam Kaplan was too late. As he backed away from Dani, Jack Carvall dived at his legs and tripped him up. The gun went flying from his hands. Carvall grabbed Sam and held him to the ground. Beth leaped for the gun. So did Susie.

At that moment the lights in the den went out. Sam and Carvall wrestled each other on the floor. Another scuffle went on a few feet away; Beth was in the middle of it, searching for the pistol. Susie saw another body fly into the fracas. She couldn't tell who it was—only that it was a man; friend or foe, she knew she'd be no match for him in a fight. She decided that the safest place to be was behind the couch, with the kitchen door a short dash away. She grabbed Carol and darted across the floor.

She heard a high-pitched scream—it sounded more like Beth than Dani, but she couldn't be sure. She stared from behind the sofa, her eyes adjusting slowly to the darkness. She saw Dani cowering in front of the TV set. She saw Beth lying on the floor, and Carvall sprawled on top of Sam Kaplan. In front of her, standing beside the coffee table, was a tall man holding Sam Kaplan's pistol.

It was Casey Wright.

33

Murray Glick and Andy Sussman ran toward the old house, stopping when they got to the driveway. They'd parked the Dakota a half-mile down the road so they could approach silently. They'd seen a red Trans Am with black racing stripes parked about fifty yards away. Murray was still wearing his headphones; he heard the beeps get louder. He stopped when he saw Sam Kaplan's Buick by the front walk. He took the phones off and rested them on his shoulders. "Voilà," he whispered. "The gang's all here."

They walked up to the front door. It was locked; Murray had just begun to pick it when the shouting began and the lights went out. "Stay here," he told Andy. He dashed around the back and peered through the window. He saw the scramble on the floor—he could tell from the silhouette who had ended up with the gun. He ran back to the front door, where he'd left Sussman.

"Where are they?" Andy asked.

"Shh." Murray went to work on the front door; it took him only a few seconds, the lock was old and easy to pick. "There's a living room on the other side. They're all in there—Casey, too. Hang on."

Murray slipped inside and crept down the hallway. He found a closet several feet from the kitchen door; there was a shallow cabinet at the back of it. He opened it and felt his way down the side until he found the breaker switch, then returned to Andy.

"Did you see Susie back there?"

"I thought I saw her behind the couch. Hang tight." Murray sprinted over to Sam's Buick. He ran his hand under the bumper, pulled out the bug he'd planted and slipped it in his pocket. He hurried back to Sussman and gave him the headphones. "Put these on." Murray tapped on the bug. "Hear that?"

"Barely. It makes a little thud over the signal."

"Listen hard. There's a fuse box inside, in the closet next to the kitchen. The fuse to the den is on the right, second from the bottom. Casey hit it a minute ago—it's the only one in the down position. When I give you the signal, flick it back on. When you hear me come through the window, flick it off again."

"Why don't you just go in through the kitchen?"

"That's your escape route. Worse case, you can grab Susie and get the hell out of here."

"Gotcha."

Murray led Andy back inside and pointed him toward the closet, then stole back around the house to the den window. A shade was pulled; there was a gap of five or six inches on the bottom. Murray squinted through it. He could see Casey Wright, standing in front of the television, holding the gun. Murray nudged the window; it was closed tightly—it probably hadn't been raised since last summer. He looked around for something to break through it. He saw an old Weber barbecue kettle, rusted and filled with snow. As gently as he could, he cleaned off the cover and scooped out the inside. He set it down, crouched against the window and listened.

". . . and get this straight," Casey was saying. "I am NOT going to have this weekend fucked up—"

"Your WEEKEND—is that all you can think about?" cried Dani. "You KILLED someone, all you care about is your ski race—"

"I didn't kill anyone—"

"Hey, what's a little bribery?" Carvall said. "Kidnapping, altering federal documents—"

"Put a lid on it," Wright said tartly. A trace of moonlight spilled through the window, outlining his bearded profile and muscular torso. "Now take a deep breath, troops, and pay attention. What we have here is a case of Rumor Control. Get it? Not murder. Not kidnapping. Not bribery—"

"Oh, please!" said Dani. "I saw everything! Beth just explained the rest—"

"Oh you did?" snapped Casey. "And just what the hell kind of a witness are you? A runaway princess who shacked up with the head ski instructor for a few weeks? Got a little jealous? Hopped into bed with a Smokey just to get even—"

"Why, you BASTARD! I never—"

"Hey, I'm just getting warmed up. It seems this North Shore Princess doesn't get along with Daddy too well, either. She's afraid the old man's gonna cut her off. She's hysterical. She concocts a harebrained story about him getting involved with crooked real estate out here—I'm sure Daddy'll be real supportive about that."

Dani shrunk against the wall behind the television, almost invisible in the darkness.

"Shall we even go into this kidnapping nonsense? Beth, have you been forcing the little princess to stay here?"

Beth alternated glances between Dani and Carvall. Her lip was still bleeding slightly, but she seemed to have regained her composure. "Forced? She was always free to go whenever she pleased. She called me to begin with."

"Isn't that interesting?" said Casey. He pointed the gun at Kaplan. "Well, Sam, I have wonderful news for you. Your daughter's safe and sound—the two of you can go home in a couple of days. Unless, that is, you want to run to the police. Start spreading these wild stories about an avalanche victim being murdered, and real estate fraud in your own company. Of course, we'd have to respond to those charges in the most complete and personal fashion—"

"Casey, you have just the most amazing opinion of yourself," Dani said. "Like I'm really going to go back home and be a good little girl." She glared at her father. "And I'm NOT going back to him."

Casey rubbed his beard. "My, but I do hate to get involved in family spats—"

"Dammit, Casey," said Carvall, rubbing the bruise on his cheekbone, "we can't just let 'em go. Why do you think we kept her here in the first place—"

"That's your problem. You can't grease the old man, Jack. He disappears, they'll have real cops in here, not some cartoon gumshoe."

"Yeah? So what do we do about the other two?"

"What other two?"

"Carol and that reporter. They heard everything." Carvall

looked nervously around the living room. "Where the hell'd they go?" He limped toward the couch.

Outside, Murray edged against the window. He reached for the bug.

"Beth, get the damn lights back on," Carvall said. "They couldn't have got out."

Murray tapped on the bug three times. He grabbed the barbecue kettle. He waited five agonizing seconds. He saw the living room lights flicker on, along with the television. As Casey jerked his head toward the kitchen door, Murray hurled the kettle through the window, then leaped through the broken glass, his gun drawn.

The lights went out again.

Murray could see Casey lurch toward him. Wright fired the pistol wildly once in his direction, but Murray had dived off to the left. Glick held his gun with both hands, but he didn't fire— there were too many people in the room. From the corner of his eye he saw Sam Kaplan lunge toward Casey. There was another shot; this one went straight toward the ceiling.

Murray darted across the room, just as Casey smacked Sam in the face with the butt of his gun. As Kaplan collapsed on the carpet, the kitchen door opened and Andy Sussman ran into the room, toward the sofa.

Casey spotted Murray in the darkness; for a brief moment their eyes met. Wright pointed his gun squarely at Glick. Murray started to fire, but held off; Andy was in his gunsight—there was no margin for error. He leaped to his right, just as Casey fired a shot. Glick felt a hot flash in his left shoulder. He held back a cry of pain as he fell behind the coffee table.

Casey aimed again.

Out of the corner of his eye, Murray saw Andy disappear behind the couch. He had a clear shot now. He squeezed the trigger. He hit Casey in the right hand, then fired another round and nailed him flush in the arm.

Casey dropped to the floor. His gun fell loose and slid toward the coffee table. Beth lunged at it.

"Don't!" Murray yelled. "Stay back, baby, it's all over." He froze Beth, then hobbled over and picked up the gun with his injured left arm. "Andy!" He turned toward the couch. "Hoops! Get the lights on."

Sussman crawled out from behind the sofa, with Susie right behind him. They stepped warily into the kitchen. A few moments later the lights flickered on again.

"Bueno," said Murray. He surveyed the scene in front of him. Casey Wright lay on the floor, blood streaming from his right hand and arm. Beth, holding her right hand, had crawled back toward Carvall. Sam Kaplan, woozy and bleeding from the chin, was propped up against the base of the television. Dani was on the other side of the room, unharmed but sobbing softly. Carol Bevins had crawled out from behind the couch, but was ready to jump back at a moment's notice.

"Andy, call an ambulance—"

"I'll do it," Susie said, hurrying back into the kitchen.

Murray looked at his left shoulder. The blood was trickling through his parka, staining the whole left side of it a dark red. He could sense the strength draining out of his left hand. He was feeling faint. He bit his lip; he clutched the Colt with his right hand.

"Jesus Christ, Murray," Andy said. "Are you—"

"I'll be fine. Here." He handed him Kaplan's gun. He turned toward Dani, who had collapsed on the floor behind them. "It's okay, darling. Everything's fine now."

"Who ARE you?" sobbed Dani.

"Name's Murray Glick. I'm a friend of your mom's. I'm here to take you home."

"I'm here to take her home," sputtered Sam Kaplan.

"I don't WANT to go home. He's a murderer."

"Listen to me, dammit, I'm your father!"

"Sam," said Murray. "Take it easy—"

"Tell her I didn't have anything to do with this," Kaplan snarled, blotting the blood from his chin with his coat sleeve.

"I don't believe it—"

"Dani, he's right. He may not be Father-of-the-Year, but his picture's not in any post offices, either."

Susie returned from the kitchen. "They don't have 911 out here. I called the police. They'll have an ambulance over in a couple of minutes."

"Good," Murray said. "Just in time for a bedtime story."

"Spare us," growled Carvall.

"Sorry. Nothing I like better than a captive audience." Murray looked at Dani. "Listen closely, sweetheart. You know most of this, except for a few small details." He dabbed some blood from his wounded shoulder. "Let's start with Rick Allanson. Loyal forest ranger. Staunch defender of the wilderness. Seems he had some qualms about rubber-stamping the lease of a pristine mountainside to the Sunburst Corporation. Didn't care who he pissed off."

Dani held back a sob.

"Enter Casey Wright: a hotshot ski instructor, trying to work his way up to the executive suite. Comes to his attention that the boardroom cowboys have a problem. A dirty little job that needs doing. Casey said, Let me carry the ball! Or the bag, as it were."

Down on the floor, Casey lifted his head a few inches. He was bleeding from the arm, his face was pale. "I just expedited things," he said. "For the good of the company. The reports would have been written the way we wanted eventually." He rolled toward Carvall. "I didn't tell you to kill the guy, Jack."

"Chrissakes, Casey, he saw us. The sanctimonious sonuvabitch, I had to deal with him."

"Ah," coughed Murray, "and next we come to Jack Carvall." Outside, a siren could be heard in the distance. Murray struggled to stay upright. "Mr. Carvall, it turns out, is quite the entrepreneur. Now we can't begrudge Jack a little free enterprise, can we? Surrounded by all this wealth. Why not make a small investment in Sunburst Village? Get to know a few ski lassies up close and personal. Only the Village Deli had an even better use, didn't it, Jack?"

Murray stopped and faced Dani. He could see the color drain from her face.

"So I sold a few sandwiches," Carvall said. "I made a nickel or two—"

"But nothing like you cleared in a couple of quick hours for altering those Impact Statements, right? How much did they pay you, Jack?"

Carvall started to move for the kitchen, then saw that both Andy and Murray had their gun barrels pointed at him.

"Enough to retire safely on," Susie said. "Enough to leave the Forest Service, anyway, which is what you were planning to do in a couple of weeks."

"As soon as you'd laundered all the bribe money through Sunburst Concessions," said Murray.

Carvall glowered at Susie, then at Murray.

"But you fucked up, Jack, didn't you?" Glick continued. "Because Rick Allanson found out. He was determined to stop you from tearing up those Environmental Impact Statements. Trouble was, Rick made a mistake. A deadly mistake. He shared his discovery with the adorable little girl he'd fallen in love with."

"That's a lie!" Dani cried. "I'd never hurt Rick."

"Not intentionally. But they found out about him, didn't they, Dani? How did that happen?"

"I don't know . . ."

"Who'd you tell, Dani? Who could have stopped him?"

"I didn't . . . I didn't tell anyone . . . I just told—" Dani stopped and stared at Beth.

"You told your best friend, didn't you? You told Beth."

Dani choked on her tears. She gazed straight at Beth.

"Of course, there were a few things that Beth never told you, Dani. You never knew that the Village Deli had an absentee owner by the name of Jack Carvall."

Dani stared at Beth in disbelief.

"And that Carvall had a girlfriend named Elizabeth."

Beth folded her arms. Her eyes met Dani's for an instant.

Outside, the drone of the sirens was getting closer.

"Beth," said Dani, in a whisper. "I trusted you."

Murray could feel his left arm tingling and getting numb. His throat was dry. "A fatal error," he said. "Beth told her boyfriend that Rick was going to blow the whistle on him. Two nights later, Jack broke into Rick's apartment. He injected him with knock-out drops, dragged him out. Twenty-four hours later, Rick is found buried in an avalanche. Nice and clean, right Jack?"

Carvall grunted and stared at the floor.

"Only Dani saw it all. She was petrified. And who did she turn to?" Murray looked at Dani. "If you'd just called the police, Dani, you'd have saved us all a lot of trouble."

"Rick told me the police were in on this; it was all one big conspiracy. That's why he didn't go to them in the first place." Dani's eyes were red, she was weeping again. "Beth said I couldn't tell anyone. If I exposed Carvall, they'd kill me."

"Who?"

"Carvall. The cops." She looked over at her father. "Him."

"That's a LIE!" groaned Kaplan. "Dani, how could you believe that? How could you believe I'd have anything to do with Casey Wright?"

"You wouldn't have anything to do with ME," Dani cried. "Just because I moved out here for a couple of months—"

"Shacking up with that crooked-ass ski bum." He leaned toward Casey. "I TOLD you he was no good. I was right."

"Great! Congratulations! So you were right—look where it got us—"

"Don't blame ME for this, young lady—"

"All right, okay," wheezed Murray. He wobbled backwards. He heard the ambulance; it was just a few hundred yards away.

"Murray," said Andy. "You want to lie down?"

"Nah." Murray coughed and wiped some blood off his shoulder. "Keep the gun trained on them," he said, struggling for breath. "Let me finish." He wheezed again. "Dani, Beth claimed your father was behind all this?"

"She told me about his plan. She showed me phone records of calls from Casey's desk to my father's office."

"So what?" Sam said. "All that means is someone made some calls—it was a big frame-up."

"Take it easy," said Murray.

"It's all a lie—"

"I know it is." Murray turned to Dani. "So you went into hiding. You were afraid of Carvall. Afraid of the police. Afraid of your father. How long did you expect to stay here?"

Dani shrugged. "Beth said only another week or so."

"Sure." Murray's voice was fading. "Until the race was over. Until Sunburst took over the west ridge and the ranger station closed down. Beth and Jack could sell the deli, take their blood money and skip town." He looked over at Beth. "Hey, Beth. What were you going to do with your best friend then?"

Beth sniffled; she looked straight at Dani. For just a moment, her icy resolve softened. "I never would have hurt you, Dani. I mean it. I was your friend."

Dani closed her eyes in disbelief.

"It's the truth!" Beth looked over at Carvall. "He would have killed you in a minute! He was ready the next time it snowed, I had to beg him—"

"What a pal," Murray rasped. "You couldn't hide her forever, you knew that. Even if you'd have gotten rid of me—"

"Dani," Beth said, "I thought if we could just wait it out a few more weeks. Until you got over Rick, then we could talk. No one was suspicious. The investigation was dead."

"But you KILLED him," Dani said, crying softly.

"You barely knew him!" Beth's eyes turned steely again. "You'd have forgotten him, just like everybody else." She dropped her voice to a whisper. "When you were ready, we'd have told you."

Dani's cheeks flushed with anger; she stood face to face with Beth. "I would never, EVER, let you get away with that!" She clenched her fist and lunged at Beth, but Murray, staggering between them, pushed her away.

"Mur—" said Sussman, as Glick struggled to keep his feet, but Murray waved him back and looked directly at Beth.

"So, what then? " he said, his right hand trembling against the Colt. "Dani won't play. You and Jack are ready to cruise. Still begging for mercy?"

Beth held her wounded arm. She glanced at Carvall. She looked back at Dani for just a split second. "Dani, we wouldn't . . . if we didn't have to. Just another week, you would have understood . . ."

"What then!" Murray said.

Beth looked at Carvall. She bit her lip and stared at the floor. The room was silent.

"Damn you," said Dani. She walked over to her father's side. "Daddy," she whispered, and broke into tears.

"Yeah, yeah," said Sam. "I'm sorry, Dani." He struggled to his feet. He limped to his daughter's side and put his arms around her. "I am sorry. Believe me."

The sirens blasted. The ambulance screeched to a halt. Two paramedics rushed into the den, along with two state troopers. The cops looked around for a moment. They saw Andy Sussman pointing the gun at Carvall and Beth. They saw Casey Wright lying on the ground in a pool of blood. They saw Murray Glick fall gently to his knees, still clutching his Colt .38 Detective Special.

"Howdy boys," Murray said, coughing. "Just in time." He aimed his wounded arm at Sussman. "Andrew, get our friends up to speed on the proceedings. And get me a glass of water.''

Sussman started toward the kitchen, then stopped.

Murray dropped his gun. He grabbed his shoulder. He fell to the floor, his breathing forced but steady. There was a wide, Cheshire cat grin on his lips as he passed out.

34

Streams of sunshine dappled through the blinds of the private room at Sunburst Peak Hospital, casting slants of light and shadow on the patient who was propped up on the bed, reading the *Rocky Mountain News* and chewing on an unlit cigar. "I see Neiman Marcus had a stock split," grumbled Murray Glick. "That'll knock the hell out of sweater prices. Did you know, Hoops, I was wearing a brand-new cashmere pullover last night? Light brown, two hundred dollars, on sale last President's Day. Ruined, totally. The parka, too."

"I'm sure Sam and Barbara Kaplan will gladly replenish your wardrobe, Mur." Andy Sussman munched on a piece of stale rye bread, the last remnants of Murray's institutional breakfast. He had prepared himself for a gruesome sight when he walked over to the hospital. Last night Murray had been barely conscious as the ambulance roared off; his left arm looked like a candidate for a tourniquet. Andy had expected to find his friend lost in a jumble of catheter bottles and slings and beeping cathodes. Instead, he'd found Murray lying among a dozen red roses. Standing over him, bussing him on the cheek, was Sara Felder. She had just finished spooning Murray his breakfast, which seemed unnecessary seeing as his right hand was perfectly functional.

"Got to fly," Sara said, rearranging the roses on the bedstand. She patted Murray on the hand. "See you at five, okay?"

"Don't leave on account of me," Sussman said, presenting Murray with his own get-well gifts, a month-old *Playboy* and a box of Slim Jims.

"No, no, not at all." Sara explained to Andy that her group

lessons were about to start and she was loaded with work now that Casey was indisposed, more or less permanently, according to the rumors that she'd heard from the ski office. "From what I understand, there's going to be an administrative opening in the ski school, even if he does pull through." She winked at Murray. "What a prince—goes through all that just to to get me a promotion."

"And you doubted my sincerity," Murray rasped.

"I'm touched." Sara turned to Andy. "How's Susie doing?"

"Oh, she's fine. She'll be over in a few minutes."

"Tell her I said hi. I'm so sorry about what happened the other day. I had no idea until Murray told me. How about coming down for a semi-private tomorrow? It's on the house."

"We've got the race coming up Sunday. I'll be busy with interviews and setups—"

"Stay an extra day! How can you leave powder like this?"

"I think my bosses want me back in New York—"

"Well, you've got an open offer. Both of you." Sara turned back to Murray and kissed him on the cheek. "Feel better, you big lug." She waved goodbye to Andy and skipped off down the corridor.

"You know, Mur," Andy said, as Murray chewed on his cigar and continued to grouse about the effect of Neiman Marcus' stock split on the price of designer jeans, "I came here determined to wallow in sympathy for you. I don't suppose you could possibly slump back a little? Look pallid, a weary groan, maybe?"

"Sorry, Hoops. Just my natural resiliency. How do you think I get my staying power in this business."

Sussman stole a cigar from the pocket of Murray's bathrobe and ripped off the cellophane. "In that case, I may just return to the state of extreme agitation that resulted from my wife being abducted and nearly killed after following your instructions. After, in fact, we both rearranged our lives in order to assist you on this caper of yours."

"A million thanks, Hoops. I thank you. Dani Kaplan thanks you. Carol Bevins and Brian Ellsworth thank you. Unknown generations of wilderness lovers—"

"I'm drowning in gratitude—"

"Hello, hello!" said Susie Sussman, walking into the room with another bouquet of flowers. "How's the wounded sleuth?"

"Arrgh," moaned Murray. "Aaagh. Hullo, Suse."

"Ooh, aren't these pretty?" Susie looked at the roses. "Andy, did you bring these?"

"A certain female ski instructor brought them by first thing in the morning."

"Aha." Susie leaned over and smelled the flowers. "Mmm." She placed her bouquet of carnations next to them and inspected Murray's arm. "Looks like they did a clean job. How'd you sleep?"

"Not too great," Murray whispered. "Got a few winks in this morning."

"Aw, poor guy. How's it feel now?"

"Still sore." Murray's voice faded into a mumble. He slid down the bed and placed his cigar on the breakfast tray. "Right where the bullet came out. I guess I'll live."

"The odds are considerably better than he lets on," Sussman said. It occurred to him that Murray seemed to grow weaker and more vulnerable in the proximity of beautiful women. "The doctor says he'll be playing tennis by next weekend."

Murray groaned and held his arm.

"Listen," Susie said, "I checked on Casey Wright—he's just down the hall. Word is he'll make it." She turned to Murray. "He lost a lot of blood, but you didn't hit anything vital. There's someone from the sheriff's department outside, waiting for the doctors to let him in for questions. Carvall and his girlfriend are in custody."

Murray managed a grin. "Susan, I'm just astounded by your ferocity on this case. I want you to know that if you ever desire to seek the more active side of the law as a permanent vocation—"

"Don't push it, I just don't like loose ends." Susie straightened the collar on Murray's pajama top.

"You're a peach, Susela. I always knew those sweet feminine instincts would shine through."

"Believe me, this is a great test of my self-restraint." Susie flashed a sinister grin and made a mock grab for Murray's throat. "Incidentally, O Great Master of Illusion, there was one thing I never did figure out."

"Fire away, chief."

"In your manuscript, you said Beth was smallish, with short brown hair."

Murray reached for his box of Slim Jims. He took one out and nibbled on it, as if he couldn't possibly anticipate where Susie was leading.

"Murray, she's a flaming redhead."

"This is true, Susan."

"So why the discrepancy? If you'd described her accurately, I might have made the connection when I saw her in the village. I'd have figured the whole thing out and called Andy. Maybe saved you a trip to the infirmary."

"Ah, Susela." Murray tapped the beef jerky on his tray. "I was confronted with a situation that called for dramatic license. I already had Sara, who as you well know, is endowed with mesmerizing locks of crimson."

"I didn't realize there was a quota."

"Susan, a world-class literary sleuth requires variety in his ladies. A proper interspersal of redheads, blondes, brunettes—"

"Murray!" Susie reached for his throat again, but she saw the catheter bottle jangle and the bed shake and decided that a good-natured karate chop might be misinterpreted by the nurse who was bracing herself for active duty across the hall. "Glick, you are a total piece of work!"

"I do my best."

"Incidentally," Susie said, as Murray continued gnawing on his Slim Jim, "I think we're going to burn that manuscript tonight."

"Burn it?" A crocodile tear slid down Murray's cheek. "My life's work?"

"I think it's the humanitarian thing to do," Andy said. "For the good of the publishing industry and the detective business. Not to mention several people who don't wish to be the subject of a slightly suspect narrative."

Murray shrugged with his good shoulder. "Ah, go ahead. I'd never have time to finish it anyway. As soon as my arm heals, I gotta get ready for the spring cruises. There's a sale at Northbrook Court in two weeks, two for one on unfaithful spouse investigations. That oughta keep me busy."

"You're sure?"

"Absolutely."

"That's your only copy of the manuscript?"

"Typed up at sixty words a minute on my trusty Olivetti. I figured I'd get a laptop computer with the advance." Murray yawned. "A brilliant literary career nipped in the bud." He leaned back in the bed. "I think it's naptime."

"Andy, he's getting sleepy," Susie said. "Let's go. Someone owes me a new pair of skis; why don't we do some shopping?"

"Sounds like a plan." Sussman turned to Murray, who was fading fast. "Anything we can bring you this afternoon, Mur?"

"Nah," mumbled Murray. "Oh, maybe a cigar lighter."

"I'll see if I can smuggle one in."

"And some Hostess Twinkies."

"I'll check with the nutritionist. Have a nice nap, buddy." Andy took Susie by the arm and led her out the door.

"See you this afternoon," Susie said.

"Be good, kids." Murray slid back in bed. He closed his eyes as Andy and Susie walked out the door.

Outside the hospital, Andy walked his wife back across the parking lot to the Mercury Cougar they had rented for the rest of the week. "There was just one other thing I wanted to clear up," Susie said, as she stumbled around a snowbank, "although I couldn't bear to assault Murray's virility in his bedridden state."

"I think Murray's virility came through intact."

Susie tossed her head back, shaking the snowflakes off her neck. "I was just wondering about 'L'Affaire de la Barbara.' We never did get that that settled."

Andy laughed as he unlocked the Cougar's passenger door.

"You're not the least bit curious?"

"Sure, Suse. But what can I say? It's Murray's word against Mrs. Kaplan's. You pays your money, you takes your chances."

"And I suppose you believe HIM?"

Sussman reached into his pocket and pulled out a quarter. "Here. Heads it's the sleuth, tails the dame." He flipped the coin high in the air, but his toss was errant. The coin looped backwards and came down in a snowbank in front of the Cougar, sinking out of sight. "Oops," shrugged Andy. "Looks like it's destined to be one of life's sweet mysteries."

"Oh, foo!" Susie kicked some snow at her husband, jerked the door open, and slid into the front seat.

Andy joined her, gave her a peck on the cheek, and put the key in the ignition. "Murray's right, you really were the tiger on this case."

"I'm just trying to tie things up," Susie said, brushing the snow off her boots. "My curiosity was piqued, I don't know how I'll ever sit behind a desk again after all this excitement."

"Right."

"No, really. A break from the routine every once in a while doesn't hurt."

Andy took Susie's hand and checked her pulse. "What's gotten into you, babe? For a while I almost thought you were enjoying this."

"I wouldn't describe it as enjoyment." Susie snuggled next to Andy. "I didn't appreciate having a gun pointed at me, or being kidnapped on the middle of the ski slope. But honestly, I'd been pushing paper for so long, it was actually refreshing to be doing something active."

"Like risking your life for Murray Glick?"

Susie wrinkled her nose. "I was thinking of the girl."

"Of course." Andy rubbed his wife on the neck. "You know, honey, I have this theory about people our age, in our situation."

"Really, now."

"You're dying to hear it."

"Does this car have a radio?" Susie said, reaching for the ignition.

Andy pushed her hand away. "My theory is, when you don't have certain responsibilities, such as—and this is just a random example—raising a family, you tend to look for other, less traditional ways to seek stimulation and achievement and satisfaction in life. As a result, you end up taking needless risks and going after unnecessary thrills, instead of opting for a path that would be much more satisfying in the long run."

"I see." Susie took Andy's hand. "That's your theory?"

"I spent all night conjuring it up. What do you think?"

"Interesting," Susie said, snuggling toward him again.

"Interesting? That's all?"

"Well, it beats doing it for the grandparents."

"Uh huh. I don't suppose I'm making any progress in convincing you."

"Convincing me of what?"

"Don't be coy."

Susie kissed Andy on the cheek. "It's possible you might be," she said. "Remember, I was never diametrically opposed to this 'other path' that you're referring to. It was just a matter of a time that would be advantageous for you and me and a third party to be named later.''

"I see. Susan, darling, could I speculate that recent events might help convince you that said time might be closer at hand then originally anticipated?''

"Anything's possible.''

"Remember, also, that I'm facing two weeks this summer on the Grand Inini River in the middle of the godforsaken Guianian jungle. Chances of survival marginal. I barely made it through this, after all.''

"I'm sympathetic, believe me,'' Susie said.

"So?'' Sussman started the car. He pulled out of the hospital parking lot, with Susie still clinging to his side.

"So, Andrew, I thought maybe we'd go shopping for some new skis first. Which, of course, will be charged to a certain invalid friend of yours.''

"Sounds reasonable.''

"Then you'll get your interviews done early. I'll go shopping for a delicious Italian dinner. After which we'll repair to our cozy hearth. Build a hot, roaring fire in the den, stoked with the pages of a certain manuscript, guaranteed to be excellent kindling.''

"That does sound extremely promising. What then?''

"And then,'' said Susie, whispering in Andy's ear, "then, we'll see.''

"See what?''

"We'll see what we shall see.'' Susie kissed Andy on the cheek.

"What's that supposed to mean?''

Susie giggled and kissed Andy on the back of the neck. "Get thee to a ski shop, lover.''

"Right away,'' said Sussman. He leaned back in the driver's seat. "We'll see,'' he mumbled to himself, as Susie found the radio and turned up a country and western song. "I love you, darling,'' he said, pulling her close with his right arm and steering with his left. "I just can't bear the suspense.''

35

Snowflakes sprinkled down from an ash-gray sky, clinging for a moment to the bandages on my left arm, then falling harmlessly to the ground. A few yards in front of me, the greatest skiers in the world were gathering for the Sunburst World Cup Downhill. The crowds clustered at the bottom of the course and filtered up the slope along the boundaries, whooping and hollering as their favorites passed above them on the chairlift. CBS cameramen readied themselves at key positions along the run. I could see Andy Sussman standing with Kevin Cumberland in a cordoned-off box twenty yards behind the finish line. Susie was right behind him, in the first row of the makeshift bleachers.

They'd discharged me from the hospital an hour ago—well, not exactly discharged me. The doctors had insisted I stay through the weekend for observation, but I'd made friends with a cute little nurse on the midnight shift. I'd offered her a discount on the Christmas Caribbean cruise and a free bottle of champagne. She'd made a few adjustments on my chart, slit the plastic bracelet off my wrist, and led me down through the service elevator and out the back door. The American Medical Association might not approve, but hey, I'm a restless guy. There's work to be done, criminals to be brought to justice.

And this case was over.

After I left the hospital, I walked over to the police station and dropped in on Craig Gustafson. He wasn't going to have much time for tying flies the next few weeks. Instead, he'd be tying together a murder and kidnapping case against Jack Carvall and his girlfriend Elizabeth, and helping the FBI with fraud and bribery counts against Casey Wright and some unnamed co-conspirators. It burned me just a little to learn that Casey would probably plea-bargain his attempted manslaughter charge down in return for identifying the three-piece suits that had funded the bribery scheme. It would be one lead slug unaccounted for, but I wasn't about to protest. I'd been hired to find a girl. I'd found her, and solved a murder as well. Craig Gustafson could take it from there. I made my visit brief. I gave him the facts. I shook hands, bid him farewell, and caught the shuttle back to the village.

I didn't stay for the race. I thought about making my way through the crowd and grabbing a front-row seat. Sara could have gotten me one easily, but of course she'd insisted that I stay in the hospital until the doctors gave me the green light. If she saw me on the slopes, she'd probably call the cops and have me sent back to my room in a straitjacket. And she'd look gorgeous doing it.

Sara will come back to an empty hospital room tonight. She'll cry when she sees the empty bed, but she'll smile, too. She'll understand. Last night she told me that she might chuck it all next winter and cruise the Caribbean with me. The west ridge expansion is history, now, and so are all those new ski school jobs. But she won't leave. We all have our niches in this world. Sara Felder will be framed forever in my memory gliding down a ski slope beneath a clear blue sky, with a trail of kids behind her—and maybe one admiring detective. I'll be framed in her memory with a kind word, a cockeyed smile, and a Colt .38.

I thought about walking over to Andy and saying a final good-bye before the race started. He'd been an invaluable help to me. Maybe he was a little burned at the way I'd brought him into the case. Maybe, this time, I'd gone too far. But what the hell, friends are friends. He'd get over it. I considered bluffing my way past the CBS security guys and bidding him adieu, but he was busy with his production, I'd just be a distraction.

His job was just beginning. Mine was over.

I wandered toward the edge of the bleachers at the bottom of the slope. I got as close as I could to the stands. I bought myself a hotdog and a pretzel. I wanted a cold beer, but it was too much to manage with my sling.

I stood by the concession stand and looked at the finish line. I saw Susie Sussman. I stared at her for at least five minutes, waiting for her to glance my way. Then, for just a fraction of a second, our eyes met. A less-insightful person might have thought that she rolled those sensational brown eyes in exasperation; a person less tuned to the nuances of a beautiful woman might have thought that she shook her pretty head in disgust. But I knew that there was a smile trying to force its way through, and I knew it came straight from the heart.

I waved at Susie, I blew her a kiss. I thought I saw her wink.

Then I turned around and walked away from the mountain.

The Sunburst Airport is a lonely place right now. Every living soul who's ever been on skis is over at the downhill, waiting for the race to begin. There's only a skeleton crew here. A single Rocky Mountain Airways prop plane taxis down the runway. A handful of passengers wait patiently in the terminal. Loners, like me. Probably a few salesmen on their way to a job, maybe some tourists who need to get back to work tomorrow and couldn't get a later flight.

Sure, I wish I could stay and see the race. I think of Andy and Susie and Sara. They're going to have one helluva party tonight. Believe me, I'd love to be part of it.

Then I think of Dani Kaplan. And a tearful Barbra meeting her and Sam back in Chicago.

I think of Rick Allanson.

I think of all the Rick Allansons whose lives are at stake, waiting for someone, somewhere, to intervene on the side of justice.

I give the flight attendant my ticket and climb aboard the airplane. I'm Murray Glick, private investigator. I don't look back.